THE QUEEN'S COUNCIL

Realm of Wonders

ALEXANDRA MONIR

DISNEY · HYPERION

Los Angeles   New York

For my mother and daughter:
The real Scheherazade, my beloved mom ZaZa, who inspired my
storytelling with her music;
And Jordan Rose, my little girl and queen of my heart.

First Edition, October 2023
10 9 8 7 6 5 4 3 2 1
FAC-004510-23229
Printed in the United States of America

This book is set in Bodoni Classic, Wiescher-Design, Lawrence, Fenotype, Yana, Laura, Worthington/Fontspring; Franklin Gothic; Janson/Monotype
Designed by Marci Senders
Illustrated by Scott Altmann
Interior illustrations by Akeem Roberts

Library of Congress Control Number: 2023934745
ISBN 978-1-368-04821-7
Reinforced binding
Visit www.DisneyBooks.com

SUSTAINABLE FORESTRY INITIATIVE

Certified Sourcing

www.forests.org
SFI-01681

Logo Applies to Text Stock Only

PROLOGUE

The Cave of Wonders was waiting.

Years had passed since the silver-haired woman paid her last visit, the same day she added an unassuming gold lamp to her collection of treasures. Her eyes had gleamed in the surrounding darkness that day as she whispered an incantation: *"Only for the diamond in the rough."* She'd placed the lamp atop a thousand-stone tower and then she was gone, letting the Cave and its magic seal up beneath the sand. A world of riches lay buried in her wake, and it seemed she might never come back to claim them.

Until now.

She appeared after nightfall in the shadow of the dunes. Lifting the hood of her burgundy cloak, she revealed a face remarkably unchanged from how it looked decades ago: the same piercing silver-flecked dark eyes, creaseless skin, and long hair plaited in the style of her girlhood. The only difference today was her purpose.

The woman glanced up at the stars before lowering to her knees in the sand. She bowed her head, letting the desert grains cover her skirts and run through her fingers as she murmured in the old, forgotten language—the one Agrabah would always respond to. And the ground began to shake.

Sand whipped through the air, swirling around the woman, who used her cloak as a shield against the onslaught. The grains spun before her, funneling into a tornado, until every last piece came together to form an unmistakable shape: a tiger's head, with sharp sandstone for jaws and teeth and a gaping mouth lit by fire.

The woman stepped forward and the tiger opened its mouth wider, revealing a glowing staircase within that beckoned her closer. *Welcome back, old friend.* She climbed inside.

The staircase spiraled more than a hundred feet down. Midway through the woman's descent, the tiger took a great, heaving breath that sent her pitching forward, sliding down the last stretch of steps. The faint glimmer of gold turned into an ocean of it as she landed on the cave floor and stepped through a gilded arch.

Mountains of gold coins soared up to the ceiling, beside trunks spilling over with diamonds, rubies, and pearls. Marble statues, some wearing glittering crowns and jeweled headpieces, towered above her. The lamp was gone, of course, but there were golden cups and plates, vases and urns, swords and shields, all strewn together in a priceless heap. It looked as though all the world's treasures had been collected in this one place, all of them hers. But none of these were what she had come here for.

She moved deeper into the cave, wading through the sea of riches until, at last, she found it: the one thing in this space that didn't sparkle. It was an austere structure of stone three times her size, designed to look like a temple and fronted by a line of alternating statues and pillars. She moved carefully down the line before stopping at the last statue.

From inside her cloak, she retrieved a small vial filled with dark red liquid. She lifted the glass top and turned the vial upside down, letting the blood drip onto her hands. She smeared her fingers across the stone, as if creating a macabre painting, and waited. And then, from behind the statue—a young man emerged. A man with soft black hair, eyes the color of night, and a determined gaze.

The woman reached out her hand, pulling him from the shadows and into the light.

. . .

Miles away from the Cave of Wonders, in an empty stretch of desert, a different man dug frantically through the sand. He had no concept of how far he was from the object of his obsession, and so the hunt continued, even after day turned to night and the last drop of water from his canteen had run dry. The darkness added another obstacle to his search, and the man kicked at a mound of sand in frustration, sending grains flying up into the air. Then, at last, something appeared . . . though it wasn't what he expected.

A flash of yellow materialized before him, remaining there like a rift or a tear in the sky. It hovered in the air, a floating chasm, and the man reached for it, captivated—

And drew his hand back sharply, as if he'd been burned. His eyes rolled back in his head; his body froze. When his eyes finally focused . . .

They were a glowing, fiery yellow. Yellow as the rift in the sky.

CHAPTER ONE

The coldest room in the palace was the one where Jasmine stood now, flanked by her father's viziers as they watched the mordeshu perform the washing of the corpse. She had never been summoned down here before, to a room without color, without windows—without a heart. There was nowhere to look but at the body, almost unrecognizable on the stone slab. Stripped of his royal turban and robes, he could have been anyone. But he was everything.

Jasmine clenched her fists, digging her nails into her palms to keep from breaking into tears. The others at court could afford to wear their grief openly, but not the princess. She would have enough people thinking her unfit to wear her father's crown based on age and gender alone. The last thing she needed was to prove their fears right by sobbing like an orphaned child—even though that was exactly what she'd just become.

The mordeshu ran the cloth over the sultan's upper body, leaving a soapy trail over arms that had just yesterday hugged Jasmine warmly after he promised that they could spend the next morning discussing plans for her upcoming wedding to Aladdin. But instead, when morning came, it was with the sound of screaming. The night had painted their world black, taking away a sultan and a father. Instead of a wedding, now there would be a funeral—and a coronation. Two occasions she felt entirely unprepared to face.

Just as we are born naked into this world, so we must leave it, covered in only the simplest cloth.

The words of Jasmine's tutor echoed in her mind as the mordeshu draped her father in a kafan, the white cotton shroud worn by the dead, and arranged the sultan's hands in prayer. Then he stepped back, bowing his head to Jasmine. It was time.

The viziers stepped aside and Jasmine inched forward, her heart lodged in her throat. For a split second she had the wild urge to flee, to escape this den of death and pretend none of it was real. But then she reached him, and all she wanted was to stretch these final moments, to make them last long enough that there would be no *after*. The tears she'd been fighting came spilling out as Jasmine knelt by her father's side, kissing his cheek one last time.

"Good-bye, Baba."

She was just rising to her feet when she felt it—a cold hand, shooting out and seizing her wrist.

"Jasmine."

She froze.

"Look at me."

Jasmine stared down in disbelief at the hand gripping her wrist, lined and weathered like her father's. With goose bumps prickling across her skin, she slowly lifted her gaze.

The sultan's dark eyes were wide open.

"Someone is coming, Jasmine." His thick brows knit together in an expression closer to fear than anything she'd seen before on her father's face. "Someone is coming, and I won't be here to protect you."

But Jasmine could barely make sense of his words. All she could register was the sound of his voice, the sight of his lips moving. *Alive* again . . . or something like it.

"I need you to be vigilant. Trust no one," he urged. "Do you understand me?"

"N-no! What do you mean?" Jasmine's voice shook. "Who's coming?"

"Find the book," the sultan continued, as if he hadn't heard her. "It will guide you where I cannot. Protect yourself and defend our people." His voice grew faint. "I'm relying on you now. My daughter."

Jasmine cried out as his hand slipped from hers.

"Wait! Please, Baba, don't go—"

"Your Highness!"

A sharp voice broke the spell. Startled, Jasmine glanced behind her at the grand vizier, Arman. When she turned back to her father, his eyes were closed, his body lifeless once more.

"You were shouting." Arman eyed Jasmine strangely as he offered her his arm. "Perhaps you should sit."

She didn't move, staring from Arman to her father's body and back again.

"You mean you didn't see . . . ?" Jasmine's voice trailed off as she silently answered her own question. Of course none of them had seen the sultan momentarily wake from the dead. There was no trace of a reaction from anyone else in the room. Clearly, she had imagined the entire thing.

But then Jasmine glanced down at her wrist, and her heart nearly stopped.

There it was—an indentation on her skin. A mark from her father's desperate grip.

. . .

Today wasn't the first time that Jasmine had sensed something supernatural within the palace. With so many storied figures having lived and died between these walls over the past centuries, it was only fitting that they would make their presence felt. She recognized them in the strange ring of light that sometimes skimmed across a sculpture of one of her ancestors in the Hall of Monarchs, or when her pet tiger, Rajah, would suddenly look up and growl at thin air—as if seeing something that shouldn't be there. Eerie as it was, she had always found it strangely comforting to live with ghosts in her midst. It meant that even in her solitary childhood, she had never been alone.

It was only recently that she had begun to feel something darker lurking among them.

"Are you . . . all right, Your Highness?" Jasmine's handmaiden, Nadia, watched her through the mirror, her face creased with concern as she helped Jasmine change into a black mourning dress.

Jasmine stared numbly back at her. The truth was, she couldn't even remember coming back up to her bedroom, or how long Nadia had been there with her. The last thing she recalled was being down in the lifeless room with her father. Seeing his eyes open one last time, with that look of uncharacteristic fear.

"No," she admitted. "But I'll have to be."

She glanced up, her eyes finding the portrait she always turned to for comfort. Two raven-haired women were woven into a magnificent tapestry on the wall, one sparkling with youth and the other elegant in middle age: the mother Jasmine couldn't remember and the grandmother she never got to meet. She knew every stitch of their faces by heart.

In her loneliest moments, Jasmine had imagined them watching and guiding her from beyond, like a secret council of her own. The two women shared the same enigmatic smile, and sometimes it felt like that smile was meant just for her—like it was trying to tell her something.

What would you say to me now? she asked them silently. But of course, there was never any answer. She looked away from the tapestry and back to the mirror, where Nadia was threading black ribbon in Jasmine's hair.

A knock sounded at the door.

"Jasmine?" The voice was warm and familiar, the voice she loved best—but it was missing its usual carefree spirit as Aladdin called out, "Jasmine, I'm here."

The sight of him in the palace was always a beam of light in the dark. Jasmine felt a wave of relief as she opened the door and Aladdin swept her up in his arms, wrapping her in a tight embrace. She buried her head against his chest, closing her eyes and breathing in the comforting scent of him as he murmured into her hair, "I'm sorry . . . I'm so sorry—"

He drew back abruptly, and that was when Jasmine noticed his red-rimmed eyes, the black tunic with a hole in the sleeve that she'd never seen him wear before. She reached for him again, but he kept his distance this time, dropping to his knees in a deep bow instead.

"Your Majesty," Aladdin whispered. "Sultana."

A jolt of shock ran through her.

"N-not yet," she said. "Not until the coronation."

But he was right. The title was hers.

"Even then, you don't need to call me that." She pulled him back up to his feet. "Call me what you usually do. Jasmine, or Princess, if you must."

Aladdin grinned at the all-too-literal nickname he'd given her when they first met, a nickname that had stuck. Still, there was something uneasy in his eyes as he said, "Things are going to change now, though, aren't they? Should I even . . . be here?" *In the monarch's bedroom.*

"Yes—and yes." Jasmine tried to smile back as she took his hand in hers. He kissed her fingers gently, but she knew him well enough to see the worry behind his expression. He was afraid of losing her. Jasmine wanted to reassure him, to tell him he was the one bright spot left in her life. But after the morning she'd had . . . she couldn't find the words.

"Apologies for the interruption, Your Royal Hi— Your Majesty."

Jasmine and Aladdin looked up to find Arman hovering in the doorway.

"They're all waiting to hear from you."

Jasmine nodded bravely, tightening her grip on Aladdin's hand. They followed the vizier down the white marble staircase that led from the palace's private upstairs wing to the Grand Atrium below, the glittering hub from which an endless parade of formal rooms extended. These gilded halls were as familiar as her own skin, but today she felt like a stranger, out of place amid the splendor. The silk curtains and plush carpets were too rich in color, the golden pillars and sculptures too dazzlingly bright—all wrong for a day like this one. And as they made their way toward the throne room, Jasmine could have sworn she heard a hissing sound following them.

"Do you hear that?" she murmured to Aladdin. "Behind us."

He glanced back, and then shook his head. It was gone, or maybe it had never been there at all. Now there was a new sound, a mournful hum of voices drifting toward them from the room ahead. Arman stopped in front of the gold-paneled double doors and gave Jasmine and Aladdin a pointed look, reminding them of protocol. She dropped Aladdin's hand; he took a step back. And then Arman opened the doors to a sea of black.

The throne room was packed with palace courtiers and staff, cabinet ministers and guards, most of them scarcely recognizable with their grief-sunken eyes and dark mourning clothes. A hush fell over the crowd as they all turned to stare at Jasmine.

She didn't think she could meet their eyes without joining in their tears, and she couldn't—wouldn't—cry. Instead, she looked straight past the crowd to the long carpet ahead, which beckoned like an outstretched hand, leading to a towering golden lion's head.

The sultan's throne sat just underneath, as regal and intimidating as the animal itself.

The audience dropped to their knees one by one, and it took Jasmine a moment to recognize the falling dominoes for what they were: her subjects, bowing to their new sovereign.

"Go on," Arman murmured behind her.

Barely breathing, Jasmine made her way up the red carpet, past the rows of bowed heads lining her path. The sultan's enormous velvet-backed chair sat empty, waiting, but she couldn't bring herself to take his seat. Not yet. She stood beside it instead, her hands planted firmly at her sides to keep them from shaking.

"Long live Sultana Jasmine of Agrabah!" a voice in the crowd shouted. "Blessed be her reign!"

Another voice took up the cry, and then another, and Jasmine finally let herself look out into their faces.

"Long live Sultana Jasmine of Agrabah!"

"Blessed be her reign!"

It was the moment she'd always known was coming—except no one had prepared her for it happening twenty years too soon. She had pictured this scene plenty of times as a young girl, imagining herself taking the throne as a wizened older woman with years of experience and triumphs behind her, the people of Agrabah rejoicing as they addressed their new sultana for the first time. Instead, when Jasmine looked at them now, she saw reflections of doubt. The strangeness of a woman—a young one, at that—leading what had always, always been a man's realm. That doubt was there in the puckered expression her court ministers shared, as though they had all drunk from the same sour cup. It was there in the halfhearted chants of her name, lacking the pride and vigor that always accompanied the cheers for her father. Of course, she couldn't blame them. She wasn't him.

The faces of Jasmine's court watched her expectantly, waiting for her to speak, to do *something* sultana-like. She cleared her throat, catching Aladdin's eye at the back corner of the room. He gave her an encouraging smile.

"Thank you, all," she began. "I know you loved my father the way I do. The way I did." There was a sharp pang in her chest, and she sped up her words. "I'll be counting on each of you to help me preserve the sultan's memory, not just for our lifetime, but for all lifetimes to come. And while I know that I have much to learn, and my ascent comes at a precarious time for Agrabah, with the recent... frightening occurrences in the city"—Jasmine paused, the memory of her father's frantic, late-night meetings the week before he died bringing a fresh wave of panic—"I pledge to you my commitment and devotion to our kingdom. To continue building on all the great progress the sultan created for Agrabah, and to return us to a safe and wondrous world."

She meant every word, yet she could see from the faces staring back at her that her speech hadn't convinced everyone. The doubt was still there... and Jasmine understood why.

The sultan had proven himself on the battlefield back when he was crown prince; he'd earned the people's love and reverence before he'd ever taken the throne. Meanwhile, as much as Jasmine had longed to leave the palace gates, in all her eighteen years she'd barely been allowed outside. The comparisons were inevitable, and yet impossible for her to match.

I'll have to find my own way, Jasmine realized as she gazed out at the crowd. *To turn my differences into strengths and prove myself a true leader.*

Maybe she too could be a diamond in the rough.

CHAPTER TWO

A tense silence permeated the air as Jasmine waited for her cue. Was she supposed to say more? Dismiss the crowd? She looked to the crown ministers before remembering: She was in charge now. It was up to her.

"Thank you again." Jasmine cleared her throat. "Please, take the day off from your duties to grieve and take care of each other. The ministers and I will keep you informed of the funeral arrangements once everything is settled."

She gave her audience a short wave and stepped off the dais, following the carpet-lined path to the double doors ahead and the promise of solitude that awaited. The crown ministers edged forward, trying to catch her attention, but Jasmine kept moving. She needed to be alone with her thoughts, especially as her father's words from earlier—real or imagined—played on a loop in her mind.

Someone is coming. Find the book.

"Jas—Your Majesty! Wait."

Nadia caught up with Jasmine just as her hand closed around the heavy door handle.

"I'm supposed to do that for you," she whispered, cheeks flushed.

Jasmine took a quick step back, letting her handmaiden open the door. She had never been one for rigid protocols, but she could see that her usual informality was out of place in this moment, this room. As soon as the two of them were through the doors and alone in the Grand Atrium, Jasmine could breathe again.

"You did well in there, Your Majesty," Nadia said. "The sultan would be proud."

Jasmine swallowed the lump in her throat. "Do you think so?"

"I'm certain, Your Majesty."

"Please don't call me that." She gave Nadia's arm a gentle squeeze. "I've always been Jasmine to you, and that's who I'll stay."

"Are you . . . sure?" At Jasmine's nod, the handmaiden continued, "It's just that I—I can't quite believe I went from serving my friend, the princess, to the *sultana* overnight." She shook her head in amazement, and it occurred to Jasmine how Nadia's life had changed along with her own. Working for the sovereign would mean a higher rank and responsibilities, and higher wages to support herself and her parents. As much as Nadia mourned the sultan, there was pride in her new position.

"In front of everyone else, then, you can follow the rules. But when it's just you and me"—Jasmine managed her first real smile of the day—"break them."

"All right, Jasmine." Nadia grinned back. "Now, let's go before those doors open and your ministers and subjects come swarming."

"I was headed to the Hall of Monarchs, actually." Jasmine

nodded at the gold-pillared archway peeking out from across the atrium's wide swath of marble. "There's no need to come with me. I won't be long."

"Of course." Nadia gave her a quick curtsy. "I'll see you at tea."

Jasmine waited for her to go, and then continued through the arch into a torchlit corridor. The hall was only one kilometer long, yet it always seemed like another world in here: darker than most of the palace, with no windows to provide any sunlight, and quieter too. Tall alabaster sculptures of Agrabah's past leaders lined the carpeted floor, while the burgundy-painted walls were hung with tapestries and paintings illustrating their many victories.

"I share their blood," she murmured, a swell of determination rising within her. "If they could do it, so can I."

Still, one truth proved impossible to ignore. Of all the dozens of sultans depicted in the Hall of Monarchs . . . not one was a woman.

Jasmine stopped in front of the last sculpture created for the reigning monarch. It was a life-sized likeness of her father, and she knelt before it, clasping the smooth, sculpted hand.

"What happened to you, Baba?" she whispered. "What were you trying to tell me before? Please—don't leave me like this."

The torchlights flickered. A sudden breeze rippled over the back of her neck, even though she was standing in a hall without windows. Soft footsteps sounded behind her, and Jasmine held her breath, every muscle in her body tensing with anticipation. *Baba—*

"Your Majesty."

Her hopes came crashing down to the floor. It was only Arman, and he wasn't alone. The captain of the sultan's army and the second-most-powerful figure in Agrabah, Commander Zohar, towered before her. He had the face of someone who rarely cracked a smile, with eyes that seemed to notice everything—eyes sharp enough to cut glass. A jagged battle scar ran from Zohar's left cheekbone down to his chin, where he wore his dark brown beard tied with gold braid at the end, denoting his high status. The commander had always been a more serious foil to the sultan's whimsical spirit, and Jasmine's mood sank lower at the realization that he would near constantly be in her presence now.

"Yes?" she said as the men bowed to her.

"You shouldn't be wandering alone, Your Majesty," Zohar said, a warning edge in his voice. "The heir must be protected. Especially while we are waiting on your father's cause of death."

Jasmine felt the floor lurch beneath her.

"What do you mean? Arman said it was a heart attack."

"That is what the court physician believes," Arman said hastily, shooting a glance at the commander. "Of course, until we have the final word from the court physician, we simply need to be . . . on guard."

On guard for what? Jasmine stared at the two men, and the meaning behind their words hit her square in the chest.

A possible killer.

She shook her head, warding off the fear before it could fester. The idea of it was impossible. The sultan was beloved, and the only man who had ever wanted him dead was long gone. Her ministers were just being overly cautious; that was it.

"Come with us," Zohar said, more of an order than a request. "Agrabah law states that the accession council must meet within twenty-four hours to proclaim the new monarch. This verbal declaration will hold only until a more official coronation can take place."

"And after the accession council, you'll stay for the sultan's—ah, the monarch's—weekly dinner with the crown ministers," Arman added.

"The dinner hasn't been canceled?" Jasmine looked from the commander to the vizier in disbelief. "It hasn't even been a full day since my father died. Surely you don't mean to carry on as if everything is normal . . . ?"

"No one is calling it normal," Zohar said pointedly. "You will be the one sitting in the sultan's chair."

His tone made her flinch.

"It is the jarring reality of death, Your Majesty," Arman said, his expression softer. "While another's life stops, ours must continue forward. In your case, that means following the sultan's routine and responsibilities without missing a step. We must ensure a smooth, immediate transfer of power for the good of our kingdom."

"After all, wherever there is a vacuum"—the corners of Zohar's mouth twitched—"chaos is free to fill it."

Jasmine side-eyed the commander. Was this meant to be encouragement—or intimidation?

"All right. Aladdin and I will be there."

"Just you," Zohar corrected her. "The consort-to-be never takes part in government dinners."

"Isn't that my decision?" Jasmine raised an eyebrow. "I am sultana now, aren't I?"

"Not until *after* the coronation," he said, swiftly putting Jasmine in her place. "Aladdin may be a part of your . . . personal life, but he is no statesman. If you want to be taken seriously by the ministers who run your government, you would do well to separate your young romance from your role as our country's leader."

His voice dripped with condescension. Jasmine felt a flash of fury.

"And *you* would do well to remember to whom you are speaking," she said, lifting her chin to meet his gaze. "This isn't just some 'youthful romance,' as you call it. Aladdin is my intended husband. The future consort to your sultana. Speak of him with respect."

The commander looked far more amused than impressed, but the color drained from Arman's face at her retort. In fact, Arman seemed almost . . . *fearful* as he glanced from Zohar to Jasmine and back again. What could he possibly be afraid of? It didn't make sense. Still, Jasmine lightened her tone when she addressed the commander again.

"Besides, Aladdin was always meant to play a bigger role than simply a consort. You'll recall that my father planned to have him apprenticed to Arman, and eventually serve as grand vizier himself one day."

"A fine plan, had your father lived," Zohar replied. "A son-in-law as grand vizier might be acceptable, but a husband of the crown? No."

He headed for the door, already moving on from the conversation, and Jasmine hurried to catch up.

"And why not? What is this rule I'm only just hearing about now?"

This time it was Arman who answered her. He placed a gentle hand on her shoulder, as if softening the sting.

"The role of grand vizier requires you to put the personal aside to see clearly and advise the sovereign correctly. You must look at them as a monarch first and a person second. Even if Aladdin were capable of that, which I'm sure we can all agree is unlikely, is that even what you would want?"

Jasmine dropped her gaze. *Of course not.* She'd fallen in love with Aladdin for his heart, and for the way he made her feel so blissfully, freely *herself.* Her true self, beneath all the layers that made up a princess. She would never want their relationship tangled up in the dynamic between sovereign and vizier.

A part of him would be relieved to hear it, Jasmine realized. Aladdin had never been comfortable around "the cloaks," the high-handed crown ministers who surrounded her father. And as she glanced up at Commander Zohar, she felt the same sense of unease . . . the uncertainty about whether he was truly on her side.

CHAPTER THREE

I t was Jafar's constant presence that had likely tainted the crown ministers in Jasmine's mind. Even now, approaching the council chamber months after he had been banished for good, she still half expected to see him standing inside with the others, that glaring snake staff in his grip. Jasmine had loathed him since childhood—her skin crawled under his gaze—but it was Aladdin who'd discovered the depths of his deception. If not for him, Jafar would still be high atop his perch of power, controlling the sultan and everyone in the palace with his dark magic. So when Jasmine walked into the council chamber and saw the burgundy-and-black cloaks sweep to the floor, the assembled group bowing before her, she couldn't help wondering who else among them had a secret. An agenda.

Baba trusted him—the same way he trusted everyone else in here.

The thought seemed to suck all the air out of the room. But as Jasmine approached her new seat at the head of the long mahogany table, she reminded herself of the key difference between Jafar and the advisers who remained. These others had already proven their loyalty. Whether they'd fought for the sultan in battle or guided him successfully through political conflicts with their neighbors around the Arabian Sea, each minister in their own way had shown they could be trusted. At least, as much as she could trust anyone in a royal court.

The council chamber had a distinctly masculine flair, with dark velvet and mahogany furnishings, elaborately carved stone walls, and glass display shelves lined with historic weaponry and other collectibles set in gold, silver, and onyx. The focal point of the room was a five-paned picture window opposite the table, a glass circle framed by four diamond-shaped sections. It was all ornamental, though: The window's frosted glass was impossible to see through.

Arman held out the sultan's chair, another high-backed seat of carved wood and red velvet. It was clearly built for a king's larger frame, and Jasmine's slight figure was nearly swallowed up in it as she sat and faced the ministers.

First in the lineup was Hassan, her father's longtime minister of law. He looked almost shell-shocked at the reality of who his leader had switched to overnight: the same rambunctious little girl he used to frown at in disapproval whenever he caught her chasing her pet tiger around the palace or playing pranks on the sultan's guests. If it weren't for the circumstances of her ascent, Jasmine would have been endlessly entertained by his reaction, imagining him sputtering alone in his room at the thought of having to work for *a princess who forgets to act like one!*—as he'd said to her with a sniff multiple times over the years.

Next was Khaleel, minister of Arabian nations and one of the younger members of the council, known around palace quarters by his booming voice. He was responsible for maintaining the peace and the prosperous trade routes between Agrabah and its Arabian neighbors. Beside him stood Majid, the softer-spoken minister of the treasury and another veteran of her father's inner circle. Where the other faces were solemn as stone, Majid's eyes were warm and kind behind his glasses. He smiled at her as he bowed.

The fourth minister stood out from all the rest, with long black hair swept up in a bun and ruby studs adorning her ears. Parisa, minister of arts and education, was the sultan's last hire, and the first woman to ever serve in Agrabah's government. Jasmine held Parisa's gaze a moment longer than she did the others', trying to convey with her eyes how much it meant to her that she was here, that there was another woman in this circle of authority. Because as much as people had bowed and scraped to the sultan all his life, Jasmine knew firsthand that the real power of the country was found behind these doors, with those who advised the sovereign and, in the process, shaped a kingdom.

Flanking the four of them were the two men who ranked at the top of the pyramid, just beneath Jasmine: Commander Zohar, decorated minister of war; and Arman, minister of the court and Jafar's replacement as grand vizier.

A long scroll unfurled across the mahogany table, dotted with the cuneiform script of the old language. *The proclamation.*

"As second-in-command and your proxy head of state, I call the accession council to begin," Zohar declared. "Crown ministers, be seated."

Chairs scraped against stone as the ministers took their places around the table. This was all meant to be just a formality, so . . . why did they look so uncomfortable?

"Today, your heads of government will decide whether you are fit to ascend the throne," the commander continued, and Jasmine's head snapped up. *What does that mean?* That they could refuse her birthright? Surely not . . .

"But first, Princess Jasmine, it's important to note that you too have a choice." Zohar peered at her perceptively. "I seem to recall a time when you were adamant that no palace or royal title should have you trapped."

Jasmine felt her cheeks turn hot. He was right, of course. There were so many days when her world had felt like a gilded prison cell, with no freedom or decisions of her own . . . and yet now that the commander was offering Jasmine the ultimate choice, the only one she could fathom making was to stay.

"I did feel that way once," she admitted. "But that was before I had my father's legacy and his kingdom to protect—and before I truly understood what it all meant. I would never abandon my duty now. Besides, even if I wanted to step aside, who would be your monarch then? I'm the last in my father's line."

"Well, in that event, we would move on to the closest male heir," Hassan answered too quickly.

Jasmine stared from Hassan to Zohar as the bitter truth dawned.

"That's what you want, isn't it? You *want* me to say no. Is it really so intolerable to see a daughter on the throne?"

Arman spoke up. "There's something else, Your Majesty. Another reason for you to consider your decision carefully. It's a . . . situation we find ourselves in. One that requires a firm hand and the strongest possible leadership."

Jasmine folded her arms.

"I'm listening."

To her surprise, Arman rose from his seat then, motioning for her to follow him to the picture window. As they drew closer to the glass, she drew in a sharp breath.

So it *was* a real window. Where before a thick layer of frosted glass had kept her from seeing outside, now that she was close enough to touch the window, it was as if an invisible curtain had lifted. Jasmine could see through clearly. Except . . . only the center windowpane showed the view of the palace grounds outside.

The other four sections of glass revealed entirely different scenes.

"Where— *What* is this?" Jasmine reached her palm up to the window in fascination, but quickly thought better of it, drawing her hand back before she made contact with the strangely enchanted glass.

"A secret passed down through centuries, shared only between the reigning sultan and his heir and council," Arman confided. "That means you must keep the secret too, Your Majesty. None of what you see or hear in this room can be discussed with anyone outside it—not even Aladdin or Nadia."

Jasmine nodded.

"I understand."

"As far as we know, it's existed for as long as the palace. It shows us what is happening in real time, in all four corners of our kingdom, with the palace in the center." Arman pointed to the glass circle, which reflected the rolling green lawns and mosaic-tiled fountain outside.

"From the cities to the west and the Seven Deserts to the east..." Khaleel joined them at the window, tracing the five panes with his finger. "And from the Alborz Mountains up north to the Orostan farmland down south, this window lets us keep close watch over Agrabah's borders. It's shown us where our people are most in need—and given us the key advance warnings to successfully fight off every attempted invasion of Agrabah from countries that want nothing more than to conquer us."

"And now it shows us this."

The commander's eyes narrowed as he pointed to the bottom right windowpane. Jasmine peered closer, astonished to discover how far she could see through the diamond-shaped sliver of glass: miles upon miles of desert backed by a valley of dunes. Stationed in the middle of an empty stretch of sand was a line of horse-mounted soldiers who appeared to be either guarding their territory or waiting for something...it was impossible to say which. Especially as the soldiers were shrouded in a layer of fog, a rare sight in hot desert climes.

"What *is* th—" Jasmine started, and then clapped her hand over her mouth as the fog started to move—creeping deliberately around the soldiers and horses like it had a mind of its own. As it slithered past, the areas that had been darkened by its shadow came into the light. That's when Jasmine saw the heap on the ground.

A fallen soldier and their horse, bodies splayed in the sand.

Dead as the dust.

"What happened to them?" Jasmine asked, willing her voice not to tremble.

There was a pause, as the ministers all exchanged a glance.

"We don't know yet," Arman finally answered. "But it's been like this for weeks now. We've had to send more and more men to our borders to replace those who've died at the hands of something no one can explain. Even this window, with all it shows us, brings us more questions than answers."

Protect yourself and defend our people.

Was this what her father had meant? Why hadn't he shared any of it with her while he was alive? He had told Jasmine of a few concerns keeping him up at night—strange weather patterns, disappearing goods from the bazaars that seemed to be the work of something beyond the usual petty criminals—but nothing like this.

Commander Zohar joined them by the glass, his sharp eyes returning to Jasmine.

"We find ourselves in dark times," he said in a low voice. "Think long and hard about whether you are the monarch to lead us through it."

For the first time since the meeting began, Jasmine felt a flicker of doubt. What if he was right? If there was a violent threat out there, wouldn't *anyone* agree that a battle-tested male monarch was the far better choice?

Unless...

"Baba used to tell me that there are many ways to lead," she said, remembering the words he shared with her. "Some people are strong in their physical being, others mentally, but he would say that a battle is never won on the front lines alone. It's won through hearts and minds, through commitment and strategy. As my father's daughter, I know I have what it takes within me." She stood straighter, gaining confidence. "Besides, isn't the purpose of the royal council to fill in the gaps, to balance the monarch's strengths and weaknesses? If I didn't need help defending Agrabah, then wouldn't that mean I didn't need . . . you?"

A surprised silence fell. The commander broke eye contact first, returning to his chair with a harrumph. There was the muffled sound of Majid's warm chuckle, and a slight smile exchanged between him and Parisa. Surveying the room, Jasmine could tell she had made her point. At least for now, in this moment, she had most—if not all—of their respect.

Hassan grudgingly smoothed the edges of the scroll on the table and handed her a reed pen. Jasmine signed her name to the accession proclamation, marking her as the next monarch. Her ministers signed their assent next, their expressions an odd mix of serene and grim as they passed the pen.

Jasmine was now one step closer to the crown—though only time would tell if she was the leader who could bring Agrabah through the coming darkness.

· · ·

"The ghūls were here first."

Taminah opened her book and eight-year-old Jasmine scampered over to sit cross-legged before her. She recognized the dilapidated sheath of parchment in her tutor's hands, the faraway glint in her eyes, and she knew what they meant. The regular lessons of the day were done, and now it was time for the prickly yet fascinating Taminah to do what she did best: frighten and thrill the young princess.

"Some say they were created in the fiercest of sandstorms, strong enough to shake the foundations of our land. Others say they were born of fire, like the jinn before them. What we do know for certain is that ghūls have lurked in the shadows of Agrabah, and throughout the Arabian Peninsula, for as long as man has recorded memories." Taminah leaned in closer, lowering her voice. "You'll find their images in the walls of Agrabah's oldest caves, etched in their own claw prints. Images like this one."

She turned the book to face Jasmine, holding the ghastly illustration aloft. Jasmine recoiled from the sight—but she couldn't look away from it, either.

"What . . . what do they want?" Her voice was somewhere between a whisper and a squeak.

Taminah smiled, revealing her crooked front teeth. The tutor never seemed happier than when she was sharing gruesome tales.

"To lure us to the underworld, of course," she said. "To feast on our flesh and grow in their power."

Jasmine let out a screech, covering her eyes, and Taminah chuckled. The sound of her tutor's laugh sent a wave of relief through Jasmine, as surely that meant it was all just a story. Nothing more.

Nothing real.

CHAPTER FOUR

J asmine called her first council dinner to begin. Servants entered the chamber right on cue, as if they'd been stationed outside the room waiting for her to say the magic words. They filled goblets from their silver pitchers and heaped plates high with kabobs, lemon-drizzled vegetables, saffron rice, and stew. Jasmine hadn't been able to eat a bite since her father's body was found, and now the sight of this feast turned her stomach. She pushed her plate to the side while her ministers tucked into the spread, discussing the fateful next steps for Jasmine and Agrabah between bites of food.

"The leaders of all neighboring nations have been notified of the sultan's passing, and most are journeying here at first daylight," Khaleel told her. "We're coordinating the funeral procession to align with their arrivals. These kings and statesmen will be staying here at the palace, of course."

Jasmine took a gulp from her goblet.

"Of course."

"They won't stay long," Arman added, clearly sensing her trepidation at the thought of a half-dozen rulers and their entourages descending on her in this time of grief. "Just until after the coronation on Saturday."

At that, Jasmine nearly spat out her drink.

"*Saturday?* I knew it would be soon, but . . . shouldn't we let a bit more time go by for the country to mourn my father first?"

"On the contrary," Majid said. "The excitement of a coronation is just the tonic your people will need after the pain of losing their sultan. They could do with a reassuring display of Agrabah's strength and vitality right now."

"Besides, it's customary for the rulers of allied nations to be present for the coronation of a new sovereign," Khaleel explained. "We'll hold the funeral at the end of the week, take our day of rest on Friday, and you'll be crowned the following morning." He spoke as breezily as if he were rattling off the schedule for a normal banquet week instead of two life-altering events.

Jasmine nodded, though something else was nagging at her now.

"What about my father's body? I thought the dead weren't supposed to remain unburied for longer than one day."

"For most people, yes," Hassan answered. "But for a man chosen from above like the sultan, different rules apply. We must wait until we can give him a state funeral worthy of his legacy, with all the heads of neighboring nations present."

"You needn't worry about his body," Arman told her. "The mordeshu will guard him day and night."

"On a happier note, we're declaring a three-day holiday for Agrabah, with everything from schools to bazaars and coin exchange houses closed," Parisa said. "This way, the entire kingdom can join in for both ceremonies."

"There's one nice thing in all of this," Jasmine said wryly. "Two extra holiday weeks for the people this year."

"Two?" Parisa looked at her quizzically.

"The wedding in six weeks, of course. Baba had already declared it a national holiday."

"Ah. Of course."

There was an awkward silence around the table, which Arman hurried to fill.

"Now, our order of service for both the funeral and the coronation will follow the traditions that have been in place ever since the reign of Cyrus the First. We don't expect you to know these details, so I've set aside time on your calendar tomorrow for me to brief you."

"I'm happy to meet, but I actually do know the old traditions," Jasmine replied. Arman's eyebrows lifted in surprise. "History is my strong suit."

She had long ago taken it upon herself to read every book in the palace library, after discovering just how flimsy her education was. While the sons and daughters of palace courtiers came home from school each day brimming with new knowledge, Jasmine was kept at home with a tutor—and her private lessons in etiquette and art weren't exactly the foundation that kings were built on. Sometimes Jasmine had the sneaking suspicion that Taminah never expected her to end up on the throne at all, that she was preparing the princess to be a royal wife instead. After all, she had mentioned more than once the possibility of Jasmine having a son in the future who could rule in her stead. But one thing the older woman had done right was introduce Jasmine to books, especially Agrabah's myths and fables, in which terrors jumped from every page. Stories with heroes and demons so vivid, they could have been real.

After she had read all the stories she could get her hands on, Jasmine moved on to history texts and illustrated maps. Hers might have been an incomplete education, but those books allowed a sheltered princess to see some of the world, both real and imagined. And they gave her a window into the past.

"If we're following the old coronation customs, those always included the monarch's consort or betrothed," Jasmine said, remembering. "That means Aladdin has a role in the ceremony. He'll need to be at tomorrow's meeting—" She stopped midsentence, catching the glances between her ministers around the table. "What is it?"

"Well. If Aladdin were a royal or nobleman himself, you would be correct," Parisa acknowledged. "But as it stands now, you so far outrank him that until you marry—if you still choose to do so—he must attend as simply a member of the palace court. Otherwise, we risk offending the blood royals who are traveling for days to be here."

If you still choose to do so.

Jasmine's mouth fell open at the words coming from the last person she would have expected to say them. Did her ministers really think Jasmine might call off the wedding now that she was stepping into power?

One look around the table told her they were not only thinking it—but that was what they were all hoping.

Later, in her canopied bed shrouded by blue silk curtains, the dark night seemed to echo Jasmine's mood. She tossed and turned for hours, and had just managed to fall asleep when she heard Rajah's warning growl. The bed shifted beneath her as the pet tiger leaped off his perch, lunging toward a sound in the near distance—the sound of creeping footsteps. Jasmine sat up quickly, holding the covers tight to her chest.

"Nadia?" she whispered, even as she knew it couldn't be her. Rajah only reacted this way to a threat.

Suddenly, through her bed curtains, she saw a shadow dart past. A shadow so large, it dwarfed the tiger chasing it. And now she could hear heaving breaths, coming closer—a sound more bestial than human. Jasmine shrank back, frozen, as each snarling breath and creak of footsteps in the room sent cold waves of terror through her.

"*Guards!*" she tried to shout, but her voice sounded like it was coming from underwater, strangled with fear. No one could hear her but Rajah, whose growls turned to whimpers as the shadow kicked him to the ground. Jasmine could see the looming outline of something long and sharp now, inching toward her—the silhouette of a dagger.

She dove to the foot of the bed, dodging the knife just before it sliced through her curtains. Rajah leaped up off the floor, roaring in fury as he tore toward the intruder, giving Jasmine a moment to slide off the edge of the bed. Her feet hit the carpet and she readied her fists, ill-equipped but determined to fight back. Whatever monster belonged to this shadow . . . she wouldn't let it take her.

Jasmine looked up, bracing for the worst, but the room had grown darker somehow; she could barely see a thing. She stumbled forward, eyes searching for the intruder, for Rajah—yet there was only a brief flicker of something flapping overhead, followed by an almost imperceptible hiss, and then silence. Nothing but black.

She grabbed a lantern from her bedside table, lighting it with trembling fingers. Through the thin beam of light, she saw . . . her same old bedroom, looking immaculate and untouched, with Rajah crouched by her chaise sofa. He whipped his head back and forth before turning to her with bewildered eyes. The shadow was gone.

Jasmine sank to her knees, her heart still thundering in her chest.

"You got rid of him, didn't you, Rajah? I don't know what I would have done. . . ." She buried her head in the tiger's fur. "What *was* that—that thing?"

Rajah let out a pained groan in response, and then slumped onto the floor. That was when Jasmine noticed his front paw, swollen and bent at a sharp angle.

"It hurt you," she gasped.

This time when she shouted for the guards, they heard her. Two of them appeared in the doorway within minutes, and, to her surprise, Aladdin was right behind them. He took one look at her face and raced through the spacious bedroom to her side.

"Jasmine! What's wrong?"

He clasped both her hands in his. It occurred to Jasmine that this was the first time he had ever been inside her room in the middle of the night—and the first time he'd seen her in a night-dress, its soft fabric clinging to her curves. She should have been flushed with embarrassment, just like the guards who were currently making a big show of averting their eyes, but she was too relieved by his presence to care. Instead, she pulled him closer.

"Are you all right, Princess?" He peered down at her closely. "What happened?"

Jasmine hesitated. How was she supposed to explain this in a way that they would all believe?

"There was an intruder," she said finally. "One minute it was right there, about to attack me with a knife, and the next minute, gone. Rajah helped me, and now he's hurt. . . . Whoever or whatever was here, it was strong enough to break a tiger's paw."

"Your Majesty." One of the men stepped forward, clearing his throat. "We have a guard posted at each wing, and others patrol the grounds. No one has reported anything."

The subtext behind his words was clear enough. *You must have imagined it.* Jasmine exhaled in frustration, and the second guard quickly added, "Of course, do tell us all you can about the intruder, what he looked like or any other important detail you remember. We will investigate further."

Except she couldn't tell them the one thing the intruder had reminded her of. They would only be more skeptical and say it was all just a nightmare, that the name on her lips belonged to a man long gone, with no way of returning. Because the only other time she'd seen a shadow so big, it was Jafar transformed.

It wasn't him. I would have known. Rajah would have sensed it too. Besides, Jafar was currently locked up in a lamp deep below the desert sand. That didn't make the intruder any less frightening, though. Jafar had proven that the dark jinn of Taminah's stories could, in fact, exist. Where there was one . . . couldn't there be more?

"I didn't get a good look," she finally answered. "I just know that it seemed . . . larger than life."

While the guards still looked dubious, Aladdin's brow was creased with worry.

"Do you have any idea who would want to hurt you?"

"I don't know." Jasmine gripped his arm tighter. "Someone . . . who doesn't want me on the throne?"

"Whoever it was, they would have to be living here in the palace," Aladdin said darkly. "Someone with access to your room."

Or someone not actually living *at all.* The thought sent a cold shudder down her spine. *Something able to appear and vanish at will.*

"I'm staying here with you the rest of the night to keep watch," he declared.

The older guard looked sideways at Aladdin and let out a sound somewhere between a cough and a snort.

"Not unless you want to tarnish the princess's reputation, you're not! One of us guards will remain posted outside her door tonight and every night, until Her Majesty feels safer."

"Well, then I'll join you," Aladdin said stubbornly. "So the princess knows I'm just outside."

"It's all right," Jasmine told him. "You don't have to do that."

"I want to. After what happened to the sultan . . ." He trailed off. "Well. It will help me breathe easier too, knowing I'm close enough if you should need me."

Jasmine squeezed his hand, touched.

"Thank you, my love." She turned back to the guards. "Could one of you please take Rajah to the menagerie?"

The tiger grunted his objection and sidled closer to Jasmine. It was then that she noticed his protective stance, the way he'd stuck to her side since the arrival of the intruder.

"I'll be all right," she assured him. "I won't be alone. Go on."

After Rajah limped out of the room with the first guard, Jasmine glanced up at the second.

"One last thing. Please send for the court physician, Doctor al-Razi, first thing in the morning. Have him bring me his notes on my father's condition when he died."

CHAPTER FIVE

After the guards and Aladdin had left her room and all was quiet, Jasmine's heartbeat finally started to slow—until she remembered Aladdin was just on the other side of the wall, and suddenly it was racing out of her chest again. He was so close . . . and aside from a smattering of guards, they were the only two people awake in the palace.

She couldn't have fallen asleep even if she tried.

Jasmine tiptoed closer to her bedroom doors, pressing her ear against the wall. The guards were trained to be silent, but not Aladdin. Sure enough, she only had to listen for a minute or two before she heard the rustle of his clothing, the sound of his exhale. Jasmine grinned and tapped lightly against the wall. *I'm here.*

There was a pause, and then he murmured from the other side, "Good night to you too, Princess." She could hear the smile in his voice.

"I wish you were in here," she said. "With me."

Maybe it was the excitement from her scare, or maybe it was

the wall between them that had her feeling bolder than usual. She heard him take another breath, then a step closer. She could picture him so clearly, pressing his palms against the white stone wall, the dimple forming in his cheek as he said her name. *Smiled* her name.

"Soon," he whispered. "When we're man and wife, we won't have to spend another night apart."

The thought sent a delicious shiver through her.

"Well, now I'm not sure I'll ever sleep tonight," she quipped.

"We can stay awake together, then," he replied. "With our third wheel, of course." He rapped at the wall, and Jasmine laughed. She reached her hand up to the stone as if she could feel Aladdin through it.

"Till the sun rises."

"Till the sun rises," he echoed.

She heard him slide down to sit with his back against the wall, and she followed suit. They were sitting back-to-back now, the thick stone wall between them. And before long they were talking about everything and nothing, his voice her comfort in the dark.

· · ·

Jasmine blinked as sunlight streamed through the curtains, stirring her from her position curled up on the Persian carpet. She must have fallen asleep in spite of herself after whispering through the wall with Aladdin till dawn. She smiled at the memory.

A knock sounded at the door, too soft to be his.

"Jas—Your Majesty? Doctor al-Razi is here to see you. I've brought Rajah back too."

"Oh, good." Jasmine hoisted herself up from the carpet. "You can bring them in. Thank you, Nadia."

The first thing she noticed when Nadia opened the door was the bandage around her tiger's paw. It was the only mark of last night's events. He seemed otherwise content, though even more attached to Jasmine than usual as he rushed to her side, nuzzling her shoulder while she crouched to inspect him.

"Did Bahman at the menagerie say anything about the injury?" she asked, glancing back up at Nadia.

"He told me it's nothing to worry about. Just a sprain from landing a jump poorly, most likely." She gave Jasmine a questioning look. "Is that what happened?"

Jasmine hesitated.

"I don't know."

It could have been just a nightmare. Rajah could have gotten hurt some other way, like Bahman said.

In the bright light of morning, it was tempting to wonder if she had dreamed it all. And with the stress she was under, after the things she'd seen in the council chamber yesterday, it was hardly a stretch to believe that Jasmine's mind would run away with itself.

She glanced through the door. Aladdin was gone; he must have slipped away quietly before daybreak. Instead, Agrabah's most renowned physician and polymath stood before them, eyeing the tiger warily. He wore a simple white cotton robe and tunic, always keeping his brilliance hidden behind plain clothes.

"Come in, Doctor al-Razi." Jasmine motioned him inside. "Don't worry, Rajah's very friendly. Aren't you, Rajah?"

The tiger gave a noncommittal grunt. Doctor al-Razi stepped in gingerly, then gave her a deep bow.

"My deepest condolences on your loss, Your Majesty. It was the honor of my life to serve your father."

"Thank you, Doctor. I know how much he appreciated you."

"Before I share the report you requested, I must remind you that only you as next of kin can view or hear the contents." He looked meaningfully at Nadia, and she gave a quick curtsy.

"I was just on my way out."

Once the two of them were alone, the doctor pulled a sheaf of parchment from his cloak pocket. Jasmine reached for it nervously, suddenly unsure of what she hoped to find. Was there anything in this report that could possibly reassure her when the worst had already happened?

She held her breath as she read, poring over the sultan's medical notes until the familiar turned foreign. Under the heading *Current Conditions*, where she expected to find nothing more than a mention of her father's mild arthritis, Doctor al-Razi had listed:

- *Heart palpitations*
- *Headaches*
- *Sleep disturbances*
- *Hallucinations*

The paper crinkled in Jasmine's shaking hands as she stared up at the doctor.

"He never told me any of this," she whispered. "He gave no sign of being unwell. . . . *Hallucinations?*"

"These were all new symptoms that the sultan developed in the weeks before his death," Doctor al-Razi explained. "Also . . . he was adamant about not sharing any information that might frighten you."

Jasmine's heart thudded in her chest, her mind flashing back to the grim scene in the council chamber window. Those strange deaths had apparently been occurring for weeks, and yet her father had hidden them from her too.

"Baba overprotecting me, as always." Jasmine shook her head, aching for a way to go back and undo it all. "What were they? The hallucinations, I mean."

Doctor al-Razi shifted his weight, his face troubled.

"There was no making sense of them. He spoke of—of seeing demons infiltrate the palace grounds. Of a book hidden within the walls that he was desperate to find." At the look on Jasmine's face, Doctor al-Razi placed a gentle hand on her shoulder. "It's not uncommon, Your Majesty. Even kings among us revert to children at the very end of their lives, troubled by nightmares and imaginations running wild. I wouldn't advise reading into any of it. You'll see in my notes that it was the combination of these symptoms and his physical state when he was found that led me to rule his cause of death a heart attack."

Find the book.

So then she hadn't imagined it. He really had spoken to her. And if that was real . . . so was last night.

"Was there any sign of—" Jasmine took a shallow breath, steeling herself. "Any sign of struggle at the end?"

"No, nothing like that." The doctor paused. "Only a head injury consistent with his fall."

Jasmine's insides clenched.

"What? What fall?"

"Oh—oh, I am sorry, Your Royal Highness, I thought you knew. The sultan's body was found steps away from his bed. Based on his condition when I examined him, it was evident he had gotten up when his symptoms worsened in the night, and then—"

"Don't say any more," Jasmine interrupted, turning away. "I understand. Thank you, Doctor." She couldn't bear to imagine her father calling out for help in the middle of the night, or the even more frightening possibilities currently swimming in her mind. It dawned on Jasmine now what she'd been hoping to find: proof that the sultan's heart had simply stopped beating in his sleep, and nothing more. The doctor might have believed his own words of reassurance, but Jasmine had a sinking feeling the truth was far more sinister.

Something had clearly been tormenting her father just before his death. Was it the same *something* responsible for the men and horses she saw through the mirror, their bodies contorted in the sand? The same shadowy figure that had come so close to attacking her in her sleep?

These couldn't be mere coincidences. And with a plethora of royal guests descending on the palace, and a public funeral and coronation imminent—she knew she had to find out the truth.

CHAPTER SIX

J asmine didn't have much time before the guests would begin to arrive, and she needed to start looking for answers. A visit to the crypt would allow her the chance to see her father—and perhaps his spirit would have another message for her. But the mordeshu would be there, eerily silent, watching her. If word traveled back to the ministers that she had been trying to communicate with her dead father, she would lose even more of their confidence. Still, there was one other place she could try that just might hold the key. . . .

She opened her bedroom door and stepped out into the plush-carpeted corridor, Rajah following at her heels. The two nearly collided with the guard posted outside Jasmine's room, and when he looked up from his startled bow, she recognized him as Payam, one of the guards who had been tasked with keeping a closer watch on her father in the aftermath of Jafar. *Quite a serious young man,* she remembered the sultan once commenting about him. *Which makes him an excellent guard, but not exactly a barrel of fun.*

Baba, he isn't supposed to be fun. Jasmine had laughed. *He's here to protect you.*

True, the sultan had conceded, a twinkle in his eye. *But never underestimate a good sense of humor. It makes even the longest days fly by.*

Jasmine swallowed the lump in her throat and forced a quick smile.

"Morning, Payam. I'm off to the library," she fibbed.

He moved as if to accompany her, and Jasmine waved him off.

"Thank you, but there's really no need."

She could see the conflict playing out on his face, unsure of whose orders to obey.

"But—but the sovereign shouldn't be—"

"I have Rajah with me. I'm not alone," Jasmine reminded him. "Besides, it's only the library. I'm sure a paper cut is the biggest threat there." She grinned, but he was too apprehensive to smile back.

"Well . . . if you insist," he said, with one more glance at her and Rajah.

"I'll be just fine. See you soon, Payam."

Jasmine headed toward the grand staircase, still watching him out of the corner of her eye. As soon as she saw Payam turn his head, she darted away from the stairs and toward the sultan's suite, motioning for Rajah to be quiet as he followed. The household wing of the palace was like a chain of decorative rooms, with the monarch's bedchamber the crown jewel in the chain. Nearly the size of a ballroom and appointed with the finest furniture, Persian carpets, and art from across Arabia, it managed to be both a picture of opulence and a cozy retreat, the place where Jasmine got to see her father as Baba instead of the sultan. It was normally a hub of activity in the mornings, with guards, servants, and viziers filtering in and out, and the contrast today felt like yet another sign of the world turned on its axis. It was so empty, so quiet. Jasmine felt a tightening in her chest as she pushed open the filigreed golden door.

She wasn't sure what she'd been expecting—blood on the floor, a stripped bed—but she certainly expected *something* to mark the loss of life that had taken place in here. Instead, it was as if nothing had ever happened. The chambermaid hadn't missed a day. The bed was freshly made with the sultan's monogrammed burgundy linens and piled high with embroidered pillows, while the sash curtains on the floor-to-ceiling windows were tied back, showcasing the view of the sand dunes and a blue sliver of the Tigris River beyond. The sultan's private dining alcove was even set for his next meal, with velvet cushions spread on the floor for companions, and silver goblets, plates, and flatware waiting on the table. Strangest of all was the fresh incense wafting through the suite, which Jasmine found burning in its brazier on top of the marble fireplace.

"Baba?" she whispered.

She felt him in here. *Alive* in here.

Jasmine crept forward to his writing table, Rajah padding behind her. A long alabaster box sat at the center of it, carved with the sultan's royal seal. Her breath caught as a memory hit her like a tidal wave: ten-year-old Jasmine, curled up with a book at her father's feet while he worked through the piles of parchment in the box, full of official correspondence from his ministers and satraps, the governors who ruled neighboring provinces in the sultan's name.

"One day, Jasmine azizam, this will be your job too," he had said, peering down at her with a serious expression. "It's the most important work a mortal could ever do: taking care of an entire kingdom and its people. Is that something you can see yourself doing one day? Ruling just like your Baba?"

"I only have to do it if you don't have a son." Jasmine had shrugged off the question with all the carefree obliviousness of a child.

An inscrutable expression had come over her father then. He opened his mouth to say something and stopped, as if thinking better of it. And then he reached down to squeeze her shoulder.

"There will be no son, Jasmine," he had said. "*You* are the one."

Back in the present, tears were spilling down Jasmine's cheeks. If only he were here—not as a ghost or a vision, but as her solid, warm, breathing Baba. She squeezed her eyes shut, imagining what he would say: *Go on, azizam. The present is the perfect time to begin.*

She lifted the lid off the box, expecting to find a mountain of sultan business that was now hers to finish. But there were only a few pieces of folded parchment left inside. Jasmine picked up the small pile, glancing at the names written in her father's hand on the outside of the parchment—and she froze.

There was only one name. Hers. *They were all addressed to Jasmine.*

Jasmine's fingers tripped over themselves in her haste to unfold the first piece of parchment, and she could hear her heart pounding in her ears as she began to read:

There was a door to which I found no key
There was a veil past which I could not see
Some little talk awhile of me and thee
There seemed and then no more of thee and me.

Jasmine stared at the words, disappointment seeping through her. What did it even *mean*? Was it a poem? A riddle? How could her father's last message be so cryptic?

She unfolded the next two pages, and her stomach dropped. It was the same four lines, scribbled over and over, like a compulsion—and dated just before he died. But one of the pages included additional lines.

One thing is certain and the rest is lies
The flower that once has blown forever dies.

Just underneath, with his handwriting growing more jagged, he'd written:

Take this flower,
Take this flower.
T

Goose bumps rose on her skin. *What flower?*

Was this one of the hallucinations Doctor al-Razi had spoken of?

She traced the final letter *T* with her fingertip, the interrupted word, wondering what had stopped him from completing it. Was he writing this when the end had come for him?

"He knew," she whispered to Rajah. Her father must have sensed he was dying, and he'd left her this incoherent warning. But as she studied the words over and over again, they began to look like more than just a warning. An answer, maybe, to a puzzle she was meant to solve . . . if she only knew what the puzzle was.

"Your Majesty."

Jasmine's heart jumped in her throat as Rajah let out a low growl. They weren't alone.

She turned and felt a flash of indignation at the sight of Payam.

"I told you I didn't need anyone to come with me—"

"To the library," he said pointedly. Jasmine's face grew hot.

"I *was* on my way there, I only stopped here first. To . . ." She let her words trail off; she didn't owe him an explanation. This was her father's room, after all.

"To remember," he guessed, his voice softer.

Jasmine looked up in surprise.

"Yes." She paused. "And what brings you here?"

"I thought I heard something. We've been instructed to continue monitoring the sultan's suite, to make sure nothing is . . . amiss." His eyes briefly flicked over to the alabaster box, and Jasmine tightened her grip on the three pieces of parchment in her palm.

"Only me."

She waited for him to take the hint and leave, but he stayed planted, a mask of a smile on his face. Her search would have to continue later. And as Jasmine turned for the door, she felt Payam's curious eyes on her back.

CHAPTER SEVEN

To tell them or not? That was the question echoing in Jasmine's mind later that afternoon, as she made her way from the Grand Atrium to the council chamber for her next meeting with the crown ministers. Surely her advisers needed to know her theory that something had *happened* to the sultan, something she couldn't yet explain, but something far removed from anything natural . . . didn't they? Shouldn't they be alerted to the almost certain danger Jasmine was in? But then she remembered the way the ministers had looked at her during that first meeting, how few of them seemed to believe in her. All she had to do was voice her vulnerabilities and they would go racing back to the idea of finding the nearest male heir.

I would be safer, no doubt, if they did, she thought. Yet if there was one thing she knew, a fact instilled in her since birth, it was that Jasmine was destined to be the first female ruler of the kingdom—and that meant something, not just to her but to every other girl across Arabia. It meant too much for her to give up in fear.

She would have to solve the mystery herself—and, until then, remain quiet about all she had seen and heard.

The sight of the long scroll unfurling across the council chamber table, bearing the names of every prominent royal and ally currently on their way to the palace for the funeral and coronation, was enough to temporarily wipe the secrets from her mind. Jasmine pored over the list as her ministers gathered round, full of their reminders about who ranked above whom, who owed a debt to Agrabah and whom the sultan had owed in return. She stopped short at one name in particular.

"Not Prince Achmed! We can't possibly have invited *him*."

She shuddered at the memory of his sneering face—even though the ironic fact was that Jasmine had this revolting prince to thank for her meeting Aladdin in the first place.

The sultan, growing desperate as he watched his daughter turn down every suitor that came calling, had made it his mission to get her engaged to an eligible royal by her eighteenth birthday. Jasmine could remember asking him time and again why it even mattered. "Why should I even need a husband when I'm sultana of Agrabah?"

The sultan had looked at her sadly as he said, "Jasmine, azizam. That is the very *reason* you need a husband. The people have never before known a woman ruler. If you want them to accept you long after I am gone, if you want to keep uprisings at bay, you must have a powerful man by your side."

She had scoffed at her father's words, but her father forged ahead with his great hope: Achmed, the prince of Batana. Rumors swirled that his palace of jasper and marble rivaled all others throughout

Arabia, complete with precious jewels encrusted in the windows and walls—something that sounded more ridiculous than impressive as far as Jasmine was concerned. They said his kingdom was rising to great heights of prosperity under his father's astute leadership, that noble young ladies were clambering over each other to be the handsome prince's bride. But as the sultan told Jasmine in delight, "The only lady he deems worthy enough is you!"

She had grudgingly agreed to meet him, not that she had much choice in the matter. As soon as he paraded up to the palace with an entire army and a swarm of courtiers and nabobs riding behind him, not to mention an actual *animal menagerie*, Jasmine instantly knew she couldn't spend a day, much less a lifetime, with this man. Anyone who had to puff themselves up to that extent wasn't for her. It was the same reason she had initially rebuffed "Prince Ali," until he revealed who he really was. An unpolished but true gem would always be her choice over the flashy and ostentatious pretenders.

Sure enough, their conversation was dull as old nails, consisting mostly of Prince Achmed boasting about his kingdom and palace, his "accomplishments," and how lucky Jasmine was that he had plucked *her* from all the young ladies whose fathers were begging him to marry their daughters. (Never mind the fact that Jasmine was heir to Agrabah's throne—oh no, *that* had nothing to do with his interest in her.) "Together, you and I will be the royal couple that everyone around the world dreams they could be."

"I'm afraid I don't share that dream," Jasmine had said bluntly. "I'm sorry if you wasted your time coming here."

She'd never been one to hide her feelings, after all. But her response incensed the prince. "I've never been so insulted in all. My. Life!" he sputtered. "*No one* turns down Prince Achmed! What kind of ungrateful, foolish, uncouth princess are you?"

Jasmine had to fight back giggles as she watched him storm out of the palace in a huff, tossing his cape with dramatic flair. But her smile had slipped as soon as her father entered the room, despair etched across his face.

"If not him, you must pick someone," the sultan had said without a trace of humor. "And soon. I say this for your own protection."

That was the night Jasmine hatched her plan to disguise herself as Nadia and escape the palace. She hadn't known how long she planned to stay away—maybe an hour, maybe forever—but she knew she would suffocate if she stayed a moment longer in this golden cage, under this pressure.

And then she'd met Aladdin in the marketplace, and her whole world opened up, her life exploding into color. If anyone had asked her that day or in the months since if she would consider inviting Prince Achmed back to the palace for any reason, Jasmine would have laughed out loud.

"I don't want him here," she told the ministers now, returning to the present moment. "Especially not when I'm burying my father."

"Snubbing the prince of Batana would be a grave mistake," Commander Zohar said sharply. "If you are as committed to Agrabah as you say, then you should know how crucial the alliance is between our two kingdoms—an alliance that has already been weakened, I must say, by your rather harsh rejection of the prince."

"He deserved it."

"Even if he did, it was still a political misstep," Khaleel said, speaking up. Jasmine's face turned hot at the reprimand. "Agrabah would be a far less prosperous country without the business and trade Batana brings us. The fact is, we need them."

"All right," Jasmine said, relenting. "I'll see if I can smooth things over with the prince. It certainly helps that I don't have to endure any more of his offensive marriage proposals now that I'm about to be wed." Her smile faded as she took in her ministers' expressions. "What is it now?"

"About the wedding," Parisa said carefully. "We took a vote, and, well, it was a nearly unanimous decision. We all feel you would be wisest to postpone the marriage for at least one year."

"What?" Jasmine's mouth fell open. "Why? And who are you to take a *vote* on my marriage?"

"It's a matter of public interest and concern now," Hassan said. "We're already asking the commoners of Agrabah to accept a new sovereign who is different from anything they've ever known. Add a man of the streets as their king consort, and we could be facing a revolt."

"I disagree. I think it would only strengthen our ties to the people—or the 'commoners,' as you call them—if they saw themselves represented in the next king consort," Jasmine insisted.

"And what of the aristocrats? The landowners whose taxes pay for the upkeep of our kingdom? How do you think they would react to having to bow to a man like Aladdin?" Zohar countered.

"It wouldn't be forever," Arman said hurriedly. "We're not asking you to call off the engagement entirely. It would only be a strategic delay, to give all the people the time they need to get used to Aladdin."

Jasmine turned away from the table. She didn't want them to see her thinking, debating this dilemma in her mind.

When we're man and wife, we'll never have to spend a night apart....

How could she put him off when their love, their future together, was the light she'd been holding on to during the darkest of days?

Then again . . . that line of thinking was Jasmine reacting from the heart, which was exactly what her ministers both expected and dreaded from her leadership. She knew instinctively that no one in this room had much confidence in her ability to make the kind of tough, necessary decisions for the good of the kingdom that her father had been so capable of. If she chose Aladdin over their advice, would she be proving them right?

Being a selfless leader meant putting her own dreams to the side in order to be the ruler her kingdom deserved. And if the people needed time to get used to the idea of Aladdin, time for the country to stabilize before she wed someone so unexpected . . . then she would give them that time.

"All right," Jasmine said, turning back to face them. "I'll do it."

CHAPTER EIGHT

The news weighed on Jasmine's mind all through dinner. Aladdin didn't question why she was so quiet at the table or why she hardly touched her food, no doubt connecting it to the funeral coming up in the morning and all the heavy tasks that hung over her. While the funeral filled her with dread, it was the thought of hurting Aladdin that sent a stab of guilt through her every time she looked at him. But she knew the conversation couldn't wait.

It wasn't until they were walking hand in hand up the grand staircase to their rooms that she finally gathered the nerve to say it.

"My crown ministers gave me some advice at our meeting today," Jasmine began, not looking at him. "About us."

She felt Aladdin's hand stiffen in hers. "Oh?"

"Yes, they feel it's important that we move our wedding date to—to next year," she blurted. "They insisted that it's too much change, and too many ceremonial occasions, to put the kingdom through in such a short time. But it's only a little delay, and then we'll be married."

Jasmine was careful to gloss over the ministers' snobbish comments about Aladdin, and to end her news on an optimistic note. But when she finally met his eyes, she found his usual spark dimmed. He sensed the truth she wasn't saying. Jasmine's heart twisted.

"It's only temporary," she said, echoing the same reassurance Arman had tried on her.

"A year," Aladdin said. "At the least."

"I'm sure it wouldn't be any longer than that."

They'd reached Jasmine's bedroom now. He opened the door for her, and she motioned for him to follow her inside. While she moved toward the balcony, he hung back.

"Jasmine," he said suddenly. "Are you still . . . sure about us?"

The question stopped her cold.

"Of course I am," Jasmine whispered, turning to face him. "Remember last night, everything I told you?"

"I'll always remember it." He looked down at her, ruefully. "But here we are now."

"I don't have any doubts about you," she assured him. "Only the timing."

"Then are you sure about this?" Aladdin asked, gesturing at the palace around them. "Taking the throne and giving up all the things you used to dream of, like traveling the world together?" He paused, softening his tone. "You just seem . . . different today. You're changing already."

Jasmine felt her defenses rise at his words.

"I'm only growing up, and maybe you should too. We always knew this would happen someday. I was born into a life in which

I'm meant to rule. Not all of us have the freedom to be as carefree as you."

Aladdin stepped back, stung.

"You mean not all of us have as little to lose."

Jasmine winced. "No, that's not what I meant. I just . . ." She sighed, pacing beside the bay windows. "You have to know, I still want the life we were planning before. A marriage filled with travel and adventure, beyond the roles we were both born into. Children when we're ready for them, instead of just to produce an heir." She turned to look back at Aladdin. "It's not my fault things turned out so different from what we planned."

Aladdin joined her at the window, his expression contrite.

"I know." He wrapped his arm around her. "I miss him too."

Jasmine blinked back sudden tears.

"I owe it to my father and my country to do my duty, to be the best sultana I can be. It just seems like the only way I can make everyone happy is by being a copy of my father, and I'm simply not him. I don't know anything about being a leader."

"You're more ready for this than you think. You've spent the better part of eighteen years watching and learning from the sultan." Aladdin paused. "You just need time to mourn two people first."

Jasmine glanced up at him questioningly.

"Two?"

"Your father, of course, but also the Jasmine you once were," he said. "The woman you might have been, if life hadn't changed overnight."

She drew in her breath.

"You're right. That is what it feels like—like that old Jasmine is gone."

"I know. When my mother died, I thought my life was over too," he confessed. "The childhood part definitely was. I had to grow up fast if I was going to survive on the streets as a ten-year-old, with no one but Abu." He grinned sheepishly. "But I had no idea what was coming."

"She would be so proud of her boy if she could see you now," Jasmine said. "If anyone deserves to be at my side when I take the throne, it's you: the man who saved my father, and all of us, from Jafar."

"I would do it all a hundred times over for you, Jasmine," he said, looking at her in the way that always brought a delicious flutter to her chest.

The two of them clasped hands, the tension evaporating between them. Jasmine gazed out through the window, past the lantern-lit gardens and sparkling crystal fountains of the palace grounds, toward the sand dunes and mountains towering in the distance. They were promises of thrills waiting to be discovered . . . if she could only get to them.

"Do you remember what you said when we first met, when you thought I was a handmaiden?" she asked Aladdin. "You told me the palace was your favorite view in the whole world."

"It was the most amazing sight I'd ever seen, that's for sure. After you, of course." He ruffled her hair playfully. "To see those white-and-gold-domed roofs towering over the city, the castle rising from the dunes . . . it was a wonder, especially from where I was sitting. It still is."

"My favorite view has always been this one." Jasmine's expression turned wistful as she nodded at the window. "You wanted to get in, while I was desperate to get out and see the world. And now . . ."

"Now you're locked in," he finished, his smile fading. "And everyone wants me out."

"Well. Hardly everyone," she reminded him.

Jasmine turned away from the view, refocusing on her betrothed. She wrapped her arms around Aladdin's waist and pulled him close, feeling the strength of his muscles as his arms encircled her in turn.

"That's one good thing about becoming sultana," she murmured.

"What's that?" His breath was warm against her ear. Jasmine closed her eyes as he nuzzled her neck.

"I can choose you, again and again," she said. "They can all say what they want now, but when I am crowned, it's up to me. And I promise, one day we will be married."

Aladdin's face lit with a grin. He tilted his head toward her, and Jasmine held her breath, pulse quickening in anticipation of his kiss. But just as she was about to feel the aching sweetness of his lips on hers, a voice sounded from the doorway.

"Excuse me, Your Majesty—"

Aladdin and Jasmine sprang apart just in time. Payam was standing before them.

"Apologies for the interruption. I arrived for my evening guard

61

post on this floor and got concerned when I heard a man's voice in Your Majesty's room." He stared at Aladdin.

"Not to worry. It's only my— It's only Aladdin," Jasmine said with an awkward laugh.

"I was just leaving." Aladdin lowered his voice, eyes shifting to the door. "Unless—will you be all right tonight?"

"I think so. Hopefully whatever I saw last night is long gone, and I've got Rajah here, who seems to take his guard duty as seriously as Payam now."

Across the carpet, Rajah lifted his head at the sound of his name and gave Jasmine a protective nod. Aladdin still didn't look entirely convinced, and Jasmine gently nudged him forward. "We have a long day tomorrow. Go on, get some much-needed sleep."

"If you're sure." Aladdin kissed her hand. "Good night, Princess."

"Good night," she called after him.

The door closed behind the two men. She heard Aladdin's footsteps fade down the hall, and then she was alone, with no one but Payam outside the door to hold back the dark.

CHAPTER NINE

The day of the funeral began with the sound of hoofbeats marching on the palace at dawn. Jasmine woke with her muscles clenched. *I'm not ready. Not ready to say good-bye, not for any of this—*

But she could hear Nadia's footsteps already entering the room, the clatter of plates and silverware on the breakfast tray. The day was starting, and there was nothing she could do to slow it.

"Good morning, Your Ma—Jasmine."

Nadia set the tray down on a low oak table in the bedroom's dining alcove and then drew back the curtains of the surrounding windows. It was a colorless day, with rolling gray clouds looming over the mountain range, hiding the peaks from view. There was something strange about those clouds . . . They were thick, like smoke.

The hoofbeats grew louder now, accompanied by the sound of voices. Jasmine swung her legs over the bed and hurried to join Nadia at one of the arched windows, a still-sleepy Rajah padding after her. The two girls peered through the glass at the spectacle unfolding on the Great Courtyard below, where a contingent of red-and-white-uniformed men thundered through the palace gates on camels and mules. They moved as a pack, surrounding and shielding a magnificent elephant carrying a billowing golden tent on its back.

"Red and white." Jasmine leaned forward, trying to catch a glimpse of who was inside the tent. "That must be the king of Azra."

Even Rajah was glued to the window as Jasmine and Nadia watched the men dismount and Agrabah's ministers sweep forward to greet them. The royal tent slid open, and Arman and the ministers all lowered into bows as the king emerged, his jeweled crown dazzling against the dark silk of his mourning robes. But now the gray fog from the sky seemed to be creeping up from the ground, blanketing the cobblestone courtyard, so that when the ministers kneeled, they appeared to be sinking into a dark cloud. Jasmine blinked, unnerved by the sight.

"Looks like there's a storm coming," she murmured.

"Hopefully it's just more of the odd wind and fog we've been getting lately. A storm is the last thing we need, with all these guests," Nadia said. "Come, let's eat. We have a bit of time until you need to be downstairs."

Jasmine couldn't muster up much of an appetite, but she forced herself to take a few bites of fruit and lavash while watching the influx of guests descending on the Great Courtyard. There was the prince of Kanan riding in on a thoroughbred Arabian steed, its jewel-adorned bridle and saddle matched only by the finery on the prince himself. The duke of Rakash arrived looking far older than she remembered him, his demeanor almost frail as he sat astride his horse, while the crown prince of Merwan galloped through the gates with his usual flair, a dozen military medals gleaming on his chest.

"We can really host this many people in the palace?" Jasmine asked, shaking her head in amazement as the new faces filling the courtyard continued to multiply. And then she remembered the sprinkling of conversations she'd heard over the years about a time when the Palace of Agrabah was the beating heart of high society, when the gates were regularly flung open and the ballroom awash with dancing figures. A time when her mother was still alive.

After his wife's death, the sultan ceased nearly all entertaining, and the guest suites in the northeast wing had sat empty ever since. Jasmine couldn't remember the last time she'd wandered those abandoned halls. That was one good thing about all these sudden visitors: They would bring those rooms back to life.

Suddenly the floor began to rumble beneath them. Jasmine looked up sharply as the end table next to her chair began to shake, followed by the sound of clarions blaring, drums beating. The cacophony transported her back to the last time a guest had made an entrance like this: "Prince Ali," making the mistake of thinking he needed to impress her by imitating the other prince who had brought a lavish parade up to her doorstep. The insufferable Prince Achmed.

"Don't tell me this is how Achmed arrives for a *funeral*," Jasmine muttered, rolling her eyes.

"You invited him?" Nadia asked, looking astonished.

"Believe me, it wasn't my idea."

The two of them watched through the window as the cause of the ground's rumbling quickly became clear. A row of white Arabian steeds, bridled and saddled all in gold, surrounded Prince Achmed and his equally overdecorated horse. The prince dismounted and proceeded to parade his long, spindly legs across the courtyard, waving and preening at the gathered crowd as if they were all there to honor him.

"I can't watch." Nadia made a face, covering her eyes with her hands.

"I would actually be embarrassed for him, if he weren't so loathsome," Jasmine remarked.

Luckily, Achmed was forced to cut his mortifying display short when the final arrivals came riding through the gates, their horses' hooves kicking up dust in his direction. While Achmed sputtered in annoyance and stomped back to his horse, Jasmine studied this last group: a younger pair dressed in matching damask robes flanked by four liveried attendants. The girl, who looked about Jasmine's age, wore a jeweled coronet circling her auburn hair, while the young man beside her wore a crowned turban over long black hair that was tied away from his face like a horse's mane. And suddenly, with a cry of delight, Jasmine realized just who they were.

"Shirin!"

All royal protocol flew from her mind as Jasmine pushed open the window for a better look. It really *was* them: Jasmine's old friend, Princess Shirin of Numan, and her younger brother, Prince Rashid. The sight of them brought a wave of memories flooding back from their last visit three years ago, when they accompanied the Numani king on an official visit. She'd found Rashid to be stiff and reserved, but his sister was the polar opposite. She and Jasmine were instantly inseparable—two princesses who'd each grown up in a strange bubble, finally finding a kindred spirit in each other. They'd exchanged regular letters in the intervening years, so Shirin knew all about Jasmine's adventures with Aladdin and the Genie; she had cheered from afar at the news of Jafar's banishment. Meanwhile, Shirin confided in Jasmine about her father's declining health and her secret doubts about Rashid as the future king, interspersed with colorful stories from the court of Numan. And now she was here.

Shirin looked up, catching Jasmine's eye at the window. The two smiled at each other across the palace grounds, and Jasmine felt a rush of gratitude. The days to come wouldn't be easy, but with allies like Aladdin and now Shirin at her side, everything looked far more bearable.

. . .

"Your Majesty." Arman rapped at her door. "It's time."

Jasmine turned from her dressing table at the sound of his voice and took a deep breath, rising to her feet. Nadia smoothed the creases of Jasmine's black embroidered gown and carefully arranged the sheer black veil to frame her face.

"It'll be all right," Nadia whispered, clasping her friend's hand. Jasmine squeezed her palm in return.

They met Arman in the corridor, his face as somber as his mourning robes. The three of them plus Rajah descended the grand staircase in silence, where Jasmine found Payam and a trio of armored guards waiting at the bottom. There were two men to march behind her, two in front. As they took their places in this strange new formation, she felt more like a soldier going into battle than a sultana in the making.

They proceeded through the Grand Atrium into Crystal Hall, the palace's sprawling foyer that appeared more than double its size due to all the carved mirror work adorning the walls. Intricate patterns of crystal wove around mirrors of all shapes and sizes and dripped from chandeliers, promising a glittering display everywhere one looked. But today, as they entered the hall, Jasmine felt the room's light start to dim—and grow darker with their every step. It was almost as if a shadow had followed them inside ... or maybe it was that strange fog, seeping into Crystal Hall and obscuring its shine.

Jasmine shook her head, trying to clear her mind of these implausible thoughts. And then she saw something in the glass opposite her—something that stopped her midstride.

Instead of her reflection, the long oval mirror revealed a dark dirt path set in a forest of leafless trees. Brass bottles were strewn on the ground, with red smoke curling from their lids, like trapped vapors fighting for escape. Jasmine moved closer and then recoiled suddenly, as if the glass had pierced her skin.

A woman appeared in the mirror, standing still with her back to Jasmine. She had long black hair that fell to her waist in waves, and her posture was ramrod straight as she gripped one of the bare trees. Suddenly she turned her head—and revealed vacant holes for eyes. A white skull for a face. A cry lodged in Jasmine's throat as she watched the skeletal head continue turning, swiveling *all the way around*—

"Your Majesty!" Arman's firm hand on her shoulder brought Jasmine gasping back to reality. "What is it? What distresses you?"

She blinked at the mirror. The glass was normal now, its crystal embellishments returned to their innocent shimmer. The dead woman was gone, and in her place was Jasmine, wearing a long mourning dress of black lace and a terrified expression.

"I—I think I saw . . ." Her voice trailed off as she wondered how to even explain it. Could the mirror be another enchanted window, like the one in the council chamber? But if it were, then why had no one else seen the same vision in the glass?

Her thoughts flashed back to Doctor al-Razi's medical report, to the confounding messages scribbled and hidden away in her father's desk. *Hallucinations.* What if the sultan's crown wasn't the only thing she was inheriting? What if his affliction—or madness—was hers now too?

"It was nothing." Jasmine said, trying to pretend she never saw it. "Just . . . my grief."

"Of course." Arman's face softened. They continued on to the palace's main entrance, with Jasmine keeping her eyes down to avoid any other illusions or ghosts that might be following them. When they reached the bronze double doors, Arman paused, and the guards halted behind him.

"Are you ready, Your Majesty?"

No. "Yes."

Jasmine straightened her shoulders, lifted her chin, tried to ignore the panic bubbling in her stomach. Arman pushed open the doors, and she followed him and the guards out onto the landing, entering a Great Courtyard teeming with people. They were congregated around the long reflecting pools that stretched out in front of the palace steps, a mix of foreign and familiar faces as visitors mingled with palace courtiers. The chatter froze on their lips when they saw Jasmine appear. Most of them were quick to bow or curtsy, but there were a handful of figures here who outranked her—at least until the coronation—and following her ministers' instructions, Jasmine made her way to them first.

She began with the king of Azra, who was inspecting her curiously.

"Welcome to Agrabah, Your Majesty." She greeted him with a curtsy. "We are honored by your presence."

"The honor is mine." The king lifted her hand and brushed his coarse lips against it. "Your father was a great man. It has been a privilege to rule my kingdom alongside his."

"Thank you. I know my father felt the same, and I look forward to maintaining the special relationship between Agrabah and Azra."

Jasmine smiled at him, about to move on to her next royal guest, when she heard the king say, "I must have forgotten how *young* you would be, Princess. Has there ever been a sovereign of such tender age?"

Jasmine paused. He might have been simply making idle conversation, or maybe this was his way of paying her a compliment, but she had a feeling it was something else. He was sizing her up, and he didn't see a leader.

"Perhaps you also forgot the boy king of Egypt," she said,

keeping her tone sweet as honey. "I am eighteen—ten years older than Tutankhamun was."

"Ah, yes. Of course."

The king smiled back, and Jasmine wondered if it really had been her age that he was skeptical of . . . or something else.

She next greeted the duke of Rakash, whose eyes welled with tears for her father, and the crown prince of Merwan, his chestnut-colored hair and white teeth gleaming nearly as bright as the silver and bronze rings adorning each of his fingers. And then she found herself in the dreaded position near Prince Achmed of Batana, his upturned face watching her pointedly. She plastered on a polite smile, forcing herself to curtsy and greet him like a proper princess who didn't thoroughly detest the man.

"Thank you for coming, Prince Achmed. We are grateful for your support."

"Yes, I should think so." Achmed sniffed. "I had every mind not to come, after I was treated *so* inhospitably on my last visit." His beady eyes sharpened on hers. "But as my father said, the sultan shouldn't be punished for his daughter's mistakes. If my father says he was a decent ally who deserves the presence of the prince of Batana at his funeral, then he shall have it." Achmed heaved a dramatic sigh and then looked at her expectantly, waiting to be praised. Jasmine was ready to tell him what she thought *he* deserved when she remembered her ministers' words and bit her tongue.

"We do appreciate it. And I hope we can put any . . . unpleasantness behind us and work together as allies from here on out."

With that, Jasmine moved quickly down the line of guests until she finally reached Princess Shirin and Prince Rashid. The two princesses broke from formality when they saw each other, throwing their arms around one another instead.

"I can't believe you're here!" Jasmine cried, hugging her friend tightly. "I thought you had to stay in Numan."

"We made it at the eleventh hour," Shirin said, wiping her eyes. "I couldn't miss being here for you, Jasi."

Jasmine smiled at the old nickname.

"It's so good to see you again." She glanced over Shirin's shoulder, where a tall, lanky boy stood in a black silk tunic and trousers, his shoulders adorned with royal regalia. "And you, Prince Rashid."

Jasmine started to curtsy just as Rashid lowered himself into a stilted bow, and she remembered with a jolt that she outranked him now. The thought was almost amusing, knowing how much Rashid had enjoyed lording his elevated status over the two princesses when he last visited. *Though maybe he's grown up since then*, Jasmine thought with a sideways glance at him.

"Our father sends his condolences," Rashid said. "His health prevented him from being here, so we've come to pay our respects in his stead."

"I thank you both."

"How are you managing with . . . all of this?" Shirin asked, her brown eyes filled with concern.

"Better, now that you're here." Jasmine caught Arman's eye across the courtyard, signaling to her that it was time for the procession to begin. "I have to go, but we'll talk more at the reception, and later tonight."

"Yes, and I can't wait to meet this Aladdin I've been hearing so much about!" Shirin stood on her tiptoes to scan the crowd, and Jasmine grinned.

"Just look for the most handsome man here. The one with the adorable monkey on his shoulder."

As she turned to join Arman, Jasmine heard Rashid echo behind her, "Monkey?" But the smile slipped off her face when she saw the crown ministers begin their march, carrying her father's coffin through the palace doors. The marble covering was left open for all of Agrabah to see his face one last time, and Jasmine froze, staring at the waxlike face that was a pale imitation of her father.

Just two days ago, you were right here. I heard your laugh, felt the warmth of your hugs. It seemed impossible that he was gone, that this motionless stranger in the coffin had once been her world. Parading her father's casket through the streets of Agrabah to the burial site would be the hardest thing she had ever had to do . . . and there was no choice but to face it.

The beat of a goblet drum pulled Jasmine from her thoughts as the court musician and poet, Rudaki, followed the coffin through the palace doors, his long black robes billowing behind him. He played a slow, percussive march and then began to sing, his voice wailing a wistful melody that tugged at Jasmine's heart.

The music was their cue to move into position for the long walk ahead, and the visiting royals and members of court filtered into line. Jasmine took her place behind the ministers carrying her father's coffin and in front of the king of Azra and Prince Achmed, wishing she could have the comfort of Aladdin or Shirin near her instead. But the princess would be walking with her brother behind the neighboring rulers, while Aladdin stood at the end of the line with the royal guards and the rest of the household. Just as the crown ministers dictated.

Arman glanced over his shoulder at Jasmine.

"Do I have Your Majesty's permission to open the gates?"

Before she could answer, they were interrupted by the sound of hoofbeats thundering into the Great Courtyard from the back of the palace. Jasmine whipped her head around, on instant alert. They weren't expecting any other guests today—and only the palace staff was supposed to know about its hidden back entrance.

A muscular stranger on horseback rode through a cloud of dust into view. He sat tall and proud on his mare, seemingly oblivious to the fact that he had entered the wrong way, that he was the only one traveling without an entourage. There was nothing to indicate that he was one of the invited nobles, no finery adorning his horse or his black cotton tunic and trousers, save for an assortment of medals pinned to his chest. Remembering her intruder, Jasmine felt a flash of fear. He might not have cast the same enormous shadow as what she'd seen the other night, but there was no way to be certain he wasn't connected to her near attack—especially when everything she'd seen had been in the dark.

"Guards!" Jasmine called, just as Arman said in a raised voice, "Your Majesty, surely you remember your second cousin Karim, son of the sultan's cousin Farhad? He's grown into quite the decorated warrior of the Caspian army."

Jasmine eyed the man in surprise. She had only the fuzziest recollections of being forced years ago to play with a whiny, runny-nosed boy who called himself her "cousin Karim" and threw raging tantrums after she beat him at backgammon. He'd gone away to school when they were eight, the same year his parents moved to another province under the sultan's rule, and Jasmine could remember her relief at being free of him. Until now.

Karim swung down from his horse and dipped into a bow before Jasmine. The cousin from her childhood memories looked nothing like this bronze man with his confident, determined gaze and eyes the color of night. Eyes like hers.

Remembering her manners, Jasmine extended a hand.

"It's good to see you again, cousin," she said politely. "When did you return to Agrabah?"

"I left my post at the gulf as soon as I heard about the sultan," he said. "But I plan to stay for a time." He flashed his teeth in a smile.

"How nice," Jasmine replied, wondering how long he meant by "awhile." She searched the faces in the courtyard until she spotted Aladdin and gestured toward him. "If you're joining us for the procession, you're welcome to walk with the rest of the court."

Karim's expression shifted.

"I prefer to walk with you, dear cousin. We have much to catch up on."

For once, Jasmine was grateful for the rigid royal protocol.

"I'm sorry, but I'm afraid I must adhere to the procession order. There will be plenty of time for us to talk afterward." She turned to Arman. "Let's go."

Karim looked to Arman for confirmation, a move that instantly annoyed Jasmine, before he grudgingly moved to the back of the line. Arman nodded at Commander Zohar, who called out, "As you were!"

At the sight of the coffin, all thoughts of Karim, Prince Achmed, and the rest of the morning's disturbances fled from her mind. She stepped back into position, taking a shaky breath, as the ministers began the march forward.

The procession moved as one toward the palace's tall golden gates, Rudaki's singing growing louder and more plaintive as they drew closer. The gates parted, and Jasmine's breath caught in her throat when she saw the mass of mourners waiting at the bottom of the long stairs that led from the palace to the streets below. It was a crowd of thousands.

The guards formed a shield around the procession as mourners rushed toward Jasmine and the ministers, reaching out their hands to touch the coffin, tears streaming down their faces. There was something jarring, surreal, about watching those who had never really known her father sobbing freely, while Jasmine was forced to stay strong and maintain a stoic facade. It took every ounce of strength for her to keep it up, to bite her lip and hold back the tears.

Rudaki led the crowd in a new song, an elegy for those loved and lost, and that's when the people of Agrabah filtered into the procession. The men and boys formed one line, the women and girls another, as they all sang together to the percussive beat of Rudaki's drum. And as Jasmine looked around her, at their people, joined in this moment of collective grief and love—she felt a surge of pride for her country.

I will rise to the task before me, she silently promised her father.

I will give my all to Agrabah, and we will continue to prosper in peace. I'll be the kind of sultana they will love . . . the way they loved you.

The procession spilled into the cobbled streets, with more and more of the sultan's former subjects running to join them as they passed the empty stalls of the bazaar and the colorful domed buildings of merchant houses and inns. They made their way onward to the desert, where the vast stretch of sand led to Sultan's Peak: a mountain range where every monarch had been buried since the dawn of time. The blazing desert sun beat down, turning their bodies slick with sweat, but not even the children complained as the crowd of thousands walked the winding path up to the peak overlooking the jeweled rooftops of the kingdom.

Jasmine's lower lip trembled as the viziers lowered the sultan's coffin into the dirt, positioning him to face Mecca. Standing beside his grave, she tried to keep her voice from shaking as she recited one of Rudaki's poems for her father.

"Look at the cloud, how it cries like a grieving man;
Thunder moans like a lover with a broken heart.
Now and then the sun peeks from behind the clouds
Like a prisoner hiding from the guard—"

Jasmine's voice faltered as she caught someone staring at her with a strange look in his eyes, something unnerving that she couldn't name. It was her newly returned cousin, Karim.

She cleared her throat and continued to recite, but it was impossible to ignore his stare. It sent a chill running through her veins . . . turning her blood cold.

CHAPTER TEN

The wind howled outside the palace, wailing against the sultan's death like in the words of Rudaki's poem. The grieving was more subdued inside the ivory banquet hall, where a somber funeral reception took place for the court and royal guests. White roses and glowing candles were the only decoration, the quiet strumming of a harp the only music. And for the first time, Jasmine took her place on her father's marble-and-gilt-edged banquet throne.

She kept her hands clasped in her lap and sat up straight, trying not to fidget, not to let the massive chair swallow her up, as she thanked the guests who approached one by one to offer their condolences. Just as the duke of Arza stepped up to speak to her, she spotted Arman and Karim deep in conversation at the back of the hall. The sight filled her with a prickly sense of unease. What could the grand vizier possibly have to say to this relation they barely knew?

Someone is coming.

Her father's warning shot through Jasmine like a lightning bolt. She gripped the sides of her chair, watching the crowd with renewed focus, even as the irony of the warning dawned on her: She was staring at an entire *roomful* of people who had come to the palace from afar. The sultan might have been referring to Karim . . . or he could have just as easily meant Prince Achmed, or any of the other new faces in front of her.

Across the room, Karim nodded at something Arman said, and then turned for the door leading to the palace interior. Jasmine drew a sharp breath. She met Aladdin's eyes across the room, where he was trapped in a dull-looking conversation between two palace courtiers, and beckoned him toward her.

"Will you take over for me?" she asked under her breath when he joined her. "There's . . . something I need to do."

"Of course. I'll be right here."

Jasmine squeezed his hand in thanks, and then drew Shirin into their circle.

"This is Princess Shirin of Numan, one of my closest friends. She'll keep you company in the meantime."

Aladdin bowed gallantly before her.

"Pleased to meet you, Your Royal Highness."

"Same to you, Aladdin. I've been *quite* curious about you since Jasmine first mentioned you in her letters." Shirin winked over her shoulder at Jasmine as she rose from the marble throne. The crowds parted as Jasmine moved toward the door, her black skirts sweeping behind her.

"Your Majesty, allow me to—"

Jasmine held up her hand, cutting Arman off as he appeared in front of her. She'd never had a reason to doubt him before, but now she felt a touch of suspicion. Her father's words floated through her mind yet again. *Trust no one.* Arman was the last person she would have expected him to mean, the steadfast adviser and confidant who helped the sultan rebuild after Jafar's betrayal. Her father *couldn't* have meant him.

Then again, maybe everyone had a price . . . a line they could be pushed to cross. Just because Arman was loyal to the sultan didn't mean he would be loyal to her.

"No need to follow me," she told him before pushing through the doors.

A long colonnade bridged the palace's formal state rooms and the more private chambers behind them. Jasmine could make out a tall, broad figure striding ahead, carrying a lantern and peering intrusively through the passing doors. Her face turned hot with indignation.

"Cousin," she called, her voice echoing sharply across the stone walls. "You seem to be lost. Come back to the reception with me."

Karim paused, and then turned to face her.

"Thank you, Your Royal Highness, but I'm just fine here. I'll rejoin you all shortly."

Jasmine frowned at his presumptuous response.

"You don't understand. This wing isn't open to the public."

"I'm not the public, am I?" The lantern cast a glow across Karim's face, highlighting the way his thick black brows shot up in amusement. "And I seem to remember so many fascinating treasures here from my childhood. Secret passageways, jewels that could change their shape, enchanted lamps . . . Won't you show them to me again?"

Jasmine's heartbeat sped up as he spoke. *How does he know?* She'd never shown her cousin any of the palace treasures, and she couldn't imagine her father doing so either. Not to mention the enchanted lamp hadn't even been in the palace all those years ago, when Karim last visited. The Genie was a shared secret between Aladdin, Jasmine, and the sultan—or so she'd thought.

"I'm afraid not," she said stiffly. "This is a home, not a museum, and we are in mourning. I'm sure you understand."

"But, cousin, don't you see?" Karim stepped closer to her, his face twisting into a smile. "This is also home to me."

Jasmine froze.

"What are you talking about?"

He paused, letting her imagination fill the silence.

"I mean that we are family," he finally said. "In more ways than one. And family must stick together in times like these."

"You hardly knew my father or mother," Jasmine pointed out. "We hardly knew *you*. Certainly not well enough for you to go looking through our things." She took a breath, collecting herself. "It was . . . kind of you to come, but now that you've paid your respects, please don't feel obligated to stay."

"You aren't trying to be rid of me, are you, dear cousin?" Karim's lips curled in a knowing smile. "I wouldn't miss your coronation for the world. But if you wish, I'll leave my exploring for another day—maybe one on which I can count on you to be my guide."

He bowed again, and Jasmine tried not to flinch as he kissed her hand. *He's my second cousin,* she reminded herself. *I can't turn him away. Not yet.*

But she could keep a close eye on him.

· · ·

The final ritual of the sultan's funeral was a visit to the sacred fire. As the banquet drew to a close and guests retired to their rooms, Arman and Commander Zohar led a white-robed man toward Jasmine. She rose from her seat at the sight of his wisp-thin frame and braided white beard, recognizing him as Sharif, the high elder tasked with the spiritual protection of Agrabah and its leaders.

"Your Majesty," he said, greeting her in his quietly authoritative voice. "Follow me to the pyre."

Jasmine fell into step with the men as they made their way down the same dimly lit corridor where she had just confronted Karim. The wall at the far end of the colonnade was decorated in an elaborate turquoise-and-gold mosaic pattern, and Jasmine watched in surprise as the high elder swept his pale hands across the painted tiles, pressing down firmly on two of the mosaic's interconnected spirals. And then the wall split apart—jutting open to reveal a small, dark room. Jasmine's mouth fell open.

In all her years at the palace, she must have walked past this same wall thousands of times and never thought twice about it. Now she wondered what else there was in her home that she hadn't seen before, how many other secrets were lurking inside.

Sharif climbed carefully over the glazed bricks through the

opening in the wall and offered Jasmine his hand. She stepped through after him, finding herself in a sparsely furnished space barely big enough to fit the group of them. There was only one seat: a miniature version of the sultan's throne, facing a burning hearth and a pail of water.

"The last sultan kindled this fire on the night of his coronation, three decades ago," Sharif said, gazing in reverence at the still-leaping flames. "A higher power has kept the same fire lit all this time, as a mark of the universe's approval of the sultan's reign. Tonight, as his successor, you will extinguish the fire—before lighting it anew on the night of your own coronation."

Jasmine stared at the dancing bursts of orange and red in the hearth. Despite the heat in the room, her insides felt like ice at the prospect of destroying her father's sacred fire. And then she suddenly remembered the opening line of the message he left her: *There was a door to which I found no key.*

Had he been alluding to this hidden, keyless room? But then, what was the *veil past which I could not see?*

"Your Majesty." Sharif raised his voice slightly. "Do you understand?"

"I . . . yes."

Jasmine hesitantly reached for the pail of water and stepped forward, until she was close enough to feel the fire's warmth against her face.

"Now," Sharif called from behind her.

But just as she lifted the pail, Jasmine saw something in the hearth—something that made her stumble backward, water spilling over the sides of the bucket.

A face. A woman's face, flickering in the flames. Her eyes were impossibly wide, her mouth frozen in a scream.

Jasmine squeezed her eyes shut. When she opened them and looked back, the face was gone, the flames nothing more than fire. The moment had passed, too quickly for her to distinguish the face. But she knew instinctively that it was someone she'd never met before.

"Try again," the high elder said, placing a firm hand on her shoulder.

Jasmine glanced behind her, catching the look Commander Zohar sent Arman. A look that seemed to say, *Just as I suspected. Our new sultana can't even manage the simplest task.*

She tightened her grip on the pail handle, and this time kept her eyes fixed just above the flames. If the face reappeared, it wouldn't stop her this time. And then she flung the water into the fire, watching as its thirty-year dance came to an abrupt end.

The color left the room. Smoke curled up from the embers, and Jasmine wiped the moisture from her eyes. She hadn't even realized she was crying.

"Well done, Your Majesty," Sharif said, bowing his head. "The heavens approve. In three days' time, the fire will light anew—and this time, it will be for you."

CHAPTER ELEVEN

Fridays were normally quiet in the palace, just as they were throughout Agrabah. It was a day of rest for most of the staff, and a chance for the sultan and Jasmine to have time for just the two of them. *Baba Dokhtar,* he would cheerfully call it, the father-daughter day she looked forward to every week. Sometimes they would play hours of backgammon in his suite, the sultan chuckling with pride every time Jasmine beat him. Other times, they would gleefully disguise themselves as merchants and ride out to the desert, even as the cavalry of guards riding behind them clearly gave away the ruse. But no matter what they did, the sultan always used their time together to share with her the business of running the kingdom, the rewards and judgments he'd handed down during the week. It occurred to Jasmine now, as she awoke on her first Friday without him, that he had been preparing her. Every time he'd told her the reasons for one decision or another, whether he'd said yes or no to a subject's plea, he was giving Jasmine a road map to follow when it was her turn to rule.

He believed I could do it. And if he believed . . . then so do I.

Jasmine stretched and swung her legs over the side of the bed, getting up with renewed purpose. Rajah gave a little grunt of protest and burrowed his head back under the quilt, clearly expecting the leisurely Friday morning he was used to. But there would be no time for rest in the palace today—the crucial final day of preparation before she was crowned.

On cue, a knock sounded at Jasmine's bedroom door.

"Come in, Nadia," she called, reaching for her dressing gown in the hanging wardrobe opposite her bed and slipping it on.

Nadia wasn't alone, and she wasn't carrying the usual breakfast platter either. She followed Payam and the minister of the treasury, Majid, into Jasmine's suite, all three of them carefully eyeing the velvet-lined tray in Majid's hands. At the sight of the tall round object draped in white cloth on the tray and the white gloves worn by both Nadia and Majid, Jasmine's heart started clanging in her chest. This was it: her father's crown.

Her crown.

"Good morning, Your Majesty." Majid lifted the white cloth from the tray with a flourish. "Here it is: the most valuable possession in the palace treasury. Today you will practice walking in the crown and reciting your vows without letting it slip." He paused. "Considering the crown weighs five pounds, that's not as easy as it seems."

"And I will practice dressing your hair around it," Nadia said, her cheeks pink with anticipation at touching such finery.

Jasmine stared at the crown's towering frame of gold, silver, and red velvet, studded with thousands of diamonds and rows of identical white pearls. The largest diamond of all, a brilliant yellow stone, shone at the apex of the crown, surrounded by a sunburst of white diamonds. Even as a princess, she hadn't touched anything so exquisite before.

"All right," she said, catching her breath. "Let's try it."

She bent her head, hearing Nadia's excited gasp as Majid lifted the crown. And then the heavy weight was bearing down on her, the precious metals digging into her scalp. It took every ounce of Jasmine's coordination to stand up straight without letting the crown fall.

Nadia clasped her hands together, her eyes welling up as Jasmine faced the two of them. Majid bowed his head solemnly, and when he looked up, he gave her a smile that was full of warmth. *He believes in me,* Jasmine realized, the thought flooding her with gratitude.

"I also have a copy of your coronation vows for tomorrow." Majid reached into the pocket of his cloak and handed her a sheaf of parchment. "I'll leave you to your preparations now. Payam is on guard outside your room, so he will keep watch over the crown and return it for safekeeping as soon as you're ready."

"Thank you, Minister."

Once they had left, Jasmine reached for Nadia's hand, and the two women took slow, cautious steps until they were standing before the long oval mirror.

"Just look at you, Jasmine," Nadia marveled. "You look every bit the sultana."

"Even in my dressing gown?" Jasmine joked. But she too couldn't look away from the reflection in the mirror. There was no denying the difference the crown made. She felt less like a child playing dress-up and more like the real leader of a nation.

As Nadia began tying back the window drapes, Jasmine noticed the thick gray haze hanging heavily over the dunes in the distance again, with flecks of sand falling from the sky like snow.

"It looks worse out than yesterday," she remarked, an unspoken worry knotting her stomach.

"I know. When I went to get your tray, I heard them saying in the kitchens..." She hesitated, and Jasmine motioned for her to go on. "They were saying that an entire farmland in the Orostan region saw its crops wiped out in the sandstorm last night. Some of the animals were found buried beneath the sand too. It's awful."

A horse and its rider, splayed out on the ground. Dead in the dunes.

Jasmine closed her eyes to block out the memory of what she'd seen in the council chamber's enchanted glass. *What if they were connected?*

"Is it true? What will happen to the people of Orostan?" she asked in alarm. "I've never known Agrabah sandstorms to cause this level of destruction."

"It could be just a rumor," Nadia said. "The kitchen cooks might have gotten it wrong, and the ministers haven't told you anything. If something was amiss, wouldn't the sultana need to know?"

Jasmine felt her shoulders relax slightly as she remembered her childhood tutor once telling her how the staff loved to gossip belowstairs. This Orostan story could easily be just an example of that, a chilling tale to pass the time. But as she gazed out the window—at the gray haze stretching wider, creeping lower, while sand swirled in the sky—she had the prickly feeling something bad was coming. Something connected to the ominous series of events that had been following her since her father's death.

. . .

After a long morning spent reviewing all the intricacies of a coronation, Jasmine finally had a chance to unwind with Aladdin and Princess Shirin over lunch. Nadia was just about to remove the crown from Jasmine's head when she was interrupted by the incoherent chatter of Aladdin's pet monkey, Abu, announcing their arrival. Jasmine held her breath, suddenly nervous to discover whether Aladdin would look at her differently now that she was wearing the crown.

He walked through the door, handsome as ever in his mauve tunic over cream-colored pants, with his dark hair slicked back. He stopped in his tracks at the sight of her, his eyes widening and then warming with emotion. A slow smile spread across his face, and he winked at her before bending on one knee.

"My sultana," Aladdin said, making the words sound like music. "I've never seen anyone who belongs so clearly in a crown."

Jasmine's heart seized. She pulled him upright, taking his face in her hands. He wasn't threatened or wary, or reacting in any of the typical ways she would have been wise to expect from a man watching a woman claim unprecedented power.

Then again, there was nothing typical about Aladdin.

He leaned down, pressing his forehead to hers. Jasmine stood on her tiptoes, raising her lips to his, when—

"Oh! Sorry, I didn't mean to— Oh, *woooow*."

Jasmine and Aladdin pulled apart with a shared laugh at the sound of Princess Shirin's sputtering.

"Foiled again," Aladdin whispered in her ear.

"Jasi," Shirin breathed, her cheeks flooding with color as Nadia led her into the room. "I mean, Your *Majesty*."

"Please, not that." Jasmine grinned. "Nadia and I already had this conversation. To the three of you—and Abu and Rajah too, of course—I am simply Jasmine."

The animals stared back at her, sufficiently unimpressed, before scampering off to play on the balcony. Shirin circled Jasmine, staring at the crown from every angle.

"It's incredible. You look incredible." A strange look briefly flitted across her face, gone as quickly as it appeared.

"What is it, Shirin?" Jasmine asked.

"Oh, nothing. It's just . . ." She lowered her voice, glanced down. "The way my father's health is looking, I realized, well . . . I might be seeing my little brother in a crown like yours sooner than we thought."

"I'm so sorry." Jasmine wrapped her arm around her friend. "I know how close you are to your father. And, nothing against Rashid, but you're the eldest child of the king. You have a far better way with people, and—"

"And Rashid is a boy," Shirin said flatly. "That's all that matters." After a moment, she added, "You're lucky, Jasi. Not that your father died, of course, but that you are a firstborn daughter who actually gets to succeed."

Jasmine fell silent as Shirin's words sank in. She was right, of course. This was an opportunity, not just for Jasmine but for all the girls of Agrabah, to see themselves as so much more than they had been taught to dream. If she did her job well, she just might prove to the world that women could be leaders too . . . even if there was a younger male sibling waiting in the wings.

"I wish things were different for you too, Shirin. But maybe someday soon, as we continue making progress—they will be." Jasmine smiled encouragingly, and though Shirin smiled back, the expression didn't quite reach her eyes.

"I should practice my vows," Jasmine said, casting about for a change of subject to lighten the mood. "You've always been the best performer I know, so I hoped you might give me some pointers. Remember those palace pantomimes you insisted we put on the last time you were here?"

Shirin burst into laughter. "Don't tell me *that* was your idea of a good performance."

"Well." Jasmine chuckled. "I said you're the best performer I know. I just don't happen to know many performers."

Shirin playfully lobbed a throw pillow at her, and Jasmine's shoulders shook with laughter as she dodged it. Aladdin looked over just in time to reach out his arm and rescue her crown before it toppled.

"I think that's your cue," Nadia said, eyeing the crown nervously. "Let's finish rehearsing so we can store it safely until tomorrow."

Nadia and Aladdin took their seats on the floor cushions while Jasmine handed Shirin the parchment containing the order of service. Shirin cleared her throat, returning to a more serious expression, and began to read.

"Before the anointing, our new sovereign must justify her claim to the throne. Your Majesty, do you possess the divine qualities worthy of a sultana and head of state? You may name them for us now."

Jasmine stood up straighter, remembering the most important words she would likely ever speak.

Nežād. "I hail from the most noble descent, as the only child of Sultan Hamed Bobolonius the Second." *Gōhar.* "I possess innate worth, far beyond the material." *Kherad.* "I bear the wisdom of my ancestors." *Dād.* "I live by the highest standards of justice."

Saying the vows aloud in her bedroom, surrounded by three of the people she loved most, Jasmine felt a surge of confidence. The words rolled off her tongue. The crown fit. She might not feel fully ready yet for such a great leap, but she was ready to begin, to take her first steps.

It was only when she heard Rajah's sudden, repeated growls coming from the bedroom balcony that Jasmine stopped midsentence.

There it was again: Rajah's warning snarl, followed by the sound of metal clashing against metal. Aladdin took off for the balcony and Jasmine quickly lifted the crown from her head, setting it back on its tray before rushing outside behind him.

She exhaled in relief as soon as she looked over the balcony railing. It was only Prince Achmed, Prince Rashid, and Cousin Karim, the three of them sitting astride their horses and putting on a show of swordsmanship for onlookers on the grounds below. Achmed wore another one of his fussy suits that looked entirely out of place for riding, a maroon silk brocade ensemble with gold frills at the sleeves, while Rashid was dressed in a dark caped tunic and trousers, and Karim in the blue uniform of his regiment. For a moment Jasmine wondered if one of the men had challenged another to a duel, but she could hear them calling out to each other jovially, looking too friendly for a fight. Which made no sense. Why would the high-and-mighty Prince Achmed socialize with her untitled cousin, for starters?

Behind her, Shirin groaned. "*Boys.* No doubt they think this display will attract all the noble ladies." She rolled her eyes, and Nadia laughed beside her.

"It's all right, Rajah," Jasmine soothed the tiger, bending down to stroke his fur. "They're harmless."

Rajah grumbled in response before resting his head back on his paws.

"I don't know if I'd call Achmed harmless," Aladdin said, narrowing his eyes as he watched the prince below. "I saw the way he treated people when he rode through the marketplace."

"That's true. But he'll be gone soon enough—and if he's not, Rajah can always have another go at him," Jasmine joked. She turned to Shirin. "Did you and your brother already know my cousin?"

"It's possible we've met before," Shirin said with a shrug. "Although I'm sure I would remember if we had. Karim seems . . . interesting, doesn't he?"

"Not particularly." Jasmine eyed Shirin. "What is it you find interesting about him?"

"I don't know. Maybe it's how confident he is, without having a reason to be. He doesn't have a title or a palace or anything, but just look at him." She gestured below the railing. "He's easily outshining both princes out there."

"That's not hard to do," Jasmine quipped.

"A man doesn't always need things like a title or a fortune, anyway," Aladdin said, exchanging a knowing glance with Jasmine. "I learned that in a roundabout way."

"Of course," Shirin said quickly. "I just meant . . . well, he's different."

Karim chose that moment to look up from his horse. He raised his eyebrows at the sight of the women on the balcony and lifted his palm in greeting.

"Good afternoon, Your Royal Highnesses," he called out, ignoring Aladdin and Nadia altogether. Jasmine couldn't help noticing that he had yet to call her Your Majesty, even though he must have known that was the correct form of address for her now. It was almost as if he couldn't bring himself to acknowledge his cousin as the new monarch.

"Enjoying the show?" Achmed asked, preening up at the ladies.

"Hardly," Jasmine couldn't resist replying, and Shirin laughed.

"Oh, we'll change that," Karim answered. He turned back to the men. "Ready for a rematch, Princes?"

Shirin leaned her arms over the railing, watching them with an amused smile, but Jasmine's attention had shifted to someone else.

Commander Zohar was striding across the courtyard below, his expression serious as he headed for Cousin Karim. He stepped between the three horses, halting the men's games, and then leaned in to say something in Karim's ear. Zohar and Karim nodded gravely at each other—as if agreeing to something. And then the moment was over as quickly as it had begun, with the commander stepping away and her cousin and the princes returning to their antics.

"What was that?" Jasmine looked from Aladdin to Shirin and Nadia, wondering if any of them had noticed the brief exchange. "What reason does Commander Zohar have to talk to Karim?"

"Could it be about the seating arrangements for tomorrow?" Shirin suggested. "I know my brother was awfully displeased at not being seated in the kings' row up front with Achmed. Maybe Karim made a fuss too."

"You might be right. He didn't look too happy to be walking at the back of the funeral procession yesterday," Aladdin commented.

"Well, that's ridiculous of him. I haven't seen the man in a decade, I don't know why he would be so entitled." Jasmine shook her head and took Aladdin's hand. "Come on. Let's go inside."

She had more important things to do than watch three arrogant men play at fighting. It was her last night as Princess Jasmine, her last day of being known primarily as a daughter. Soon she would say a further, final good-bye to her father by stepping into his coronation robes and taking his place. She would be anointed, in a sacred ceremony that promised to transform her from the princess she was now to the great ruler she could be.

It would all happen in just a matter of hours.

CHAPTER TWELVE

Her last dinner as a princess was spent with the crown ministers, parchment and reed pens in hand, as they talked through the final to-dos and reminders before the coronation day ahead. Normally Commander Zohar ran the council meetings, but he was oddly quiet tonight, letting Parisa and Hassan do most of the talking. There was an unmistakable buzz in the room as they reviewed the choreography of tomorrow's events, an excitement so palpable, it seemed to take up its own space. Jasmine felt herself getting caught up in the emotion of it, goose bumps rising on her skin when Parisa, standing in for the high elder, pronounced her "Jasmine the Great, Jasmine the First: exalted Sultana of Agrabah." It wasn't until Arman was escorting her to the grand staircase after dinner that Jasmine spotted Cousin Karim skulking into the palace from the back gardens, and the uneasiness in her chest returned.

"What were you and Karim talking about yesterday?" Jasmine asked, turning to Arman. "How is it that you and Commander

Zohar both seem so ... familiar with my cousin, when he is a near stranger to me?"

"He was only asking for directions to the library," Arman answered. "There was a book he wanted to find, but I told him it wasn't the appropriate time. And he did, in fact, keep up an occasional correspondence with your father over the years. The sultan would dictate his replies for me or Jafar to write, so I suppose I do feel like I know the boy."

"What?" Jasmine stopped in her tracks. "Baba was writing to him? Why wouldn't he have told me?" And then another thought occurred to her, like a trickle of ice down her back. "You said he was looking for a book. What was it?"

Arman lifted his shoulders.

"He didn't tell me the title. And I suppose the sultan didn't see the correspondence as significant enough to share with you. I know he felt for the boy in recent years, after his parents died, and so the sultan and Commander Zohar secured Karim a position in the Caspian army. A position he's entirely earned now," Arman added approvingly.

It all sounded innocuous enough. Still, Jasmine couldn't shake the feeling that something wasn't quite ... right. And what were the chances that he too was looking for a mysterious book?

"Can I see their letters?" she asked.

Arman gave her a sideways glance before nodding.

"I'll have to collect them from the archives after the coronation, but yes, if you wish. Of course, we only have the letters from Karim. Your cousin has all of the sultan's replies."

"That should be enough," Jasmine said. Enough for her to hopefully get a sense of who this cousin of hers was—and if she was right to be suspicious of his reappearance in her life.

. . .

There was a scratching in the walls that night.

Jasmine lay awake, listening, as the usual creaks and sighs of the centuries-old palace gave way to something else. Something different.

Just a mouse, she told herself. *Or maybe a group of them, traveling up from the scullery.*

But it wasn't the light pitter-patter of mice, or even rats. It was a fervent *scritch-scratch-scratch,* as if someone were trapped within the walls and trying to claw their way out. A sound that made Jasmine's skin break out in a cold sweat, her heart thudding in terror.

"It's just my imagination," Jasmine muttered to herself, stuffing a pillow over her head. "Back to sleep. Tomorrow is too important."

But then she heard a voice, whispering.

"There was a door to which I found no key, there was a veil past which I could not see . . ."

Jasmine scrambled upright. Her eyes searched the dark for the voice—a woman's voice.

"Wh-who's there?" she called sharply.

The only response was a quick intake of breath from outside her bed curtains.

Jasmine's heart stopped. She looked around wildly for Rajah and found him awake and upright at the foot of the bed . . . listening too.

With shaking hands, Jasmine drew back the bed curtains and reached for the small oil lamp on her dresser. It took her three tries to light the wick in her panic, but finally the lamp flickered to life.

"Who's there?" she repeated, her voice wavering, as she stepped down from the bed. "What do you want?"

"Some little talk awhile of me and thee . . ."

There was something hypnotic about the voice, almost soothing, even as it frightened her. Jasmine crept forward, following, but every time she thought she was getting close to the voice, the sound faded; there was no catching up.

"There seemed and then no more—of thee and me . . ."

"Did my father send you?" Jasmine stammered. She aimed her lamp frantically at different sections of the room, illuminating the dark with a thin beam of light. But all she saw was the same furniture, the same art adorning the walls. Everything was as it should be—until her light found the mirror.

A stranger's face stared back at her. A *woman's face,* with unblinking dark eyes and long black hair falling past her waist. She wore an amber gown that must have been beautiful once, but was now torn in different places, as if someone had taken a knife to it and slashed indiscriminately.

"Who are you?" Jasmine whispered, and her stomach dropped as the woman in the mirror mouthed the words along with her. She scrambled away from the mirror, clapping her hand over her mouth in terror. When she dared to look back—the woman was gone. So was the voice.

Jasmine stood deathly still, afraid to breathe, waiting. But the only sound in the room now was of her heartbeat, pounding in her ears.

The floor creaked behind her. Jasmine jumped; a scream lodged in her throat. Then she felt soft fur brush against her legs, and she let out a long exhale. It was only Rajah, urging her back to bed.

Rajah would have known if there were any danger, just as he had jumped to protect her three nights ago. He always knew. *Unless . . .*

What if it was all in her mind?

In the days before his death, her father had complained of hallucinations disturbing his sleep. . . .

What if she was next?

Returning her gaze to the mirror, Jasmine found a sight almost as frightening as the strange woman. It was her own trembling reflection, looking too terrified, too unsteady, to lead a nation. Was the high elder about to crown a sultana on the verge of losing her mind? Or . . . were the visions real, and was something otherworldly coming for her?

Which would be worse?

Jasmine turned away from the mirror, desperate to look anywhere else. As she moved, her lamp's beam landed on the portrait of her mother and grandmother. Slowly, the tension left her body as Jasmine remembered who she was.

I am one of them: a powerful, capable woman. And no ghosts—not in the palace or in my own mind—will stop me from taking my place as ruler of Agrabah.

CHAPTER THIRTEEN

Jasmine gazed up at the sunrise from her balcony on the morning of her coronation, watching the rooftops of the kingdom move from shadow to light. She had spent the rest of the previous night tossing and turning, managing only snatches of sleep before dawn broke. But now, standing beneath the bright desert sun with the coronation day stretched out before her, it was easier to set aside last night's fears. *It was just a dream, a reflection of my nerves*, she told herself. *Only my consciousness trying to sort out the messages Baba left behind.*

It had to be.

"You're up early."

Jasmine turned at the sound of Nadia joining her on the balcony. She was already in formal dress for the coronation, a burgundy silk tunic over a long cream-colored skirt.

"Is it daunting, all of this?" she asked.

"Yes." Jasmine nodded, tracing the decorative carvings on the balcony railing with her finger. "Daunting, and also the greatest honor my father could have left me. I hope so much to make him proud."

And to survive. The thought flew into her mind unbidden, along with the memory of the dagger silhouetted against her bed curtains. Jasmine shivered, wishing she knew how to fight back. It was deemed uncouth and unnecessary for the princess of Agrabah to learn to fight, and so she was defenseless in the face of a sword. As soon as she ascended the throne, she was determined to learn to defend herself.

"Of course you'll make him proud." Nadia squeezed her arm. "Especially because you have the most important quality of a sultana, at least in my mind."

"And what is that?" Jasmine asked, mentally running through the key words from her coronation vows. *Noble descent, innate worth, wisdom, justice.*

"Your kindness," Nadia answered. "The fact that you don't look down on anyone. I know of no other princess or noble lady who would treat a handmaiden as a close friend, or choose a man of Aladdin's background as a future husband. You see beyond rank, and I know that will make you a beloved sultana." She smiled. "Sultana of the people's hearts."

For a moment, Jasmine was too touched to speak. She wrapped an arm around Nadia's shoulder.

"Thank you. I can't tell you how much that means to me. But truly, anyone would be lucky to have you as a friend. And I want you to rise within the palace too, if that's what you want." She paused. "How does 'future grand vizier' sound to you?"

Nadia's eyes lit up.

"Really? Is a leap like that even possible from my current position?"

"Anything is possible. If I can be the first sultana, why can't you be another first?" Jasmine pointed out. "Besides, you're as intelligent and capable as the rest of them. You've taught me so much already over the years, just by sharing the knowledge you learned from going to normal school. Once Arman retires, I know you'll be ready."

Nadia beamed back at her, just as bells began to ring out from the roof above. The sound echoed quickly, ricocheting across the kingdom as neighboring bell towers rang in response. Nadia looked at Jasmine in excitement.

"Those are for you. I heard they're ringing the bells in your honor every hour today throughout Agrabah."

"Really?" Jasmine's heart seized.

"I think it's time we start getting you ready, Sultana." Nadia motioned her inside. "Your crown awaits."

. . .

When the bells struck eleven, Arman appeared outside her door flanked by Payam and three more armored guards. Jasmine emerged from her bedroom in a crystal-embellished ivory organza dress over sheer trousers with a turquoise beaded peacock cape over her shoulders. She felt like she was floating in the dress as Nadia walked behind her, holding the train of her cape. Suddenly, Jasmine realized something was missing.

"Just a moment, please."

She turned back swiftly, returning to her bedroom and dressing table. Pulling open the drawer, she found the marble jewelry box she was looking for, with a jade cuff bracelet inside. It wouldn't match her coronation robes, but it was just the finishing touch Jasmine needed: her mother's favorite piece of jewelry.

"Ready, Your Majesty?" Arman called from the doorway.

"Yes." With one final glance behind her, she stepped out of her room for the last time as Princess Jasmine.

The group made their way down the long corridor and grand staircase in solemn silence. As they drew closer to the throne room, she could hear a hum of voices from the great assemblage of guests inside who would be taking their seats on the velvet-and-gold benches lined up before the throne. Jasmine felt her stomach flip in anticipation.

Outside the closed doors to the throne room, Sharif the high elder waited, holding a kaftan robe of red silk and velvet in one hand and a long spear nearly twice his height in the other. Jasmine's heart beat faster as she recognized the gold trim and signature jewels lining the robe, the ancient craftsmanship of the spear. These had belonged to Cyrus the Great, the first ruler of the empire. And in mere moments, she would be the first woman to feel them against her skin.

Nadia untied Jasmine's peacock cape while the high elder held out the red robe.

"Today you shed the persona of Jasmine, the princess," he said, "and step into the skin of a sultana."

Jasmine took a deep breath, slipping her arms into the pre-served silk. The material was more fragile than anything she'd worn before, and she was conscious that one wrong step, one tear of the fabric, would be a rip through history. Yet she felt stronger in the cape too, as though Cyrus were transferring his power through it to her. When Sharif handed her Cyrus's spear, she could barely contain her awe.

"Now we begin," he said with an approving nod. "Arman?"

After one last bow to Jasmine, Arman pushed open the doors. He walked the long red carpet, joining the other crown ministers who were standing behind the waiting throne. Two guards followed him, and then a hush fell over the crowd as the high elder began his walk.

"Ready?" Nadia whispered.

Jasmine nodded, raising herself to her fullest height. And then she stepped forward, Nadia holding the edges of Cyrus's floor-length robe behind her as they entered the room where hundreds were waiting to see Jasmine crowned.

They all stood on her arrival, and then each row of guests lowered to their knees to bow or curtsy as she passed. At the front of the room, Rudaki began to sing, this time a song of reverence and celebration. Goose bumps prickled across Jasmine's arms as she walked the outstretched path, closing the gap between herself and the throne. The crown was waiting there too, atop a velvet pillow that rested majestically on an ornately carved wood pedestal—another relic from the days of Cyrus.

Sharif took Jasmine's hand, leading her to the massive, gilded seat. As she took her place on the throne, she had the surreal sensation of leaving her body behind, of floating upward and watching the scene from the outside.

She looked out at the crowd lining the benches, her eyes

searching for familiar faces. Seated in the front row were all the highest-ranked royals and heads of state, from the king of Azra and Prince Achmed at one end to Princess Shirin and Prince Rashid on the other. They wore silver headdresses instead of crowns or tiaras today, in deference to Jasmine's coronation—and her position at the top. With Agrabah the center of the empire, its sultan was always known as the "king of kings," ruler above all the others. The masculine term clearly wasn't coined for a woman, but Jasmine would inherit the moniker all the same.

The second row held Agrabah's prominent landowners and their noble sons and daughters. Government officials mixed with members of the palace court in the third row, where Jasmine finally spotted Aladdin, gazing at her with a mixture of pride and awe. One face she didn't see was Cousin Karim's, even after all that fuss about staying for her coronation. *Strange*, Jasmine thought, *but a welcome surprise*. If he'd been summoned back home or to his army post early, that meant she would be spared any more of his presumptuous poking around the palace. The thought made her smile as she turned to the ministers standing on either side of her throne.

Except—someone was missing. Jasmine's smile slipped as she took in the empty space where Commander Zohar should have stood. She shot a questioning look at Arman, who responded with a slight shake of his head. From the tense looks on the other ministers' faces, she could tell none of them had a clue where he was. *How* could her second-in-command fail to be here?

Jasmine opened her mouth to speak, to pause the proceedings until the commander arrived, but the high elder was already beginning.

"The coronation of Sultana Jasmine begins a transformation from princess to exalted leader," Sharif announced. "From this day forth, she is imbued with an otherworldly power and is capable of dispensing both justice and prosperity to the people of Agrabah." He turned to face Jasmine. "Before the anointing, our new sovereign will justify her claim to the throne. Your Majesty—"

"*Stop!* There's been a mistake!"

Jasmine's head snapped up. Gasps and murmurs rippled through the throne room as Commander Zohar stormed inside. Jasmine stared in disbelief, the blood draining from her face, as he advanced toward her. *This isn't real—it's not what it looks like—*

That's when she saw the man lurking behind the commander: Cousin Karim, his eyes a dark threat. And though she couldn't say how, Jasmine knew in her gut that this day, this moment, would be her undoing.

"Have you gone *mad*, Zohar?" Sharif thundered. "You dare interrupt the crowning of our sovereign—"

"She's not the true sovereign," Commander Zohar cut in, to the sound of gasps across the room.

"Commander." Jasmine's voice shook with fury. "What is the meaning of this?"

"I am the rightful heir."

Cousin Karim stepped forward, meeting her gaze head-on. The notion was so absurd, so ridiculous, that Jasmine sputtered with laughter.

"And where did you come up with that, *cousin?* Your joke is not only in poor taste, but it defies all logic."

"He has proof." Zohar looked almost apologetic now as he

reached into his robe and pulled out a letter—its envelope bearing the sultan's familiar seal. "A letter from your father to Karim's mother."

Jasmine felt the room start to spin around her as Karim said, "Haven't you wondered why we look so much alike? More like siblings than second cousins, don't you think?"

"No," Jasmine said, choking on the word. "He wouldn't." She looked pleadingly at her ministers, their mouths agape in shock. "You knew my father like I did. You *know* this couldn't be true."

"Your mother was dead, your father alone with a baby," Zohar said. "Anyone would forgive him for taking solace in the arms of a woman."

A searing-hot anger burned in Jasmine's chest, fury like she'd never felt before. She reached for the letter in the commander's hands, determined to shred the lies into pieces. But before she could seize it, Payam and the armored guards burst to life. They launched toward Jasmine, surrounding her as if *she* were the threat in the room. She stared at them, aghast.

"What are you doing? Get away from me and throw these two treasonous men out of the palace, now!"

But Payam bowed his head and said gravely, "We cannot, Your Highness. If this man's claims are real . . . then he is the male heir. He would be sultan."

"The guard is correct," said the firm voice of Hassan, minister of law. "Until we investigate further, we cannot allow these proceedings to continue."

The words were sharp blades through Jasmine's heart. It was

only now, when the crown was slipping away from her, that she realized how much she wanted it.

Shock reverberated through the audience; within seconds, all decorum and protocols had fallen by the wayside. Princes and kings clambered out of their seats to surround Karim and the commander and inspect the letter, while young royals and nobles exchanged scandalized whispers with their seat neighbors. For once, no one objected when Aladdin sprinted from the back row to join her up front, wrapping his protective arms around her.

"It'll be all right," he whispered in her ear. "They can't do this to you."

Princess Shirin and Nadia were quick to follow him, the three of them encircling her like a shield against her humiliation. But over Shirin's shoulder, Jasmine unwittingly caught Prince Achmed's eye—and noticed he was smiling. Her hands balled into fists as she realized he was actually *enjoying* this.

The high elder, recovering from his shock, swept through the throng. He held out his palm for the letter.

"You must remember, Commander Zohar, that only I have the power to continue or call off a coronation," he said, his tone thick with warning. "I will determine if the letter is authentic."

Jasmine held her breath, one hand in Aladdin's and the other in Shirin's, as Sharif began to read aloud.

"'Dearest Dunyazad,'" he began. "'I trust this letter finds you in good health and spirits. What I am writing is difficult to put into words, as I know it will be difficult to hear, but the truth is undeniable. What happened was a mistake caused by grief, and one we must put behind us. I have to do right by my daughter, the one true child I will ever know, and focus on her and the people of Agrabah. My fervent hope is that you will understand we cannot see each other again. Of course, should you or your child ever need anything, Jafar and my ministers will be available to help you.'"

The ringing in Jasmine's ears grew louder as the high elder read. Inside she was screaming, but she forced herself to maintain an image of calm, to not show them how much the words had shaken her.

"The letter doesn't prove what you say," she argued. "At most, there was a—a minor dalliance. There is no proof the woman's child was his."

"Look at the date," Karim said evenly. "Eighteen years ago. Just months before I was born."

"I don't believe it." Jasmine gritted her teeth. "My baba wouldn't have betrayed the memory of my mother in this way. And he certainly would not abandon any child of his."

"He never abandoned the child, *Your Highness*," Commander Zohar said, emphasizing her title. She couldn't help noticing how quickly everyone had dropped *Your Majesty*, putting her back in her former place. "The sultan likely arranged the quick marriage between his first cousin and Karim's mother so that the child wouldn't be born out of wedlock. He always took an active interest in Karim and helped him make his way in the world."

"And why do you think my visits stopped so abruptly?" Karim challenged her. "Didn't you think it strange you hadn't seen your cousin in so many years?"

No. I thought it was because Baba knew I never liked you.

"He was afraid of being found out," Karim continued. "Especially as you and I started to look so much alike. And I suspect it was painful for him to see the son he couldn't claim as his own. The son he always wanted."

"Stop it. Just stop." Jasmine couldn't stand there a second longer, couldn't bear to hear any more of these words that were like daggers to her insides. She turned to the high elder. "Sharif, as you said, the decision rests with you."

The high elder lifted his hands, his expression helpless.

"Your Royal Highness, I'm afraid the letter does appear authentic and raises serious questions about your claim to the throne. Before anyone can be crowned, the ministers of Agrabah and I must sort through this matter in detail."

Jasmine's heart plummeted to the floor. Still, she couldn't give up just yet. She faced her ministers, meeting their eyes with a defiant gaze.

"You would actually consider taking the crown away from the sultan's only daughter, his only true-born child, someone the people of Agrabah know and love—and give it to a stranger with a flimsy claim?"

Majid shook his head, his expression tormented, but the rest of the ministers were unmoved . . . or too stunned by the turn of events to respond.

"My dear princess," said Hassan, the minister of law, looking at her almost pityingly. "It is an undeniable truth that any kingdom will find it easier to accept a male ruler over a female. Even if the male heir is a bastard."

The words knocked the wind out of Jasmine. Parisa opened

her mouth to speak, and Jasmine felt a flicker of hope. Surely, the only female minister would argue on her behalf. They were in this together, weren't they?

But instead, Parisa said ruefully, "I'm afraid this is the way it has always been." Jasmine was sure she detected a hint of bitterness in her voice.

Her hands trembled with rage as she untied Cyrus the Great's cape from around her shoulders, flinging the garment and spear into Sharif's arms. Then, ignoring the shouts of her name, Jasmine stormed down the same red carpet she had walked so ceremoniously only minutes ago, keeping her eyes fixed on the door ahead. This time, there were no guards to surround her or stop her. They were too busy watching over Karim as he was swarmed by curious guests.

It was as if he had already taken her place.

CHAPTER FOURTEEN

A s she returned to her room in a state of shock, it seemed to Jasmine that all the portraits on the walls were watching her. Their smiles were no longer serene but pitying; their eyes knew too much. If she couldn't slip through the floor and disappear, then the next best thing would have been solitude, to be alone with her humiliation and anger at the father who had done this to her—but the portraits wouldn't even allow Jasmine that. For once, the faces of her mother and grandmother gave her no comfort. Instead, she felt a crack in her chest at the sight of their twin smiles. She tore off her mother's cuff, flinging it at the foot of the portrait.

"How could he let this happen?" she cried. "How could *you* leave me to suffer it alone?"

It wasn't enough. Jasmine grabbed the peacock cape that she had donned so proudly this morning and ripped the exquisite fabric in half. She squeezed the torn silk in her clenched fist, as though the sultan could somehow feel her rage through it. "How could he keep that horrible secret all these years—"

Jasmine heard a whimper behind her and jumped. She had nearly forgotten Rajah—the only other beating heart allowed in the room.

Rajah nudged the fallen bracelet back toward her, a hurt look in his eyes. Jasmine sank onto the floor, burying her face in his fur, as the memory from when she was ten came flooding back. The way her father's face had changed at Jasmine's innocent mention of the possibility that he could have a male child.

There will be no son, Jasmine. You are the one.

Why had he let her believe the lie? Why not simply tell her the truth then, when she was young enough to accept it?

With a stab of irony, Jasmine recalled the countless times she had wished for something just like this: a brother to take on the role that had been laid out for her since birth. A chance to be free and see the world, to choose her own life. The same wish Aladdin had granted the Genie. But now, with her birthright slipping through her fingers, Jasmine was nowhere near ready to let it go. Especially not into the hands of conniving Karim, with those menacing eyes she could never trust. Furious as she was at her father, Jasmine knew she would never be able to live with Karim taking his place.

"I have to fight this," she whispered to Rajah. "But how?"

"There was a door to which I found no key . . ."

Jasmine looked up sharply. *Not again.* The woman's voice—there it was, singing softly, just like last night.

"There was a veil past which I could not see . . ."

Now even Rajah's ears were perked. Listening.

Jasmine stood and tiptoed forward to follow the voice, which sounded both frustratingly near and, at the same time, a world away. She trailed it to her balcony window but found no one there, only a bird perched on the railing. It was a type of bird she'd seen just a few times in her life—it had caught her eye every time with its black plumage that turned a striking purplish-blue in the light. *That's our desert bird,* the palace gardener had told her when she was a little girl. *The fan-tailed raven.*

And now the voice disappeared. There was only silence, and Jasmine found herself right back where she had started—looking up in dejection at the portrait of the mother and grandmother who'd left her here alone.

"I don't have time for this," she snapped to the empty space around her. "I don't care about some door or veil, or the rest of that confounding verse. I have a traitorous cousin I need to defeat. So unless you can help with that, just leave me be—and take your haunting somewhere else."

• • •

By nightfall, Jasmine had turned away half a dozen visitors from her door, including Nadia bearing trays of food. Her stomach was starting to grumble after going empty for nearly a full day, but all it took was the thought of Karim wearing her father's crown, that smug smile on his face, and her appetite vanished. She was pacing the length of her bedroom, trying to formulate her next move, when she heard a familiar voice on the balcony.

"Jasmine, please, come out." Aladdin's warm voice entreated her from outside.

She turned to face the balcony doors, their curtains drawn. As much as she ached to feel Aladdin's closeness right now, she couldn't bear to see the look of pity on his face, the acknowledgment of all she had lost.

"I have a surprise for you," he added.

Jasmine felt herself start to waver. She had never been able to resist a surprise from Aladdin, who seemed to always have something wondrous up his sleeve.

She glanced down at Rajah. "What should I do?"

The tiger prodded her leg with his paw, nodding at the balcony.

"Oh, all right."

Jasmine crossed the room to the balcony and opened the doors to find Aladdin floating in midair behind the railing, a mischievous grin on his face.

"Look who came back," he said, before soaring above her on a large Persian carpet woven in an intricate pattern of rich blues and gold.

"Magic Carpet!" Jasmine exclaimed. For a brief moment, her troubles faded from view as Carpet and Aladdin landed on the balcony beside her. Carpet bowed with a flourish, and Jasmine crouched down to hug the colorful fabric. It used its tassels to hug her back. "I thought you were with the Genie!"

"It seems the little fella knew we needed him," Aladdin said, handing Jasmine a folded piece of parchment from his vest pocket. The Genie's loopy blue handwriting filled the page.

Al and Jas,

Can you take this carpet off my hands? It's getting to be a real drag, just letting me walk all over it. (Ba-da-bum!)

For real, though, a little bird told me that you could use a pick-me-up. Since Carpet can literally take care of that, he's yours. Just save me a couple weeks a year for my annual World Carpet Tour, okay?

Good luck, kids, and know I'm always rooting for you,

G

Jasmine hugged the parchment to her chest.

"Thank you, Genie." She met Aladdin's eyes. "It's amazing, isn't it, how he always knows?"

"It must come with the all-powerful-greatness package." Aladdin grinned, pulling her close.

She knew he was concerned for her, but Jasmine was relieved to not find any pity in his eyes. It wasn't every day that a would-be sultana was so brutally humiliated in front of her kingdom, her identity called into question, yet Aladdin still looked at Jasmine like she was every bit a queen.

She closed her eyes against the warm sturdiness of his chest as he tightened his arms around her and kissed her hair, grateful for the lack of questions. No useless *How are you?* or stress-inducing *What happens now?* He was simply there for her, and that was all she needed.

"What do you say we get out of here?" Aladdin offered, cocking his head toward Magic Carpet. "Take a little ride and get away from it all?"

Jasmine hesitated. It sounded perfect, but . . .

"I don't want to leave while *he* is still in the palace," she grumbled.

"Just for a few hours," he coaxed her. "Everyone is going to bed now, anyway. He's surrounded by guards. What could he do?"

Magic Carpet twirled in the air in front of Jasmine, nodding eagerly for her to say yes. She couldn't help but giggle.

"All right," she conceded. "Just for a few hours." But Jasmine knew even as she said it that once she felt the wind in her face and the swoop in her stomach, she wouldn't want to be anywhere else but in the air.

Carpet flattened itself on the ground and Jasmine climbed onto its soft fabric, holding one of the front tassels like a horse's reins. Aladdin climbed up beside her, his arm around her waist. Once they were seated, the Magic Carpet began to rise...as if they weighed nothing at all.

Jasmine whooped with delight as Carpet picked up speed, soaring higher and higher. She felt a rush as they flew above the gold-domed towers of the palace, leaving today's pain behind. They skimmed the rectangular rooftops and steepled towers of Agrabah, so quickly that Jasmine only had a split second to notice the leftover flowers and flags in the windows meant to honor her blotted-out coronation, before Carpet rose higher still, racing above the clouds to join the birds and the scattering of stars. From up here, those same rooftops were like miniatures—her entire kingdom the size of a doll's house. Jasmine felt the tension in her body disappear, replaced with only the rush of flight.

They sailed beneath the moon, and it looked so close that Jasmine felt sure that if she stood, she could reach up and touch the glowing crescent. Then Carpet made a sudden swoop and Jasmine yelped, and Aladdin let out a giddy laugh, spurring on their guide to amp up the wild turns and loops in the sky. Carpet led them past the towering Zagros Mountains and bronze valleys of Agrabah, toward the lakes and vistas of its neighboring country, Azra. Jasmine looked on in wide-eyed wonder, drinking in every spectacular sight while her stomach rose and fell with the ride.

The brilliant blue Karkheh River appeared below them, its water stretching for what looked like forever. Carpet plunged down toward it, swooping so low that Jasmine could feel the water's mist spray her face. She gasped and Aladdin grabbed her hand, keeping a protective hold on her as they rode the waves. They exchanged an exhilarated smile, and Jasmine raised their clasped hands up to the sky, imagining they were two birds who shared the same pair of wings.

Carpet stopped for a rest at the top of a mountain peak, pausing them in midair. Jasmine turned to Aladdin, just as he inched closer to her. And suddenly her lips were on his, and he was cradling her face in his hands, kissing her with a passion that would have sent her soaring even if she were still on solid ground. Jasmine ran her hands through his soft black hair as he pulled her closer, so entwined in each other that they forgot where they were, forgot everything but the feel of each other's skin, the sound of their racing heartbeats.

It wasn't until minutes later that they finally took a breath, Jasmine leaning her head on Aladdin's shoulder as they gazed out at the flowing Karkheh River and the golden-brown sand dunes beyond.

"It's an incredible world out there, isn't it?" Aladdin sighed in contentment. "A world we now have the chance and the freedom to explore." He met her eyes. "If you want to."

Jasmine smiled wistfully.

"It would be wonderful, wouldn't it?"

"*Could* be wonderful," he corrected her. "No one would blame you if you chose to step down after what happened today. You and I could be free to travel the world and live the life we always wanted. You could finally be free."

Jasmine tugged at a strand of her hair, trying to put her conflicting feelings into words.

"Everything would be so different if I had grown up knowing I had a brother," she said quietly. "If I knew and trusted him, then of course, I'd have loved nothing more than to let him rule the kingdom while you and I go off on our adventures. But as much as I hate to go back, I can't abandon my duty to my people. I can't give my father's throne to this usurper."

Aladdin placed his hand over hers, lacing their fingers together.

"I understand."

"I just can't make any sense of this. I know the letter looks real, I *know* it's my father's handwriting. But I feel so clearly in my gut that Karim is lying." Her shoulders slumped. "Of course, no one would take my intuition over his proof."

"Your feelings haven't steered you wrong before," Aladdin reminded her. "Trust them."

"And even if he is telling the truth, even if my father really did lie to me for all these years, I just can't accept that my whole kingdom would so easily cast me aside for a stranger when I am the only legitimate child from the sultan's marriage." She let out a frustrated exhale. "It can't be such a crime to be born a girl."

"No, it can't." Aladdin narrowed his eyes, his expression determined as he asked, "What are we going to do to stop them?"

"I don't know." Jasmine thought for a moment, and then called out, "Carpet, can you fly us to Orostan? There's something I need to see."

Carpet pitched forward, and the wind whipped beneath them as they curved and soared through the sky. Jasmine felt her stomach flip in exhilaration, a grin spreading across her face. But as they hovered above the Orostan farmland, her smile froze.

Even in the moonlight, she could see that all the greenery was gone, covered by a layer of sand the color of charred ash. Lying there with their bodies half-buried were more than a dozen dead horses, in a scene frighteningly similar to the vision in the council chamber window.

The story Nadia had heard was true.

Jasmine and Aladdin exchanged a look of horror.

"Fly us lower, please," she urged Carpet.

She heard Aladdin's sharp intake of breath as they skimmed closer to the ground, flying just above the carnage, where the blood of the horses had stained the sand a black-tinged red. The strange and oppressive gray fog was here too, hanging low over the gruesome scene, while smoke curled through the air.

"What happened to them?" Jasmine whispered. "A sandstorm wouldn't cause . . . *this*. At most there would be dust everywhere, enough to burn your eyes and throat, but nothing that would draw this bloodshed."

"It looks a lot more sinister than a sandstorm to me," Aladdin said grimly. "Carpet, will you show us to the town? We should check if anyone needs help."

"Good idea." Jasmine gripped her edge of the carpet tighter as they flew toward the center of town. But what they found were empty, sand-covered streets and the ghost of a marketplace, with torn awnings and bare shelves. She covered her mouth with her hand, a pit forming in her stomach.

Carpet seemed just as spooked as the two of them. It flew hastily from the scene, weaving its way between deserted-looking farmhouses. Jasmine and Aladdin peered through the windows as they swooped past, finding only darkness. No candles lit, no signs of life inside.

"Where did the people *go*?" Aladdin asked, his brow furrowed.

"It looks as if they knew something bad was coming," Jasmine said with a shiver. "Something bad enough to flee."

Carpet picked up speed, clearly ready to leave this desolate place behind. As they flew over the gray-turned farmland, they spotted movement in the sand—their first sign of life.

A yellow snake, long and coiling, slithered toward the animal carcasses. At their approach, its head flicked up, beady eyes meeting theirs. Jasmine could feel the carpet shudder beneath her. The last time she'd seen a snake as large and vivid as this, it had been in the pages of a book. A wicked creature from one of the frightening folktales Taminah loved to scare her with. Jasmine peered closer, curious despite her fear, leaning over the edge of the carpet. . . .

Suddenly the snake's tongue slithered out of its mouth and its head reared back, as if to strike her. She recoiled with a gasp as Aladdin shouted, "Fly, Carpet!" Carpet didn't need to be told twice; it took off into the night sky. They could still hear the hissing down below.

Jasmine couldn't breathe, not until they reached the lights of Agrabah City and saw the familiar teardrop-shaped rooftops of monuments and towers, the clustered streets of row houses and the waving awnings of the bazaar. *Home.* The hour had grown late by now, but there was still the comforting sound of voices rising up from below, even strains of flute and sitar playing through an open window. The darkness that had fallen upon Orostan had not yet reached the heart of Agrabah, and Jasmine was determined that it never should. She would stay and fight—for herself, for her people, and for her country.

CHAPTER FIFTEEN

Jasmine dressed carefully the next morning, choosing her clothes like they were her armor. She paired a regal purple waistcoat and blouse with matching wide-legged trousers gathered at the ankle and bordered in gold thread, while Nadia dressed her hair with a diamond-studded tiara inherited from Jasmine's mother. As she surveyed herself in front of the mirror, the ensemble had just the effect she'd hoped for. There was nothing delicate about Princess Jasmine today. She looked the picture of power.

Now it was time for her to claim it.

Nadia sent for Arman, who turned up at her door minutes later. Jasmine squared her shoulders and stood tall to greet him, using her most commanding voice as she said, "I require a meeting with the crown ministers, the high elder, and Cousin Karim. Today."

"Your Highness, I can assure you that your government has been locked in discussions to sort out the issue of succession since yesterday. Once we come to more of an agreement—"

"I insist on being an active part of these discussions," Jasmine interrupted firmly. "The sultan you so loyally served believed all his life that I would go on to be his successor. Before anyone tries to betray his wishes, I have the right to make myself heard."

Arman nodded, looking slightly taken aback.

"We meet at eleven in the council chamber. I'll send for the high elder and Karim."

"Thank you. That will be all."

Step one, complete, she thought as Arman's footsteps faded down the hall. Once he was gone, she crept out the door and down the corridor until she was standing at the threshold of the Sultan's suite, another memory bubbling up to the surface.

She was twelve and standing at her father's elbow as he knelt before a curious wooden chest, in the four corners of which a disc-shaped dial was carved. Each disc was bordered by sixteen letters in the old Aramaic alphabet, with a triangular notch at the perimeter. Jasmine watched in fascination as the sultan began turning the dials.

"The inventor Badi al-Jazari calls it a 'combination lock,'" her father explained, his voice brimming with excitement. "He brought it to court yesterday, to show me before he includes it in his new Book of Knowledge. Choose the right combination of four letters, and the lock will open . . . like this."

Jasmine bent down for a closer look as her father twisted the notch on the first dial to the letter *D* and the second to *V.* He aligned the third notch with the letter *J,* and after he twisted the fourth dial to *S*—the lid swung off the trunk.

"It works!" Jasmine clapped her hands together in glee.

"Just as he showed me." The sultan gave a nod of satisfaction before reaching into the trunk.

"But why is it empty?" Jasmine asked with a frown.

"Because I have to decide on something valuable enough to lock inside," he answered, smiling down at her. "Something for you, perhaps." He rose to his feet, crossing the suite to his writing desk. Opening his marble correspondence box, the sultan retrieved a sheaf of paper, embossed with his seal and the emblem of Agrabah. "Like this."

Back in the present, Jasmine raced through the room to her father's wardrobe, all the while praying that no one else knew about the trunk—that it would still be there.

She searched on her hands and knees, rummaging through the stack of silk and velvet blankets at the back of the wardrobe until she felt it against her palm: the wooden trunk. It was still there, in the same hiding place he'd shown her years before.

"Please let the letters be unchanged too," Jasmine whispered into the empty room. And then she began to turn the dials, just as she'd watched her father do.

$D \ldots V \ldots J \ldots S \ldots$

With a loud click, the lid snapped open. And there it was, nestled in the trunk where it had been placed six years ago: a single sheet of parchment, signed by her father—declaring Princess Jasmine his official heiress and successor.

To twelve-year-old Jasmine, it had seemed the most anticlimactic, unnecessary "valuable" to store in the trunk. She'd soon forgotten all about it . . . but now she was beginning to think her father had known just how badly she might need this piece of paper one day.

It was almost as if he'd expected a challenger to her throne.

. . .

Jasmine arrived at the council chamber early, ready to claim her father's seat at the head of the long mahogany table. But first, she took a glance through the enchanted window, wondering in the back of her mind if the ministers had shown it to Karim yet too.

Where before only one of the five windowpanes showed a scene of strife, now there were two. The outer reaches of the desert and the farmland of Orostan both looked desolate through the glass, their landscapes stained by death. And suddenly this fight for the throne seemed small by comparison. . . .

She was startled by a noise behind her, and turned. Karim stood in the doorway, and when her eyes met his, they flashed darker. He looked somehow taller than yesterday, his face a picture of smug confidence that only briefly wavered when he saw Jasmine standing behind the sultan's chair. He nodded to her instead of bowing, muttering a quick "Your Highness" before taking a seat at the opposite end of the long table. Jasmine stared straight ahead, making a valiant attempt to ignore his presence.

The ministers filtered in after him. Jasmine kept her eyes narrowed on Commander Zohar for a few extra seconds, wanting him to feel in her stare what she thought of him now.

"Your Royal Highness," Arman said with a hurried bow. "I was just about to come upstairs to escort you."

"Thank you, but I don't need an escort," Jasmine said coolly. "This is my home."

He didn't respond, lending her words added significance as they hung in the air.

The high elder entered next and made a point of bowing to not just Jasmine, but Karim as well. The gesture felt like a stab in the chest, seeing the high elder validate her usurper in that way, but Jasmine reminded herself to stay calm. *Don't let them see how this is affecting you.*

She was just clearing her throat, about to say her piece, when she heard a clamor of footsteps at the door. And before she knew it, a half-dozen royal guests were marching into the room to join them.

"What is all this?" Jasmine whispered to Parisa, the minister nearest her, before bending to curtsy to the guests, who still out-ranked her after the coronation-that-wasn't.

"Your ministers and the high elder were all in agreement that the neighboring rulers and heirs should have a voice in the matter, seeing as whoever ascends the throne of Agrabah will be known as their 'king of kings,'" Parisa answered. Jasmine winced at the term that so clearly assumed a masculine ruler. "Not to mention the importance of maintaining smooth trade and diplomatic relations between our lands."

Jasmine nodded, but she felt a shot of outrage when Prince Achmed strolled in. The last thing she needed was someone like him having a say in her future.

Once every seat around the table was filled, Commander Zohar stood up to speak.

"Welcome, everyone, to a critical meeting between our nations' rulers and successors, and the government of Agrabah. Let us begin—"

"I have something to say," Jasmine announced, before any of the men had a chance to talk over her. She stood and gripped the back of her chair, beginning the speech she'd spent the past hour rehearsing in her mind.

"I understand that to some of you, the suggestion of my father's alleged indiscretion seemed credible enough to warrant pausing my coronation. But there are other more likely explanations—including that the letter was not, in fact, alluding to what you all assumed, and that my physical resemblance to this man is simply due to our being cousins. Yet there can be no other interpretation to *this* official document that my father kept safeguarded all these years."

Jasmine reached for the shawl beneath her chair, unwrapping the fabric to reveal the sultan's Letter of Succession tucked carefully inside.

"I believe that's your signature as witness, Commander?" Jasmine said coolly, holding up the parchment for her rapt audience around the table. She glanced at Karim out of the corner of her eye and was gratified to see his face turning a shade of purple. Commander Zohar coughed awkwardly.

"It is, Your Highness, though of course if I'd had any idea back then about Karim—"

"Who is, himself, only an idea," Jasmine interrupted. "I am the truth. Just as this legal document from the last, *legitimate* sultan proves."

"Whatever it may say, the people of Agrabah now know there

is a male heir," Karim said, staring daggers at her before turning to address the rest of the table. "It is already unprecedented to have a sultana instead of a sultan. Do you truly think the kingdom will accept her when they have a capable son ready to assume the throne?"

"Interesting question," Jasmine said without looking at Karim, keeping her eyes focused on the ministers and royals in front of her. "Though I have a better one. Do you think the kingdom will accept *him*, a usurper they know nothing about, when I'm the one they've celebrated as their future monarch since the day of my birth?"

There was a pause in which Jasmine felt a rush of triumph, that surely she must have won the argument. But then Hassan, minister of law, spoke up.

"We did, in fact, pose that question to all the key landowners and nobles of the kingdom who were in attendance yesterday—and their support was split down the middle between you and Karim." He cleared his throat. "As was the case here in this room, when all of us ministers met to discuss the issue last night, without the two of you present."

Stung, Jasmine slumped back in her seat. How was it even *possible* that so many of them, who had only just met Karim, could so quickly and easily take his side?

"And what about the people? I don't mean wealthy landowners or nobles, but the men and women and families who make up the vast majority of Agrabah?" she challenged.

A few of the visiting royals exchanged chuckles as Zohar said dismissively, "Their opinion holds no weight here."

That's the first thing I'll change when I'm sultana, Jasmine silently vowed. Out loud, she said, "There's something else to consider." She paused, unsure how much to say, but then the words came tumbling out.

"I fear there is a dark and malevolent force sweeping across Agrabah. The sandstorm wreaking havoc on our animals, people, and crops is...not of this world. I've seen what's become of Orostan in only a matter of days." A murmur rippled through the room. Jasmine steeled herself. "Furthermore, I've spoken to my father's physician, and ... I don't believe his death was due to natural causes. He has spoken to me from beyond the grave. Our lives, our very safety, is at stake. The people need their country's true leader—*me*—now more than ever."

The expressions around the table ranged from dubious and pitying to flashes of recognition from her ministers ... and even a hint of fear. Jasmine knew then that the number might be small, but there were at least one or two others here who believed as she did.

"Well, if she doesn't take the crown, Princess Jasmine can always be a storyteller," Achmed chortled.

Jasmine shot him a withering look as Commander Zohar said, "Assuming there *were* such a malevolent force and threat to Agrabah—how could we entrust our kingdom's safety and leadership to someone who has never fought in battle before?"

Her cheeks burned at the kernel of truth in his words, even as she argued, "I defeated a dark force once. I can do it again."

"You had plenty of help fighting Jafar," the commander reminded her. "It was hardly you single-handedly defeating the man."

"And I would have help here too—"

"Enough!" the king of Azra's voice boomed. He rose from his

chair, and the room grew silent. Once he had the table's attention, he said, "In the absence of an irrefutable heir, it seems to me that if you are to evaluate who is the rightful monarch, then you need a chance to see how each would lead. A way to measure them against each other."

Arman raised an eyebrow.

"And how would we do that?"

"Historically, these things would be decided by a tournament," Prince Rashid commented.

Karim leaned back in his seat with a cocky grin, arms folded behind his head.

"Well, I've never fought a woman before, but I suppose there *is* a first time for everything."

"Wait a minute." Khaleel drummed his fingertips on the table. "What if it wasn't that sort of tournament, but another? A series of challenges designed to test your skills, instincts, and leadership in the key areas of governance . . . such as the same six sectors represented by each of us ministers?" He jumped to his feet, warming to his idea. "By winning the tournament, either Princess Jasmine or Master Karim would secure the respect and loyalty of the kingdom, far beyond what their parentage alone commands."

Jasmine shook her head in disbelief. Was he actually suggesting that the ruler of their kingdom should come down to whoever won a silly *game* instead of automatically going to the sultan's only legitimate heir? Surely no one else would fall for this harebrained idea . . . and since when was her cousin called *Master* Karim, anyway? But to her chagrin, heads were nodding in approval all around the table. Only Karim looked less than enthused. He obviously hadn't expected to have to jump through any hoops to win the crown either.

"We could announce the tournament far and wide, encouraging visitors from all across the empire to come to Agrabah for the events," Parisa suggested. "This would put Agrabah at the very center of the world stage."

"Not to mention the visitors would fill up our inns and shop at our bazaars," Khaleel said eagerly. Jasmine could practically see the silver and gold coins dancing behind his eyes.

"And who would judge this tournament?" she asked, crossing her arms against her chest. "How could we be sure it's fair and impartial?"

"May I suggest a panel of judges?" Majid offered. "The minister who devises his or her challenge could also serve as judge, along with one of our neighboring rulers here to offer their perspective. The high elder can serve as tiebreaker."

Sharif nodded sagely.

"It's certainly a canny solution to our predicament."

Jasmine exhaled in frustration. She was outnumbered. Even the sultan's Letter of Succession had given her no advantage. Her only option was to play their game—and win.

"Fine," she said crisply. "If this is what it takes, then I look forward to proving myself the true and worthy successor of my father."

"And I look forward to proving you wrong," Karim retorted.

The king of Azra chortled in amusement.

"Let the games commence!"

CHAPTER SIXTEEN

Word of the Crown Tournament rippled its way across Agrabah within just a couple of days. From her balcony, Jasmine could see flags beginning to rise from the roofs across the kingdom, some painted with an image of her face and the name *Sultana Jasmine*, while others were adorned with bold script declaring Karim the *king of kings*. Her people were choosing sides already—and in yet another stinging blow for Jasmine, it was clear the minister of law was right. The kingdom was divided. Even after watching her grow up, after proclaiming their loyalty to both the sultan and Jasmine for all these years, it still wasn't enough. Not when there was the prospect of a male heir.

In the afternoon, a frenzied knock sounded at her door. It was Princess Shirin, who barreled into the room breathless.

"They're forming a training team around him," she blurted out as soon as Jasmine opened the door.

"What? Who?"

"Commander Zohar—he's trying to help Karim win," Shirin

said. "He knows he can't be seen actively training Karim himself since he's on the judging panel, so he's tasking others with the job. Like my brother."

Jasmine's stomach twisted. Even though she had never been particularly wowed by Rashid as a person, he was still skilled and influential enough to make for an unwelcome enemy.

"The only good news is that Rashid says we're not going home as planned," Shirin continued. "We're staying until the close of the tournament, which could be weeks from now."

"That is good news," Jasmine said, thinking quickly. "Especially because I'll need a training team now too, including someone who can help me get inside Karim's and Rashid's heads." She paused. "Will you do it, Shirin? Be part of my training team?"

Shirin's mouth opened and closed before she finally answered.

"You know I want to, Jasi. But Rashid . . . he'll make things even more miserable for me. He expects me to follow his lead. Which means rallying behind Karim." She raised her eyes to the ceiling. "Who even knows why he's backing that horse?"

"Because seeing me on the throne of Agrabah would let the world know that women can be rulers too—and the people of Numan may start to question why *you*, the eldest child of the king, couldn't be the one to succeed him. That's what Rashid is so worried about," Jasmine said flatly. "As he should be."

Shirin slumped onto the nearest ottoman, chin in her hands.

"It's all ghastly unfair. But . . ." She glanced up. "Maybe there's a way I can help you without him knowing? I mean, Rashid isn't *completely* thickheaded, he knows you're one of my closest friends, but I could pretend to be on his and Karim's side for the sake of the family . . . and then tell you everything they're up to."

Jasmine felt a flash of hope.

"That could work. You can be like my secret war council—publicly supporting Karim and Rashid, but just as an act."

"Just an act," Shirin promised, holding out her hand. The two princesses shook, sealing their agreement.

. . .

While the ministers reconvened alone in the council chamber to devise the tournament's four challenges, Jasmine made her way to the library, determined to get her hands on all the knowledge she could find that might help her win. On her way there, she crossed the royal household wing to the opposite side of the grand staircase from her and the sultan's suites, heading toward the chain of rooms reserved for other members of the family. The cream-and-pink room was Jasmine's former nursery, preserved for her future children to use one day, and the beige-and-gold room overlooking the fountain courtyard was given to Aladdin by the sultan, after he and Jasmine were engaged. She was just about to knock on Aladdin's door when she heard footsteps coming up behind her.

Jasmine turned to see Karim striding toward the third, unoccupied bedroom with Payam behind him, carrying a trunk in each hand. She stopped in her tracks.

"What are you doing up here?" she demanded, eyeing the trunks suspiciously.

"What does it look like, sister?" He stretched out the syllables with his tongue, clearly relishing the way Jasmine shuddered at the word. "I'm moving in."

Jasmine shot a pointed look at Payam.

"All of our royal guests are staying in the East Wing. Surely a room situated near the likes of the king of Azra and prince of Batana is good enough for him?"

Payam licked his lips nervously before answering, "I was instructed by Arman to find more permanent quarters for Master Karim, given the . . . situation."

Jasmine's face turned hot with fury.

"Have you all forgotten that I was nearly killed by an intruder just last week?" she snapped at Payam as Karim walked ahead of them and flung open the bedroom door. "Now is hardly the time to allow anyone new onto this floor."

"But, Your Royal Highness, what you saw—or thought you saw—was well before Karim even arrived in Agrabah," Payam said, blinking back at her. "Surely there is no connection between the two events."

"So you think," Jasmine grumbled. She straightened her spine. "Either way, this is my home first and foremost, and I don't feel safe with him so close."

"I'm afraid you'll have to take it up with Arman," Payam said. "Though I'd be happy to arrange for a second guard to patrol this floor, if that would put you at ease."

Jasmine gave a halfhearted nod. There wasn't much comfort in the prospect of yet another guard. She wasn't sure she could even trust them at this point, not after seeing how quick they were to take Karim's side.

Just then, Aladdin's bedroom door swung open. He stepped out, handsome as ever in his white tunic and red vest paired with gold-trimmed cream trousers, Abu perched on his shoulder. He grinned at the sight of her, and Jasmine felt a rush of relief. The only thing that could possibly make Karim's intrusion into her life bearable was the fact that Aladdin was here too.

"I thought I heard your voice," he said, greeting her with a bow and a kiss on the hand.

"I wanted to see if you'd join me in the library," she said under her breath. "And then I found . . . this."

She nodded at the open doorway of the bedroom beside his, revealing burnished red damask walls and dark-wood furniture that Karim was already settling his trunks onto.

"Oh." Aladdin's face fell. "I see."

Karim peered out of the doorway, his expression souring when he saw Aladdin.

"Don't tell me that room is yours."

Jasmine couldn't help smiling. Little had Karim realized that moving up to the prized family wing would mean being neighbors with her betrothed, whom he clearly looked down upon.

"That's one silver lining," she said cheerily. "You two will have plenty of time to get to know each other now. And Aladdin will be *sure* to fill me in on everything you're up to."

With that, Jasmine took Aladdin's hand and turned on her heel, leaving Karim scowling behind them.

• • •

Out of all the palace's awe-inspiring interiors, the Round Library had always been Jasmine's favorite. A marble floor painted with a lotus-flower motif gave way to three tiers of balconies lined with books, stretching up to an arched ceiling where a bronze chandelier flooded the circular space with candlelight. Bound books had still been a novelty when the sultan was young, but in the intervening years, he'd amassed a collection of nearly three thousand titles from across the East. This was where Jasmine had come to fill in the gaps in her knowledge while her nonroyal peers were sent off to school. It was thanks to the books in this room that she'd learned to read and write in Greek and Latin along with Persian and Arabic, that she could look at an astrolabe and point out the different planets in the universe. It was where she'd fallen in love with studying maps and imagining other lands, far from here—and where her tutor had found those spine-tingling tales that had captivated her years ago.

"It's the chapter you've been waiting for, Princess."

Jasmine's head whipped up at the sound of Taminah's long-ago voice, echoing through the room . . . or through her memory. Aladdin didn't seem to notice a thing, but Jasmine could have sworn she heard the sound of rustling pages, and her own childish footsteps rushing to Taminah's reading chair.

"The Story of Dahish the Ifrit," Taminah read, an eager glint in her eye. *"A tale of a jinn who chose darkness."*

"I thought all the jinn were good," Jasmine had said, furrowing her brow. *"Don't they jump out of bottles and lamps granting wishes?"*

"Mmm. Not all. You see, they have free will, just as humans do. The jinn who use their powers for good are known as Genie, while those who succumb to evil take the name Ifrit." She lowered her voice theatrically in Jasmine's ear. *"Demon."*

The young princess had jumped then, and Taminah laughed. After a beat, Jasmine giggled too. . . .

"Are you all right, Princess?"

Aladdin's voice cut through Jasmine's memory, bringing her back to the present.

"Oh. Yes, of course. I was just remembering . . ." She moved farther into the room. "I used to spend so much time in here when I was a child. When everything was simpler."

She shook her head, refocusing on the task at hand. Today, she was looking for books of an entirely different kind than the ones with which Taminah used to entertain her.

"You still seem a thousand miles away."

She hesitated, wondering if now was the time to tell him.

"Would you believe me if I told you something . . . slightly impossible?"

Aladdin gave her a sideways smile.

"Jasmine. You and I were brought together by the help of a genie, and our first date was on a magic carpet. Is there anything I *wouldn't* believe?"

"I know," she said, chuckling. "It's just that . . ." Her smile faded. "Well, even the Genie said it was impossible to bring anyone back from the dead. And yet—I know it happened. Baba opened his eyes and spoke to me."

Aladdin listened, his expression riveted, as Jasmine revealed what had happened in the underground room with the sultan's body.

"He instructed me to find a book, only he didn't tell me what kind. And he said someone's coming, and not to trust them," Jasmine confided. "It wasn't even three days later that Karim showed up with his outrageous claim. I just know Baba was trying to warn me about him."

Aladdin's dark brown eyes deepened as he studied her.

"I believe you," he said. "And I'll help you solve this. The only thing I'm unsure of is if the 'someone' the sultan was talking about is Karim. It would appear that way . . . but we've both seen how appearances can be deceiving. The palace is full of guests right now, and it could be any one of them."

"But only one has tried to do me harm," Jasmine reminded him. "The one trying to steal my throne."

"That's true. But I still think we need to be more careful with everyone in the palace. Not just Karim." Aladdin's face was grim as he added, "I'm beginning to doubt all of their intentions."

Jasmine couldn't argue with that. The two were quiet for a moment as she began to climb the spiral staircase that wound up through the balconies of books, and Aladdin followed.

"The ministers haven't told us what the tournament challenges will be yet, but I was thinking we could start by looking for books related to the different fields they're testing us in." Stepping off onto the first balcony, Jasmine began riffling through the nearest shelf. "So, books about Agrabah law, wars and trade, and so on. All the things they don't expect me to know enough about."

"What's that?" Aladdin pointed to the top balcony overhead, where a wooden wheel layered with shelves of angled books stood on display.

"My father's book wheel," Jasmine replied. "It was a gift from one of Agrabah's inventors, a rotating shelf that allows you to have multiple books open at one time."

"Why would someone need that?" Aladdin wondered.

"Baba said it was created mainly for scholars to go back and forth between texts while collecting information. But he loved to use it for his personal reading too."

She stopped still, locking eyes with Aladdin.

"*That's it.* The books on the wheel right now are the ones my father would have been reading before his death—which makes it the best place to find what we're looking for."

Aladdin grabbed her hand.

"Let's go."

They raced up the spiral staircase, anticipation thrumming as they reached the top balcony and the book wheel. Jasmine gave it a spin, holding her breath as her father's last collection of books rotated into view. She grabbed each leather-bound tome as it slid to the fore, quickly studying the title before adding it to the growing pile in Aladdin's hands. There was a volume of poetry by Omar Khayyam and an epic tale by Ferdowsi. A book of medicine and al-Sufi's *Book of Fixed Stars,* along with an updated printing of the alchemists' handbook *The Emerald Tablet.*

Jasmine and Aladdin spread the six volumes out on one of the wooden reading tables, trying to piece together the puzzle.

"Khayyam and Ferdowsi must have been just for Baba's entertainment," Jasmine said, moving those two aside. "He always did love poetry. I can't imagine either of these being of any help to us, though."

"And he likely started reading the book of medicine because of his own health troubles." Aladdin added it to the stack, on top of Ferdowsi's fiction.

"So that leaves the *Book of Fixed Stars* and *The Emerald Tablet.*"

Jasmine sighed. "One about constellations, and the other, from what I remember, being long ruminations on philosophy and creation." She glanced up at Aladdin, perplexed. "I can't imagine why he'd find any of these so urgent for me to read."

"The cover says this one is a new volume." Aladdin turned *The Emerald Tablet* over in his palm. "Maybe there's something in here you haven't seen before."

"I hope so." Jasmine stacked the rest of the books together, staring at their faded leather spines. "But I'm going to have to read them all to be sure of what we're looking for."

· · ·

Jasmine had every intention of skipping dinner at court for as long as Karim and Commander Zohar were in attendance. She couldn't stand to watch the intruder and the traitor feasting away in her dining hall, their faces ruddy as much from drink as from the high of being so close to power. But it was Nadia who talked her out of dining alone with the books she brought back from the library.

"Think of what it will say to everyone if they are at the head table with the other royals and you're nowhere to be found," she cautioned, her deft fingers moving quickly as she dressed Jasmine's hair in front of the mirror. "Don't give your cousin any more opportunities to playact at being sultan. There are enough fools in the dining hall to fall for it."

"You're right, as usual. Though I don't know how I'll stomach it." Jasmine shuddered at the thought of sharing a table with them.

"You will, the same way you'll get through every day until you take back your crown: by knowing that you are the rightful heir, and that it's only a matter of time before all of Agrabah recognizes it again too."

"Thank you." Jasmine met her eyes in the mirror, and they shared a smile. Though in truth, she didn't feel quite as optimistic as Nadia. Karim had already come so much further than she ever would have expected. Who could say how far his scheme would take him in the end?

She arrived at the banquet hall just as everyone was taking their seats around the long dark-wood tables set with gold and silver plates and ewers. The court performers were taking their positions at the head of the room, in front of the monarch's table, and Jasmine froze when she saw that her father's seat was already taken. But to her surprise, it wasn't Karim in the weighty, gilded chair. It was the commander.

Gritting her teeth, Jasmine weaved her way between the tables, hardly registering the voices calling her name or the members of court who stood from their seats to bow and curtsy. Her mind was too preoccupied, buzzing with what she would say when she reached him.

The table was filled with a who's who of Arabian royalty, and it took all Jasmine's self-control to go down the line and curtsy to her superiors when all she really wanted to do was run to her father's chair and shake Commander Zohar right out of it. When she finally made it to him and Karim—who was sitting beside Zohar, right across from Jasmine's usual seat—the rest of the table fell silent to watch.

"Your Royal Highness." Commander Zohar rose to bow, but Jasmine ignored his greeting.

"I didn't realize there was a third contender for my father's throne," she said, eyeing him pointedly. "Why are you not seated with the other ministers, Zohar?"

He flashed her one of his jarring, teeth-baring smiles.

"Perhaps Your Highness needs to brush up on the rules of succession. As the sultan's second-in-command, I am bound to serve as Agrabah's proxy ruler until the new monarch is crowned."

Jasmine sucked in her breath as she remembered. He was right. *No wonder he was so enthusiastic about the tournament.* The longer it took to crown her father's replacement, the longer Commander Zohar would wield the power. And there was nothing she could do about it.

She reluctantly took her seat beside him, turning to face the side of the table that *didn't* include him or Karim. At this point even Prince Achmed, currently picking a morsel of meat from between his front teeth, was practically a welcome sight compared to those two. Luckily Princess Shirin was there as well, and she sent Jasmine an imperceptible wink across the table when no one was looking. Jasmine had one ally nearby, at least. That was when it hit her that Aladdin was missing from the table. He used to always dine with Jasmine and the sultan . . . in the same seat Karim was occupying now.

She turned in her chair, scanning the crowded dining hall for him as the commander said, "We had to amend the seating arrangements to account for our more esteemed guests. Surely you understand."

Before she could reply, the court's musical trio launched into their first song. The soprano, lute, and tambourine drowned out any possible comeback she could make.

Jasmine tried to relax into the music, to focus on the other guests around the table, but it was no use. Surrounded by rivals, she was too jumpy and suspicious to even taste the food filling her plate.

When there was a break in the song, Commander Zohar leaned forward.

"We'll see you both in the council chamber tomorrow evening," he said to Jasmine and Karim. "The ministers will present your first task for the tournament."

Jasmine's pulse ticked faster. The commander gave Karim a slight smile as he added cryptically, "You'll be glad to have the right people in your corner to prepare you for this one."

Karim nodded and smirked down the table at Prince Rashid and then Achmed, who raised his goblet in the usurper's direction—as if already toasting to his victory. Jasmine froze. Did that mean Achmed was helping him too?

Whom do I have in my corner? she worried. There was Aladdin, of course, but he didn't know these people and their games. Shirin might be helpful if she were to succeed in getting intel from her brother and Karim. As for all the other royals around this table, and the nobles and members of court filling the dining hall ... well, she had to agree with Aladdin. Now that her father was gone, there were a scant few people here whom she could trust.

Which meant she would have to look beyond the palace walls.

CHAPTER SEVENTEEN

Aladdin arrived at her door the next morning looking like a man of the streets—the same one who had bumped into a disguised Jasmine in the marketplace last year and promptly changed her life. Instead of the sumptuous white-and-gold tunics and silk trousers and capes he now wore in the palace, Aladdin was back in his sun-faded purple vest and threadbare shirt paired with baggy pants torn haphazardly at the ankles, no doubt from all his running and jumping to escape the guards of the bazaar. Abu cooed happily on his shoulder, much more at home resting his fur on streetwear than silks.

Catching Jasmine and Rajah staring, Aladdin lifted his shoulders sheepishly.

"Nadia said to come looking like the old Aladdin, so I figured I might as well dust off the uniform." He glanced closer at Jasmine. "You look different too. Less . . . sparkly?"

Jasmine chuckled. Nadia had given her a pale-blue kaftan and chalvar pants that she wore on her own marketplace visits, embroidered simply and with no other embellishments.

"I'm so glad you kept those clothes," she said fondly.

"Can't forget where I came from," he replied with a grin. "Although I would have thought you'd be thrilled to never see these old duds again."

"You must be joking." Jasmine reached for his hands. "This is just how you looked when I first started to fall for you."

Aladdin's eyes warmed. He bent his head, pressing his lips against hers. She kissed him back, feeling the delicious rush as their lips met. But before she could get too comfortable, she pulled away.

"We have somewhere to be. There's a reason we're dressed like this—and it's not just a sentimental one."

"We're going into the city?" he guessed, a dimple appearing in his cheek.

"That's right." Jasmine pulled on Nadia's draped beige cloak. "And we're going in disguise."

• • •

Magic Carpet flew them high above the treetops, dipping behind the clouds whenever someone on the ground happened to glance up and squint at the sky. They weren't used to flying in broad daylight, but it was the only way for Jasmine and Aladdin to leave the palace without the guards or ministers or any other court spies noticing and following.

After an exhilarating few minutes in the air, they spotted the rectangular stone roofs of the marketplace below, with clotheslines hanging between them and smoke rising up from the food stalls.

Carpet sped behind the path of trees, pitching downward when Aladdin pointed out a safe place to land.

"Are you sure about this?" Jasmine had to shout to be heard above the wind as the rooftops rushed toward them. "Won't people see us up here?"

"We'll be gone before they blink." Aladdin grinned. "And inside is probably the safest spot you could be in the city. None of our enemies would set foot in a place like the broken tower."

Jasmine's breath caught as she realized where they were. Her mind flashed back to their first conversation alone, when he'd brought the girl he thought was a handmaiden up to his makeshift quarters after helping her escape an overzealous pair of guards. The broken tower was more of a hole than a home, but Aladdin had been giddy to draw back the tattered curtain and show her his view of the palace. Even though her gilded cage was the last place she wanted to see in that moment, her spirits had been lifted by this intensely charming young man from the marketplace who showed her such kindness without having a clue who she was. Jasmine smiled at the memory, lacing her fingers through Aladdin's as Carpet glided onto the crumbling rooftop. Abu scampered ahead of them, leading the way through a trapdoor in the roof to the cramped tower room where Aladdin and his pet monkey once lived, above an abandoned shopfront. Abu squealed at the sight of their old home, though Jasmine hardly recognized it.

Instead of Aladdin's single cot and thin blanket lying beside the lumpy square pillow that served as Abu's bed, there were now two rows of fine woolen mattresses lining the floor, made up with linen sheets and feather pillows. At the center of the space was a small stove and tea set, beside a table laden with breads, cheeses, and fruits. Abu made a beeline for the food, and that was when Jasmine noticed the family of three snacking underneath the table.

"Wh—where'd you all come from?" a little girl exclaimed, scrambling out from under the table so fast that she bumped her head.

"We were told it was safe here," the father called out, his expression verging on panic as he stood. A younger boy followed, clinging to his leg, and Jasmine felt a tug in her chest.

"Of course it is," Aladdin reassured them. "This place is here for you and anyone who needs it. I'm Aladdin, and this is my—er, this is my friend Nadia."

The father wiped his hands on his trousers before extending his palm to shake hands with Aladdin and Jasmine.

"I'm Babak, and these are my children, Laleh and Emad. I used to sell food and goods farmed in Orostan, but ever since my crops were destroyed in the sandstorm . . ." He let out a heavy exhale. "We've had nothing."

Jasmine's stomach lurched while Aladdin said quietly, "I know what you must be feeling. Please, stay as long as you'd like. Meals will be replenished every evening." He crouched down to eye level with the children. "Tonight's menu is fish and rice stew. I won't be here, so would you do me a favor? Will you be my taste testers, let me know if I chose the right order?"

The children's faces lit up with joy, while Babak gaped at Aladdin.

"Thank you, kind sir. You've blessed us."

Jasmine blinked back tears as she watched Aladdin point the

family toward a tall rattan trunk in the corner of the room that held toys and games, and warm clothing and shoes in a range of sizes. She had known men of all kinds, from sultans and princes to ministers and merchants, and everything in between—but she had never known anyone like Aladdin, generous even before he had anything material to give.

Jasmine reached into the pocket of her shawl, where she'd tucked a small sack of gold coins for the marketplace. She placed the sack on the table for the family beside the food, while making a silent promise.

As sultana, I will make sure no one in Agrabah goes hungry again.

. . .

"When did you do all this?" Jasmine asked, looking at Aladdin in wonder as they followed Abu down a cracked-stone staircase that led from the tower room to the marketplace below.

"Remember when I told you I had an idea I wanted to present to the sultan, and that it would cost some money?" Aladdin jumped over a pair of broken steps ahead of her, holding out his hand to help her. She gently brushed his hand aside, skipping over the steps on her own.

"I said that I trust you, and to ask him for anything you need," she recalled. "I'm so glad I did—and even more glad that he said yes."

"Me too. I just couldn't leave the streets without doing something to take care of the people who are still here." He stopped to face Jasmine, his gaze deepening. "You and the sultan changed my life. I wanted to give back some of that good fortune."

"*You* changed your life," she reminded him. "By saving us from

Jafar, and proving yourself to be the true 'diamond in the rough.'"

They shared a knowing smile.

"How many more of these do you think you can build?" Jasmine asked, looking back at the broken tower behind them. "So that anyone in Agrabah who needs food or shelter can have it?"

"There's space for another building at the far end of the marketplace, next to the rug sellers," Aladdin said eagerly. It was clear he'd already put much thought into this. "If we had the funds, we could create at least a dozen room-and-board units for people who need them."

"Let's do it," Jasmine told him. "Commander Zohar and the others might say no to us now, but once I am sultana, I'll have the final word."

Another idea was brimming in her mind too—a new role for Aladdin in her cabinet. A liaison or ambassador between the palace and the city so that the people who typically had the least say in the kingdom would have their voices heard.

She just had to get her title back first.

"Agrabah needs you," Aladdin said, as if reading her thoughts. "Let's find you a team and win that tournament."

CHAPTER EIGHTEEN

Jasmine's eyes lit up as they entered the colorful whirl of the bazaar, with all its cacophony of sounds. Merchants and shoppers filled the narrow cobblestone streets in an array of richly hued tunics, cloaks, and turbans, while market stalls draped in all different shades of fabric were brimming with wares and curiosities. From food vendors to carpet sellers, from jewelry to pottery and medicinal tea, one could find nearly everything under the desert sun here. There were even street performers, and Jasmine stopped in her tracks, riveted by a fire-breather who juggled four flaming torches before swallowing each of the flames whole.

Just then, two familiar guards rounded a corner and marched into the bazaar, knives glinting at their belts as they scanned the crowd for thieves. Jasmine hid her face in her cloak as Aladdin grabbed her arm and led them into a tiny alleyway behind the fish market stall.

"Don't worry," he murmured in her ear. "They're not looking for us." But she could tell he was a bit more nervous than he let on when he added, "Still, it couldn't hurt to wait for them to pass."

Jasmine wrinkled her nose as the fishy smells wafted toward them.

"If only we'd picked a less . . . pungent corner."

Aladdin laughed.

"Well, in the meantime, do you have any ideas about who you're looking for out there?" he asked as they waited for the guards to finish their rounds.

"I'm not sure yet. But . . ." Jasmine paused, thinking. "Well, Karim has his supposedly impressive military career and the old-guard, high-ranking types like the commander on his side. We might not be able to compete on that level, but we *could* win by playing the game a different way—by filling our team with the very people they've been trained their whole lives to look away from. People with talents and skills Karim wouldn't even know to prepare for."

Aladdin nodded slowly.

"The truest magic is usually hidden behind the ordinary," he agreed, the dimple in his cheek reappearing. "So let me introduce you to the Agrabah I know."

Aladdin peered around the corner to make sure the guards were gone, and then the two of them plus Abu darted forward, back into the hustle and bustle of the bazaar. As he led the way through the market stalls, murmuring commentary in her ear on each of the names and faces he knew, Jasmine got to see the town and its characters through his eyes. She learned that the coppersmith was once a great fighter who'd lost his arm fighting in a war in his youth, and that the woman with falcons perched on each of her shoulders was known to speak the language of animals. She got to meet Aladdin's old friend Tarek the tailor, and together they stopped to watch a drummer, trumpeter, and clarion player perform a joyful tune beneath the thousand-year-old olive tree at the center of the marketplace. It was one of the most fun afternoons Jasmine had ever spent, and for a brief moment she forgot about the pressure she was under to find her team.

Aladdin quickened his pace as they approached a large shopfront with the word TANNERY painted in calligraphy across its awning.

"If you want to learn how to fight, there's an old friend who taught me everything I know back when we were kids. I'd be willing to bet he could beat Karim in a duel any day of the week."

Jasmine raised an eyebrow.

"That description alone has me sold."

She followed him under the awning into a sprawling space lined with massive buckets nearly overflowing with paint in a wide range of colors. The buckets were manned by workers, some stirring and blending the dyes with long sticks while others dipped swaths of leather inside to dye. Everyone appeared to be working diligently . . . until Jasmine glanced up. On the balcony above, nearly hidden by hanging fabrics, two young men balanced on the rims of their paint buckets, using their sticks for a mock duel, grinning as they leaped from one bucket to the next without a spill. Jasmine gave Aladdin a dubious look.

"Don't tell me it's one of them."

"Do you trust me?" Aladdin said in response, grinning at the pair on the balcony.

Every time he had asked her that question since the day they met, Jasmine had said yes—and she'd never once regretted it. And so she said yes once again, then followed Aladdin and Abu across the tannery and up the ladder to the balcony.

"Malik!" Aladdin called.

One of the fake duelers paused his stick in midair and swiveled on the rim of the paint bucket. His mouth fell open at the sight of Aladdin and Jasmine.

"Aladdin?" The man named Malik dropped his stick and stepped off the paint bucket toward them. Aladdin pulled him in for a hug, and even Abu squealed happily as Malik reached down to ruffle his fur. Yet Jasmine couldn't help noticing that while Aladdin showed the warmth and enthusiasm of someone reuniting with a cherished friend, Malik had a slightly chilly demeanor. His companion, a man Aladdin greeted by the name Omar, seemed markedly more pleased to see him than Malik.

"I didn't think we'd ever see you again in our humble tannery," Malik said, his words pointed. "Thought you were too busy with your fancy princess in her fancy palace."

There it is, Jasmine thought. Malik clearly felt Aladdin had left him behind.

"I can never stay away for long," Aladdin replied easily, brushing off the tension. "I stopped by last week, but you were already gone for the day."

"Oh." Malik paused, letting that sink in. "And who is this?" He eyed Jasmine, who lowered the cloak from her face.

"The not-so-fancy princess," she quipped, before smiling and extending a hand. "It's nice to meet you both."

Malik's mouth fell open, his face turning bright red. He and Omar exchanged an astounded glance as they lowered into deep bows.

"The princess of Agrabah, in this place?" Malik shook his head in amazement. "Never thought I'd see the day."

"It's a wonderful place," Jasmine said, glancing admiringly at all the brilliant colors and transformed leather.

Omar flushed with pride.

"It's my father's."

Aladdin slung an arm over Malik's shoulder.

"Omar, any chance you could cover for Malik for an hour or so?"

Still half gaping at Jasmine, Omar nodded. She pulled a second pouch of gold coins from her cloak pocket.

"Thank you so much for your help," she said, handing him the pouch.

Omar's eyes widened into saucers.

"Th-thank *you*, Your Royal Highness! Wait till my family sees this!"

Jasmine felt a warm glow at his evident joy. Behind the palace gates, it was all too easy to take coins for granted, but out here she saw plainly how much she could help. *Once I have access to the treasury, as sultana, I will plan a day of giving once a week*, she determined. *I will ride through the marketplace handing out gold coins to all.*

Malik led them up to the roof of the tannery, away from any others, and that's where Aladdin told him of Jasmine's plight.

"We've all heard about this 'Master Karim' and the tournament to choose a sovereign," Malik said. "For what it's worth, Your Highness, most of us here on the ground think it's unfair what they're putting you through."

"Thank you, Malik." Jasmine gave him a wan smile. "You can probably guess why I want—*need*—to learn how to fight. I don't know yet what the challenges of the tournament will be, but I can only guess that whatever they're planning, it will be designed for Karim to shine. Not me."

"That's where you come in," Aladdin said. "You're the best fighter I know, especially when it comes to catching your opponent by surprise. Would you help me train Jasmine, in secret?"

"I would pay you, of course," she added quickly.

Malik glanced between the two of them, his expression uncertain. Jasmine was sure he was going to say no when he answered, "I do want you to win and take your father's place. It is what's right and just. But the thought of showing a woman, much less a *princess*, how to fight goes against everything I've been taught."

"Well, what if we've been taught wrong?" Aladdin countered. "Your sister, my princess—there's no good reason why they shouldn't all learn to defend themselves."

"And you don't have to think of me as a princess," Jasmine said. "If you agree to train me, you must see me as simply a student."

Malik was quiet, frowning in thought.

"Do you have any skills?" he asked her suddenly. "Anything that could be put to use on a battlefield?"

"Well, I've always been a good rider," Jasmine answered. "Better than good, actually."

"She once smoked me and the sultan in a race," Aladdin said, elbowing her playfully.

"We can work with that," Malik said with a nod, and Jasmine felt a rush of gratitude. He was in.

"How about weapons? Have you ever shot a bow and arrow for fun?"

"When I was a child, my father let me join him for target practice. Then once I grew up, we were told it was 'improper for the princess.'" Jasmine sighed in frustration. "I always enjoyed it."

"Well, maybe this tournament is the right time to revisit it. But first..." Malik unsheathed a small knife with a curved handle from his belt. "Let's begin with this."

Jasmine ran her hand along the knife's cool, smooth edge. She had never been allowed to so much as touch weaponry before, but with the blade in her hands, she felt instantly less vulnerable.

The three of them spent the better part of an hour up on the roof, with Malik teaching Jasmine the basics of knife skills and defense techniques while Aladdin played the role of opponent. She was clumsy at first, but before long she was unsheathing the blade from her cloak and pointing it up to Aladdin's chin in two seconds flat, while using her other arm as a shield.

"Well done, Princess," he said in her ear.

"You're a quick study," Malik agreed, and Jasmine flushed with pride.

"And you're both good teachers." As the sun dipped below the clouds, she realized with a jolt how long she'd been away from the palace. "Before I go, is there anyone else either of you can think of whom I should meet here in the city? Someone whose expertise would come in handy for our training team?"

Malik thought for a moment.

"There might be someone.... Follow me."

With that, he leaped over the edge of the rooftop. Jasmine turned to Aladdin in bewilderment—what was Malik doing, without a magic carpet to catch his fall? But then she saw him sliding expertly down the side of the roof, with Aladdin quick on his heels.

"Wait," Jasmine called after them, exasperated. "You do realize there are stairs?"

"Which are useless if we don't want to be questioned in the middle of the tannery when we land," Aladdin replied cheerfully. "Besides, knowing how to make a quick escape is another crucial part of your training."

While Abu swung from tree to tree and Malik scaled down the building, Aladdin chose a more ambitious move. He broke into a run, then grabbed hold of a long pole resting at the edge of the roof—and used the pole to vault into the air, landing with a perfect somersault on the next rooftop. From there, he swung on a clothesline and dropped down onto the ground, landing upright beside Malik while Jasmine watched with raised eyebrows.

"I suspect you were trying to impress me with that one," she called down.

"Your suspicions might be correct." He grinned. "Now throw down your cloak and climb over, keeping a hand and foothold on the railings. I'll be here to catch you if you slip."

"No need for that," Jasmine said. "I won't fall."

Still, she held her breath as she climbed over the edge of the roof, grasping the railing. She kicked her feet until they grazed the balcony below, using side rails to shimmy four floors to the bottom. Aladdin cheered as Jasmine landed on her feet, dust from the alley kicking up around them.

"Now just learn to do that about ten times faster, and you'll be able to escape in a pinch," Malik said.

Jasmine rolled her eyes good-naturedly. Aladdin took her hand, and they followed Malik back into the crowded marketplace. As they weaved through the throng, dodging horse-drawn carts, scampering children, and vendors balancing baskets of fruit atop their heads, Jasmine suddenly spotted the bird. A fan-tailed raven, just like the one she'd seen from her balcony, with its strangely beautiful plumes. What were the odds of seeing this creature again so soon? She didn't realize she had frozen at the sight of it until one of the fruit sellers bumped smack into her.

"Hey, watch yourself, miss!" he called out angrily. Jasmine crouched down to try to help him retrieve the fallen fruit, but he waved her away. "You've made enough trouble for me today."

As he stomped past, Jasmine looked back up just in time to see the raven flit toward a dark blue awning in the distance. She squinted to make out the letters woven into the fabric, and her mouth fell open.

"Look at the name of the shop," she whispered to Aladdin, pointing.

He followed her gaze up to the words on the awning: THE EMERALD TABLET. The same title as the book the sultan had been reading before he died.

"That's where I'm taking you," Malik said. "It's Fatimah's stall.

She's new to the marketplace, and a healer many of us suspect is actually an afsungar—someone who practices magic."

Jasmine's heartbeat sped up.

"Let's go."

The name was surely more than a coincidence. Was this whom her father had been leading her toward?

CHAPTER NINETEEN

Stepping through a navy silk curtain, Jasmine found herself in a market stall empty of shoppers but crowded with curiosities. Shelves stretching from floor to canopied ceiling were lined with worn leather books, glass bottles with different colored liquids simmering inside, and jars curling with smoke. Perched on the highest shelf, a fan-tailed raven cawed as the three of them walked inside. Then, seemingly from nowhere, a woman materialized behind the shop counter.

She had an almost ageless face: hooded brown eyes that looked like they'd seen decades of sorrows and joys, yet no creases or lines in her skin. Her ivory headdress and shawl were unadorned and simple, but the red beads around her neck were striking, matching the strands of dark red hair visible through her veil.

"Are you Fatimah?" Jasmine approached her.

The woman nodded and lowered into a curtsy.

"Salaam, Princess Jasmine."

Jasmine stared at her in surprise. "How did you recognize me?"

Fatimah turned to the other two before answering.

"You must be Aladdin. And, Malik, it's good to see you again." She stepped out from behind the counter, leaning against an embellished walking staff. Her eyes flickered back to Jasmine. "I didn't need to recognize you. I knew you were coming."

"How?" Aladdin asked. Malik gave him a pointed look and mouthed the word *afsungar*, reminding them of who—or what—she was rumored to be.

Fatimah didn't respond. She simply looked more closely at Jasmine, waiting. That was when it occurred to Jasmine how quiet the raven had become since they entered the shop. She glanced up and felt the hairs on the back of her neck stand on end.

The raven was gone. It had vanished into thin air. In fact, it dawned on her she hadn't seen or heard the bird since Fatimah had appeared.

Jasmine's pulse began to race. Fatimah was the real thing—an afsungar, a woman of magic. What's more, Jasmine felt certain she was meant to find her all along.

"My father was reading *The Emerald Tablet* just before he died," she said when she found her voice. "Is this—is your shop connected to the book?"

"I am a practitioner of the alchemy described in its pages," Fatimah answered. "The sultan was a great believer."

Jasmine's breath caught.

"You knew him? He never told me . . ."

"I've known more than one sultan in my lifetime," Fatimah said, locking eyes with Jasmine. "One day soon, I hope to say I know a sultana too." The words made Jasmine's heart swell with hope.

"That's why I'm here." Once she began, the story tumbled out quickly. She hadn't expected any of this, neither the mystic in front of her nor the intuitive pull calling her to enlist Fatimah's help. "I'm forming a small council, a select few people outside the palace to train me for the Crown Tournament. Would you consider it?"

From the corner of her eye, she saw Aladdin and Malik exchange a look of surprise at her quick decision, but Fatimah's expression didn't move. She had already seen Jasmine's request coming

"If it's magic you're after to help defeat your challenger, you must know that I only offer it to those who prove deserving," Fatimah said, her face unreadable.

"Of course," Jasmine said hurriedly. "And I don't want anyone to win it *for* me. I want to learn what you are willing to teach. Magic could be one part of a winning strategy, but it won't be the whole of it." *Maybe you can help me decipher the message from my father too,* she added silently.

Fatimah gave her a scrutinizing look, as if peering into Jasmine's soul.

"Yes," she finally said. "I will help you . . . for a time."

· · ·

Flying home on Magic Carpet, Jasmine felt like one of the many weights on her shoulders had been lifted. For the first time since losing her father and gaining an enemy in Karim, she had her sense of optimism back. Tomorrow morning, both of her new allies would be arriving at the palace for a secret council meeting and a training session with Jasmine and Aladdin. It was an unconventional group of characters, the kind Karim and the commander would scoff at, but Jasmine knew there was something uniquely special about each of them that couldn't be found anywhere else.

Aladdin and Jasmine landed on her bedroom balcony to the sight of Nadia pacing inside, her brow furrowed as she waited for them.

"Nadia, what is it?" Jasmine quickly hopped off Carpet and pushed through the balcony doors.

"They've been waiting over an hour for you in the council chamber," she fretted. "Commander Zohar is announcing the first challenge of the tournament."

"But that wasn't supposed to be until tonight!" Jasmine exhaled in frustration. The last thing she needed was to start this tournament on the wrong foot.

"I suppose they moved up the timing." Nadia jumped in front of Jasmine to stop her from rushing to the door. "You can't go like that!"

Jasmine glanced down. Of course—she was still dressed in her disguise, which was now covered in a layer of dust from the market.

After a rushed kiss good-bye and a whispered "Good luck" from Aladdin, Jasmine quickly changed into another ensemble fit for a sultana: a rich orange waistcoat and blouse trimmed in gold, paired with matching silk trousers and a long string of turquoise beads and turquoise-and-gold earrings. Then, with her head held high, Jasmine made her way down to the palace's main floor.

Entering the council chamber, she felt her confidence take a dip. The ministers around the table looked up, some eyeing her in disapproval, while Karim smirked from the sultan's chair.

"Where have you been, Your Highness?" the commander asked evenly, rising to give her a perfunctory bow along with the others.

Jasmine lifted her chin to meet his gaze.

"I was preparing for the tournament. I was told this meeting wouldn't be until evening."

"And how were you preparing?" Karim asked, cocking an eyebrow at her. "We don't even know our first challenge yet."

"By gathering some of the best resources I could hope for." Jasmine held his stare, wanting to make him squirm with curiosity.

"Well, now that you're finally here," Commander Zohar said grudgingly, "let's get started. Your first task of the tournament will determine how well each of you is able to mete out justice. The minister of law has devised a challenge that will test your instincts and your ability to take swift, decisive action." The commander nodded in his direction. "Hassan?"

The minister of law stood.

"Tomorrow, at the start of the tournament, we will bring forth four different men: two from the dungeons, two from the streets. Each of you will be faced with one thief and one innocent man, though naturally both will claim their innocence. It is up to you to use your judgment to determine which is the guilty party, and then watch as the executioner severs their hand." He gave a chilling smile. "After, you will learn if you were right."

Jasmine felt the blood drain from her face. This couldn't be real. Of all the possible challenges she'd imagined, never had she pictured watching someone get their hand sliced off at her order.

"So—so what you're saying is that if one of us happens to choose the wrong man, an innocent will lose his hand all the same?" She couldn't keep her voice from wobbling. "How is that justice?"

"*If* you choose the wrong man," Karim reminded her. "That's the point, dear sister. The rightful sultan wouldn't make the wrong choice."

She narrowed her eyes at him. He looked much too confident for the fifty-fifty odds. *Someone must have already given Karim the right answer.* The realization hit her like a punch in the stomach.

"And what if we feel the punishment doesn't fit the crime?" Jasmine asked the ministers, trying a different tack. "Perhaps the item that was stolen isn't worth losing an entire hand over."

"Then I would have to conclude that someone with this belief is too soft to be sovereign," Hassan said in a tone so sharp it nearly made her flinch.

There was no way out. *Soft* would be the end of her. If they had to play this game, she would need to figure out how to play by her own rules—and still come out the victor.

• • •

"Your Highness, there is an unfamiliar man and woman in the courtyard who claim to be your guests?" Payam coughed on the last word as he met Jasmine at the foot of the stairs the next morning, clearly having a hard time believing Malik and Fatimah were her intended visitors.

"That's correct." Jasmine smiled at his surprise. "I was just on my way down to meet them."

"All...right. Remember, the kingdom is expecting you and Karim on the Sultan's Balcony at three o'clock for the start of the tournament."

"I know." It was all she'd been able to think about in the hours since yesterday's meeting: the miserable first challenge looming ahead. *Just make it through today*, she repeated to herself like a mantra. *The next challenges can't possibly be worse.*

Waiting in the Great Courtyard, Aladdin, Fatimah, and Malik looked an unlikely trio, with Aladdin dressed in his court finery, Malik in streetwear with a bow and arrow slung over his shoulder, and Fatimah looking every bit the mysterious, elder afsungar. Jasmine forced herself to sound cheerier than she felt as she greeted them.

"Salaam, and thank you both so much for coming. Follow me to the gardens, where there are fewer eyes to watch us."

She and Aladdin led the way around the back of the palace, past the first rolling lawn toward a series of gated gardens. Malik's face was alive with wonder as they walked, and he stopped to take in every bit of scenery, but Fatimah moved as though she had seen all this before and knew her way around. Jasmine studied Fatimah out of the corner of her eye as she unlocked the garden gate. She had clearly been a guest here before, so why hadn't Jasmine met her until now? Or did she know these paths the same way she knew Jasmine was coming to visit her, by some otherworldly intuition?

Their first training session was supposed to focus on target practice, refreshing Jasmine's childhood skill with a bow and arrow. But once they were in the garden, their voices muffled by the wind whispering through the leaves, all she could think about was the daunting task before her.

"If I don't go through with this, they will see me as weak." Jasmine searched their faces, desperate. "But how can I? What if I mistakenly convict the wrong man? And even if I get it right, I don't believe *anyone* should ever lose a hand for thievery. There are a hundred other far more humane punishments I would choose, but the minister of law made it clear that would cost me the challenge."

"Going by their logic, I would have lost both my arms years ago," Aladdin muttered. "Don't they realize most people who steal in Agrabah are forced to because they're hungry? Because the kingdom has never done enough to help the poor?"

Jasmine felt the sting of his words as he spoke them. It was rare to hear Aladdin criticize her father or his regime, but occasionally he let slip what he really thought: that despite how prosperous Agrabah had grown under the sultan's rule, there was an entire subset of the population struggling in the margins, unnoticed by those with the power to help. And not for the first time, Jasmine felt a wave of regret over how oblivious she had been to all of them until so recently.

"I know," she finally said. "But Karim won't hesitate—and if he wins the crown, you and I both know what will become of the poor." She turned to Fatimah. "I need to beat them at their own game. Is there any sort of . . . spell we can use that might reverse the punishment after today?"

"I'm afraid that's not how the art of transformation works. I can only grow back that which I take away," Fatimah answered. "As I am not the executioner, I cannot change the outcome." Jasmine's face fell, and Fatimah added, "But you can. There is a way you can subvert today's stakes. Think outside the rules of the game—without breaking the rules."

Jasmine stared at her, perplexed.

"What do you mean?"

Instead of answering her question, the afsungar asked one of her own.

"Tell us, Jasmine, what are your strengths? What are you passionate about? What makes you . . . *you?*"

Jasmine exchanged a bewildered glance with Aladdin. How would any of this help her with the impossible task that was mere hours away? He shrugged and nodded at her to answer.

"I don't know. I'm passionate about people, I suppose. All sorts of people, from different walks of life, and animals too. And learning about different places, and stories. Always stories." Jasmine paused. "But what does this have to do with anything?"

"Yes. Stories." Fatimah nodded in approval, as if this were the answer she'd been waiting for. "This afternoon, you'll write your own."

Jasmine began to pace impatiently. She needed real, tangible solutions, not this metaphor-speak. Sensing her thoughts, Malik spoke up.

"I've found there are certain facial cues to look for when you're trying to gauge who is guilty and who is innocent. Aladdin and I can certainly help with that," he said wryly.

"That's true. The clues aren't just in their facial expressions either," Aladdin said. "Watch what their hands do when you're questioning them."

Jasmine listened intently as her team offered their advice, trying to memorize it all. Still, there was no telling what would happen when she was alone against Karim on that balcony, forced to make a snap decision that would affect three lives: those of the two men she was about to meet, and her own.

CHAPTER TWENTY

The Crown Tournament began with a chilling display of pageantry. Jasmine and Nadia watched from her bedroom window as the guards opened the palace gates, sending crowds flooding the entrance and swarming the Great Courtyard, faces frenzied with anticipation. It wasn't only the people of Agrabah who turned out in droves to gape at their vulnerable princess and the challenger to her throne—Jasmine counted half a dozen traveling caravans among the crowd too. While the hordes waited for the spectacle to begin, a dueling chant kicked off on the ground.

"Jasmine, Jasmine, our true sultana!"

"Karim, Karim, our king of kings!"

And the knot in Jasmine's stomach drew tighter.

When it was almost three o'clock, Arman arrived at the princess's door to escort her down to the Sultan's Balcony. Located just off the throne room, the public-facing balcony was more than twice the size of Jasmine's and one level closer to the ground. Close enough to feel the full force of the crowd's admiration or ire.

They reached the doors to the throne room at the same time as Commander Zohar and Karim, who was bedecked in a new outfit meant to portray him as a sultan. His lavish brocade kaftan bore the colors of Agrabah, rich reds and greens with patterned gold trim, while a golden-yellow belt around his waist held a dagger that looked suspiciously like Cyrus the First's. He even wore a white feathered turban nearly identical to her father's, a sight that sent a flash of fury through Jasmine. She forced herself to look at anyone, anything, besides him.

The crowd's roars reached a fever pitch as the bells rang out for three o'clock. This was it. Arman placed a hand on Jasmine's shoulder, the commander on Karim's, and they marched the contenders forward. Karim smiled broadly and Jasmine gritted her teeth as they stepped through the wrought-iron doors and onto the Sultan's Balcony.

A thunder of cheers and shouts greeted their entrance, with the dueling chants resuming: "Jasmine, our true sultana!" "Karim, our king of kings!" Jasmine forced a smile and a wave for the hundreds watching, even though her stomach was churning with fear. Her eyes combed the crowd, searching for allies, but there were so many people squeezed into one space, it was a blur of faces. And now the commander was sweeping forward to the foot of the balcony, calling the crowd to silence.

"Salaam and welcome, all of you, to the Crown Tournament of Agrabah!" his voice boomed. "As we aim to settle the unprecedented case of a princess versus a newly discovered prince, your ministers of Agrabah have come up with a historic solution: a tournament that will test their mastery of the crucial skills and traits a ruler must possess in order to lead our kingdom. Challenge number one will evaluate Princess Jasmine's and Master Karim's abilities to distinguish a criminal from an innocent and to lay down the law." He paused dramatically before raising his voice to shout, "Let the Crown Tournament begin!" to the roaring approval of the thrill-hungry crowd. Jasmine took a shallow breath, her palms turning clammy with sweat.

From a side door, the four other ministers entered the balcony, each dragging a disheveled man bound in chains. Jasmine's heart plummeted.

The men were all different ages and shades of skin, but they shared the same pleading expression as their eyes darted from Karim to Jasmine and back again. Their clothes were threadbare, no shoes on their feet, and Aladdin's words echoed in Jasmine's mind as she watched them: *Don't they realize most people who steal in Agrabah are forced to because they're hungry?* Suddenly, looking at the four desperate faces in front of her, she had a terrible flash of recognition.

The old friend of Aladdin's—the same one they had stood with under the olive tree just yesterday, listening together as the musicians played folk songs in the marketplace square. It was Tarek, the tailor.

Jasmine searched the crowd for Aladdin and was almost relieved to not be able to spot him. She couldn't imagine what was going through his mind now, seeing his own friend up here. Meanwhile, Karim wrinkled his nose at the prisoners in disgust, and a few loud voices in the audience jeered them too. But all Jasmine felt at the sight of the four men was sorrow.

"Our players will begin by casting their lots to see who goes first."

Commander Zohar handed Jasmine and Karim a pair of stone dice, and the crowd craned their necks to watch as they rolled. While Karim pumped his fists at rolling a higher number, Jasmine exhaled in relief, welcoming any extra minute between her and the terrible choice she would be forced to make.

The minister of law shoved two of the prisoners forward to face Karim.

"Master Karim, here before you stand Essam and Ziad, both from the slums of Agrabah. Both are on trial today for the same crime, yet only one is guilty of stealing a sackful of the finest meats from the marketplace—and then disobeying and *disarming* the first guard who caught him."

A gasp rippled through the crowd at the statement of the thief's brazen acts. Jasmine turned back to the balcony doors, wishing she could run straight through them and escape this. It was there, standing in the palace hall by those same open doors, where she found her team. Aladdin's and Malik's faces were frozen in horror while Fatimah stood between them, her expression grave.

Just then, Fatimah met Jasmine's eyes, giving her a slow, encouraging nod. But Jasmine could only feel her panic mounting as the men pleaded their innocence to Karim, one by one. *What will I do when it's my turn?*

Karim turned away from the prisoners and looked out at the crowd, his dark eyes determined, his confidence unwavering.

"After evaluating and hearing from both of these men, I can

clearly see who is guilty." The spectators leaned forward, everyone holding a collective breath. "Essam, for your crimes, I sentence you to lose your hand. May the pain of your severed appendage be a reminder to never steal again."

Essam let out a wail of despair that pierced Jasmine's insides, while Ziad fell to his knees in gratitude, kissing Karim's feet. Karim shook him off in disdain.

"Go," he told Ziad curtly, and the freed prisoner raced down the balcony steps.

The royal executioner marched forward, wearing head-to-toe steel armor that disguised his face. The only sign of a human underneath was a pair of green eyes flashing behind the steel mask. In his gloved hand, he carried a tabarzin: a seven-foot-long metallic battle-ax with a heavy crescent-shaped blade. Essam flailed against his chains in fear at the sight, and Jasmine felt her insides go numb. *Don't look, don't look, don't—* But she felt the ministers' eyes on her, watching to see if she could handle it, judging whether she was too "soft." Jasmine wrenched her head up, forcing herself to bear witness as the royal executioner swung the blade.

The guards pinned Essam down as the tabarzin blade smashed into his arm, cutting it off at the wrist. A bloodcurdling scream shot through the balcony, a scream that seemed to go on forever as Essam stared in agony at his severed arm, spurting blood while its missing hand lay in a mangled clump at the edge of the balcony. Jasmine felt the ground start to sway, bile rising in her throat, but she forced herself to meet Essam's eyes, to try to tell him with her gaze how much she hated this. How desperately sorry she was.

Gasps and cries mingled with applause in the crowd, along with the sound of several bodies fainting to the ground at the grisly sight. *This can't be the way,* Jasmine kept thinking as she looked on in horror. *It can't be. Not in my Agrabah.*

"Well done, Karim!" The commander and Hassan joined him, smiling in the face of the butchery. But Jasmine noticed that two of the other ministers, Majid and Parisa, looked just as aghast and shaken as she felt.

"You showed wise judgment today," Hassan continued. "Your verdict was correct: Essam was the convicted thief, and Ziad the innocent planted to trick you. Because of your strong instincts and decisive action, the right man was punished today—and now, with only one hand remaining, he may never steal again."

Hassan made a grand sweep toward the crowd, and applause broke out on cue. The guards carted a still-wailing Essam off the balcony, while one of the palace stewards rushed to sweep away the remnants of his hand. Jasmine looked wildly around her, unable to grasp that this was even happening. She had heard rumors of cruel punishments doled out in the cities and prison dungeons, but never wanted to believe they were real, or that they happened in her kingdom's name. Her father had always left matters of sentencing up to the commander and Hassan, and now she wondered how much she knew; she couldn't imagine him ever approving such a violent display. . . .

"And now it's our princess's turn," Hassan announced, with a look in his eye that made it clear he expected Jasmine to fail. The crowd fell back into silence as Arman and Khaleel dragged the last two prisoners forward in front of Jasmine, where they fell to their knees at her feet.

"And here we have Fareed and Tarek." Hassan played to the crowd, introducing the two men as if they were characters in a play rather than real-life figures on the edge of tragedy. "Your Royal Highness, during the sultan's last public audience at the palace, these two men were among the peasants lined up to ask your father for help—in the form of gold, of course. The sultan was generous enough to offer them two coins each, but *one* of these men failed to appreciate such a gesture. He was the trickiest of thieves, for it wasn't until the room was clear that we saw the priceless Golden Flagon was suddenly missing."

Jasmine drew in a sharp breath. In all the upheaval of the last week, she hadn't even noticed it was gone. The jewel-encrusted vase had been a part of the palace scenery for as long as she could remember, small enough to stow in a traveler's sack but weighed down by a plethora of diamonds, emeralds, and rubies. She couldn't imagine how a thief managed to sneak such a treasure out of the palace unseen. It would take someone diabolical to do such a thing . . . or someone desperate.

"A crime of *this* caliber, to steal from the sultan himself, is even more serious than pitiful Essam's. Serious enough to warrant, possibly . . . execution?"

Jasmine's heart stopped. *No.* He didn't mean it, he couldn't expect her to—

Of course. The terrible truth dawned on her as soon as she met Hassan's knowing yet unfeeling eyes. They were testing her with a personal edge, knowing she would see Aladdin in the prisoner in front of her. Knowing she could never bear to have anyone, much less him, killed. They might as well have simply handed the win to Karim then and there.

"Please, Your Highness." The first prisoner, Fareed, clutched the hem of her skirt. "I swear to you, by my family and everything I hold dear, I did no such thing. I would never disrespect your father, the great sultan, in such a way."

Jasmine looked into a face full of conviction. There were no shifty eyes or fidgety hands, no stumbling speech or any other signs Aladdin and Malik had advised her to look out for. She believed him. Which meant . . .

"Your Royal Highness," Tarek rasped. He was shaking as he gazed up at her, all traces of the dancing young man from the marketplace long gone. That's when Jasmine noticed how painfully thin he was. So thin that she could see his ribs through his tattered tunic. "I didn't—" He could barely choke out the denial, his eyes confessing his guilt. "I have three daughters. Their mother died, and without me, they will starve. I was only going to—"

"I know," Jasmine cut him off, anxious to stop him before he implicated himself any further. "Don't worry. You'll be all right."

"Ah!" Hassan jumped to attention. "So you are declaring Fareed the thief, then?"

"No!" she said firmly. "What I am saying is . . ."

What *was* she supposed to say? There was no right answer. Jasmine could feel walls closing in around her, suffocating her, even though she was standing in open air. Looking out at the crowd, she found a mass of wide-eyed faces staring back at her. Most of their expressions had slipped into pity. They could sense it—she was flailing.

She turned back to the balcony doors, where a pair of silver-flecked gray eyes found hers. Fatimah nodded at Jasmine, encouraging her to do . . . what, exactly?

There is a way you can subvert the stakes today. Think outside the rules of the game—without breaking the rules.

Stories . . . This afternoon, you'll write your own.

And suddenly, with a rush of inspiration, Jasmine knew what she had to do. It was a leap of faith, but if it worked, it just might be ingenious.

"I do know who the thief is. And yet I can also tell you with full certainty that if this man loses his life, or even a hand—all of us in Agrabah will be the ones to suffer."

A bemused murmur rippled through the crowd, and Karim snorted with laughter. Jasmine ignored them all, injecting her voice with a haughty confidence and playing a role now as she continued:

"Before I reveal the answer, I must first tell you, my people of Agrabah, a story."

The commander barked out a laugh.

"We don't have time for such childishness, *Princess*. Go on, make your choice and let the executioner be done with it."

"The story is relevant and true, Commander. In fact, it was one of the last things my father told me before he died," she improvised. "That's how important it was. But we'll let the people decide." She looked back at the crowd. "Do you wish to hear my—my father's story now, or after it's too late?"

"Let the princess tell us!" "Now!" they chorused. Jasmine could hear Aladdin and Malik joining in the shouts from the balcony doors too. She turned to her ministers with a pointed glance, and the minister of law fixed his cold eyes on her.

"I don't know what you think you're playing at, Your Highness," he said in a low voice. "But if you're trying to make a mockery of this tournament, all that will lead to is seeing the crown on Master Karim's head."

"Go on, then," Karim said with a cocky smile.

Commander Zohar waved her forward, his lip curling in derision.

"We will humor your foolish request. But I'm afraid this won't end the way you'd like it to, Your Highness."

With her heart hammering in her chest, Jasmine turned to face the crowd. This was it—her only chance to save Tarek and still win the challenge. Everything was hinging on this one story. A story she would have to spin out of thin air.

"Once upon a time, before any of us walked the earth, a deadly ailment spread through Mesopotamia," Jasmine began. She projected her voice, trying to make it as commanding as the traveling theater troupe that often came to perform at the palace.

"One by one, houses fell to this dreaded virus. All you had to do was breathe it in"—she sucked in her breath, building up the drama for her audience—"and within hours, you would be dead. Until one night, a man-of-all-trades by the name of Omid was visited by a dream that gave him the precise formula for a miracle cure." She took another dramatic pause. "Of course, Omid was a poor man, with no money to purchase the ingredients. Still, he was sure his kingdom would thank him for doing whatever it took to follow his dream and create the cure. Yet when he was caught stealing from the marketplace, no one listened to his pleas. No one heard him."

Jasmine took a quick glance at her audience and felt a flicker of hope. The story was working. She had them riveted.

"It wasn't until after Omid was killed that those who judged him realized how wrong they had been. Of course, they only lived mere days to regret it." Jasmine waited, drawing out the suspense, and then said, "They had caught the virus by then. And with Omid gone, there would be no cure. It took years for the sickness to run its course, for the Mesopotamian population to rebuild. And it's something my father warned me of before he died."

She raised her voice, gearing up for the grand finale.

"You see, Tarek, who stands before you all—yes, he is the man who took the Golden Flagon." Gasps from the crowd echoed across the courtyard, mixed with murmurs behind her on the balcony. Even though she couldn't see them, Jasmine could feel Tarek's anguish, Fareed's relief. She pressed on, hoping with all her might that she could tie her story's conclusion with the right ending for Tarek—and for her.

"But he is no thief," she declared. "You may know him as a tailor, but he too is a man-of-all-trades who works with his hands. He is also building something that will one day help all of us when we need it most. And if he needed our Golden Flagon to make this invention possible"—she took a deep breath—"then he shall have it. My father must have told me this story because he knew this day was coming . . . and that I as your sultana had to spare Tarek."

There was a stunned silence. The expressions in the crowd ran the gamut from wide-eyed awe to scornful skepticism. Jasmine glanced back at Fatimah by the balcony doors, wearing a ghost of a smile. She needed one more trick to push her plan over the edge . . . and she knew the people of Agrabah believed firmly in signs.

"If you don't believe me, then I call upon a fan-tailed raven." Jasmine lifted her gaze to the sky. "If this unique bird appears, and lands on the shoulder of Tarek, then that is all the proof you need that my story is true—and he must go free."

Whispers of anticipation filled the courtyard, while Tarek gaped at Jasmine like she'd just sprouted a third eye.

"Your Highness," he whispered frantically. "Please, I must tell you—"

"It's all right," Jasmine said under her breath. "You'll see." *It has to be.*

"You have three minutes," the minister of law called sharply across the balcony. "And then your game is up."

Jasmine nodded, anticipation bubbling in her stomach. She looked over at the balcony doors and, sure enough, Fatimah was gone. The bird would soon land.

The first minute ticked by, then a second . . . and no raven. Jasmine felt beads of sweat forming on her skin, each second draining more of her confidence. The uncertain expressions in the crowd seemed to reflect her own quickly mounting fear that this "brilliant" idea was about to unravel.

She saw Aladdin, Malik, and Nadia huddled together, murmuring nervously, while Fatimah was nowhere to be found. And then the buzzing from the crowd grew into a roar. Slowly, Jasmine raised her eyes to the sight of fluttering wings.

Wild cheers rose from the crowd as the fan-tailed raven flew toward an incredulous Tarek, perching on his shoulder. Jasmine clapped her hand over her mouth in delirious relief, before remembering that none of this was supposed to be a surprise to her. She beamed at the raven, and the bird's silver-flecked eyes winked back.

Across the balcony, Majid and Parisa shared an awed smile, while the rest of the men all looked thunderstruck. Karim's face had turned an almost purplish shade, and Jasmine could see spittle forming at the corners of Hassan's mouth as the minister of law descended on her, furious at having been outplayed.

"How did you do this?" he hissed. But he was drowned out by the wild cries of "Jasmine, Sultana Jasmine!" echoing from the crowd below.

"Thank you so much," she called out, resting a hand over her heart. "I look forward to continuing to show you all the just and worthy sultana I will be." She turned to the guards. "Now, unhand these men."

They were too stunned to object. As the shackles came off, Fareed sprinted away from the scene, but Tarek first bent to kiss the tips of Jasmine's shoes.

"I will never forget this, Your Royal Highness," he whispered. "I will repay your kindness, I swear to it."

"Take good care of your daughters, and teach them right from wrong," Jasmine told him under her breath. "If ever you need food or shelter, go to Aladdin's broken tower in the marketplace. You don't need to steal again."

He nodded solemnly, kissing her hand once more before disappearing from the balcony. When Jasmine looked back at her ministers and her team, she found Aladdin, Malik, and Nadia grinning at her with pride and relief—while Hassan, Khaleel, and Commander Zohar all eyed her with the same cold stare.

The commander turned on his heel to face the crowd, raising his hands to silence it.

"We're not finished yet. The judges still need to declare the winner of our first challenge."

This time, Jasmine was the one smiling while Karim gritted his teeth. The few shouts of "Karim, king of all kings!" were barely audible now over the boisterous cheers of "Sultana Jasmine!" By outsmarting the rules of the game, she had won this round. It was clear to them all.

Prince Rashid stepped onto the balcony, with Princess Shirin trailing reluctantly behind. Jasmine's spirits dipped at the sight of him. She must have blocked from her mind the fact that he was one of the judges today, along with Hassan and the high elder.

The three men huddled together for a few minutes at the back of the balcony. As soon as they returned, Jasmine knew something was wrong. Prince Rashid and Hassan were both smiling.

"While each contender for the throne displayed their skills well today," Hassan began, "only one showcased their strength and willingness to mete out justice. In a score of two to one, our winner is Master Karim!"

Karim pumped his fists in the air while Jasmine stood stock-still, feeling as though someone had just dumped a pail of cold water over her head. There was a thrum of surprise in the audience, and then the cheers of her name faltered.

Soon Karim's name was the one that could be heard across the Great Courtyard, echoing loud and strong.

CHAPTER TWENTY-ONE

J asmine watched gloomily from her seat as dinner in the banquet hall turned into an impromptu celebration of Karim's
win. The neighboring rulers leaned across the table to congratulate
him, with Princes Achmed and Rashid giving a gruesome play-by-
play of Karim's "decisive action" that led to Essam losing his hand.
In these quarters, Jasmine's triumph with Tarek and the raven was
seen as more worthy of ridicule than applause.

"Did you all see the way the peasant's fingers skittered across
the balcony?" Achmed chortled obnoxiously. Jasmine shoved her
plate away. There was no chance of her appetite returning anytime
soon with that image in her head.

The only friendly face at the table was that of Princess Shirin,
who was seated across from Jasmine tonight. Karim had apparently
insisted on sitting beside her, and kept leaning over to whisper into
her ear with a glint in his eye. It was a nauseating sight.

"Excuse me," Jasmine said, rising from the table. "I just remembered something I need to tell Aladdin."

She crossed the long banquet hall to his table three rows behind hers, where he was seated among the entourages of visiting royals. Her heart tugged at the sight of him, looking out of place among the stiff, buttoned-up strangers around the table. It occured to her that the last time she'd seen him look and act like his truest self—the Aladdin she'd fallen in love with—was back in the marketplace, leaping across buildings with Malik. With a pang of guilt, Jasmine realized that while he'd worked hard to become a part of her life, he might never feel at home in the palace, a place he'd loved from afar for so long. And if she won the tournament and they married, this would be his future.

Everyone around the table rose to their feet as Jasmine approached, bowing and curtsying, and she found herself wondering if they would still treat her this way if Karim kept winning the competitions. Or worse—if he won it all.

"Are you all right?" Aladdin whispered in her ear.

Jasmine lifted her shoulders. She wasn't sure how she was, really.

"Come for a walk with me?" she asked.

Aladdin took her arm, and the two made their way past the long tables of raucous guests and through the door. No one seemed to notice them leave—Karim was the focus tonight. Jasmine wasn't sure whether she should be bitter over that fact, or grateful for the momentary escape it offered.

They stepped out onto one of the terraced hallways, decorated with mosaic-tiled floors, lattice windows, and a small fountain pond swimming with bright orange and white carp. After double-checking to make sure they were alone, Aladdin pulled Jasmine into his arms.

"Today was cruel," he said, gently tilting her chin up to meet his gaze. "You handled it brilliantly, though. I couldn't believe the way your mind worked so quickly on the spot, how you managed to save my friend. Thank you."

"It wasn't enough, though," Jasmine said regretfully. "Karim still won."

"Who cares about that? You saved the life of someone who didn't deserve to die. *That's* what matters." He paused. "If you hadn't come to the marketplace last year, if we'd never met . . . I could have so easily been one of those prisoners today."

"I know. And I promise that as sultana, I would never let anything like that disgusting display happen again." Jasmine's fists clenched at her sides. "It's another reason why I can't let Karim keep winning."

"This was only the beginning," Aladdin reminded her. "You have three more chances in the tournament."

"Yes." Jasmine's eyes narrowed in determination. "And I have to beat him at all three."

"Jasmine!"

They turned to see Nadia rushing to catch them. She held a cloth-wrapped parcel in her arms and said, "This arrived for you just now. The man who delivered it insisted that I be the one to give it to you."

Jasmine exchanged a curious look with Aladdin before taking the parcel. As soon as she felt its weight, she knew what it was. She unwrapped the brown cloth and found something that sparkled from every angle, that lit up the night with emerald and ruby rays.

"The Golden Flagon," Nadia breathed.

A piece of parchment fluttered to the floor, and Aladdin bent to retrive it. He pressed it into her palm and she read it aloud, keeping her voice low, even though the three of them were the only ones gathered on the second-story landing. From the sounds of the booming laughter and clinking glasses downstairs, it seemed that the feast was still in full swing.

"Dearest Princess Jasmine,

"'There are so many ways I wish to express my gratitude for this second chance you have given me. I will begin by returning something precious of yours.

"'I am forever changed by what happened today and will devote myself to making an honest living from here on out: for me and my girls, and in your honor. If there is any justice in the world, we will soon see you crowned sultana.'"

The letter was unsigned, though it needed no signature. Jasmine blinked back tears as she slipped the parchment into her pocket.

"You really did alter the course of someone's life today," Aladdin marveled.

"That's the true win," Nadia said.

As she smiled back at the two of them, Jasmine felt a warm glow spread through her, replacing the bitter taste of Karim's victory. Aladdin and Nadia were right. She wouldn't have been able to live with herself if she had won the way Karim did—and tonight, she could go to bed with no regrets.

"Get some rest," Aladdin said, planting a kiss on her forehead. "Tomorrow we'll pick up the fight."

. . .

Once she was in bed, Jasmine found herself too restless to sleep. Her mind ran a million miles a minute as she tossed and turned, wondering what was next to come in the tournament, how she would ultimately defeat Karim—and returning as always to the question of her father's message.

While Rajah lay snoring at her feet, Jasmine climbed out of bed to retrieve the leather-bound tomes from the sultan's book wheel hidden underneath. She lit a candle on the table beside her and propped herself up against the pillows, selecting *The Emerald Tablet* first.

As she read, Jasmine wrote on a separate piece of parchment any lines that seemed to have a deeper meaning that might be connected to her father's final message. One sentence in particular stuck out in her mind: *That which is above is from that which is below, and that which is below is from that which is above.*

A casual reader could have easily interpreted the line to mean that the sun and moon and earth are all connected. But when she read it, all Jasmine could think of was . . . another world. A world beyond this one. Especially when later sections of the text described the principles of turning base metals into gold and predicted the future creation of an "Elixir of Life"— *immortality*—Jasmine knew her father's interest in this book ran far deeper than mere curiosity.

She could feel it.

. . .

When Jasmine's eyes finally closed that night, the voice returned. The same unfamiliar whisper from days ago, setting music to the riddle left by her father.

"There was a door to which I found no key," *it sang to a slow and haunting melody. The phantom voice drifted through the long corridors of the darkened palace while it sang, leading her somewhere.* "There seemed and then no more of thee and me . . ."

Jasmine was in the Round Library now, seven years younger. She sat nestled in one of the oversized reading chairs, beside her tutor. Taminah wasn't any older than the sultan, but her face had grown pallid, her bones frail. Her fingers were shaking as she held the book, reading to the princess with an intensity in her voice.

"'Those who cross the realms are possessed of the greatest magic. The past and future, angels and demons, the mythical and mortal—each lay claim to their own realm. Our world is but one in a universe full of them, orbiting in their own separate dimension. Yet every so often, a person or being, most often a jinn, crosses between the realms and blurs the lines between them.'" She took a breath. "'And that is how magic crept into our world.'"

"Taminah." Jasmine twisted in her seat to look at her. "It's just a story, isn't it?"

The tutor smiled slightly.

"If it were true, then perhaps I could still read to you, long after I'm gone."

"You're not going anywhere." Young Jasmine shook her head defiantly. "Baba says you're only a little bit sick."

Taminah chuckled under her breath. She rested her palm against Jasmine's cheek, in a gesture far gentler than any she'd shown her before.

"Just remember, Princess Jasmine: Sometimes what may seem impossible is, in fact, the most true."

Jasmine woke with a start, sweat drenching her brow. Her fingers were clasped tightly around something—a book, but not the one she'd been holding when she fell asleep. Instead of *The Emerald Tablet*, she held *The Rubaiyat of Omar Khayyam* against her chest. One of the books she could have sworn she'd left in a pile next to the bed.

Heart racing, Jasmine drew back her bed curtains. No one was there. Only Rajah, still curled up in his same sleeping position at the foot of her bed.

She relit the oil lamp on her bedside table and carefully lifted the book to view the page it was opened to. Somehow she knew, before her eyes could even register the words, just what she would see.

There was a door to which I found no key.
There was a veil past which I could not see
Some little talk awhile of me and thee
There seemed and then no more of thee and me.

Jasmine scrambled back against the bed frame, dropping the book like it was on fire. Had someone—a ghost—switched the books while she was asleep? Was it the ghost of her father, leading her to this page . . . or was it the woman whose voice haunted Jasmine's room? The same woman she'd seen in the mirror?

194

"Is someone there?" she called out shakily through the dark room. "Please—if you're here, show yourself."

No answer. Jasmine hesitantly reached down for one more look at the printed page. That's when she saw the black ink strokes, underlining four words of the poem: *Door. Veil. Thee. Me.* And in a flash, the code to the sultan's combination lockbox flew into her mind. *D V J S.*

Door. Veil. Jasmine. Sultan . . . or sultana.

Even though the meaning was still opaque, even though she still hadn't the slightest clue which door or veil her father was trying to draw her toward, something lifted in her chest as she looked at the words. *Hope.* He was still talking to her, communicating with her, even from another plane.

"As above, so below," she whispered.

CHAPTER TWENTY-TWO

The palace court barely had a chance to regroup from the first challenge of the tournament before Jasmine and Karim were called into the council chamber that same week to hear of their second task. *Please, no severed body parts in this one*, Jasmine thought grimly as she entered the room, making it just in time to claim her father's seat.

When Commander Zohar announced Khaleel as the minister leading the second challenge, Jasmine felt her tense muscles relax slightly. The minister of Arabian nations was a few degrees less ruthless than the others. This couldn't be *too* terrible.

"As you know, we are presently at a standoff in our trade route negotiations with Azra," Khaleel began. "The relationship between our two kingdoms is of the utmost importance, which is why it was such a meaningful gesture that the king traveled to Agrabah to honor the late sultan. And it's why he is at the center of the second task.

"Princess Jasmine and Master Karim each must plan a formal

dinner reception worthy of the king's name—on the same night," he continued with a sly smile. "One of you will have use of the formal banquet room; the other will take Crystal Hall. You will be provided with the same budget from the treasury to finance the feasts, entertainment, and decorations, and you will have three days' time to prepare. The palace staff will be divided between you to assist in the arrangements."

Jasmine raised her eyebrows, practically giddy with relief. All she had to do was plan a reception? After the fatal stakes of the last challenge, this one was almost too good to be true.

"This affair will also be where you present your intended royal consort to the court, who will co-host alongside you," Khaleel said. His eyes settled on Jasmine. "You may think you've already decided whom you plan to marry, but I advise each of you to give it serious thought. One of the judging factors of this challenge will be the suitability of your choice."

Jasmine felt her heart plummet to the floor. *This is how it starts.*

From the beginning, she'd feared that this was her ministers' aim—forcing her to choose between Aladdin and the throne—and now her fear was confirmed. Jasmine knew full well that this challenge wasn't about whether she could plan an impressive enough party, or even about her diplomatic skills. They were testing how far she would go to become sultana, if she would be willing to give up her love. And since there was no chance of Karim picking anyone from Aladdin's lower-class background, unless she did the unthinkable, Karim would hold the advantage over her. Again.

"Master Karim, since you've only just arrived in Agrabah, I suggest you take the next couple of days to get to know the local noble ladies and daughters of esteemed landowners," Khaleel added. "There is no expectation that you will propose in time for the king's banquet, only that you announce your intended."

"Not to worry," Karim said, smiling to himself. "I already have someone in mind, and I can assure you—she is a true prize."

Shirin, Jasmine realized in horror, remembering the way he'd looked at her last night at dinner . . . as if she were a present he was eager to unwrap.

"One more thing. There is another component of this challenge that even the king himself doesn't know about." Khaleel leaned across the table. "You will each use your time with him during your separate receptions to try to change his stubborn mind about the trade route. Get him to say yes." He breathed in sharply. "If this challenge goes according to my design, we will accomplish two aims: a victory for one of you, and a long-awaited resolution in our trade dealings with Azra."

Jasmine swallowed hard. How wrong she had been to think this challenge would actually be easy when it was only another variation on the first: pinning her into an impossible situation. The only difference was that this time, the treachery came dressed up in disguise.

· · ·

Jasmine and Karim cast their lots to determine who would get to use the banquet room (Karim won that roll of the dice) and which key members of staff would be on his or her side of the dueling receptions. Once the terms were set, the two set off in opposite directions of the palace to dive into their preparations. Jasmine caught the smile playing on Karim's lips as he hurried out of the council chamber, and she had the sinking feeling that she knew exactly what he was about to do first: ask Shirin to accompany him to the reception. To be his intended bride and consort—a thought that made Jasmine feel physically ill.

After a couple of hours spent with Nadia brainstorming the finest menu selections, decorations, musicians, and entertainments, it was time for Jasmine to meet her training team. They had planned to gather in the Royal Stables, a sprawling courtyard adjacent to the palace gardens, where nine horse stalls surrounded a decorative stone water fountain. While Jasmine led her black Arabian stallion, Midnight, from her stall and the horse drank from the fountain, she filled her team in on the second challenge. She stumbled over her words when mentioning the part about announcing her chosen consort, and Aladdin's expression wavered. He could see clearly just what was happening.

"They're making it impossible for you to win this one," he said under his breath. "I know what they think of me. . . ."

"Impressing the king of Azra is still the primary task," Jasmine assured him, even as she knew his words were closer to the truth. "If I can find a way to wow King Mahmoud, and also sway him over to my side of the trade argument, that should far outweigh what anyone thinks of my chosen consort." She paused in thought, brushing Midnight's mane with her fingers. "But how on earth would I segue from entertaining him in lavish style to suddenly pressing him on trade? That just seems . . . desperately awkward." Jasmine wrinkled her nose.

Fatimah, who had been listening carefully, spoke up.

"Is there a way you could weave the topic of relations between Agrabah and Azra into the reception events somehow?"

Jasmine fell silent. *How could that possibly work?* She paced beside the fountain, watching the soothing scene of Midnight lapping up water, until it came to her.

"There is nothing quite so influential in our culture as stories," she said slowly. "If I didn't know it already, the way the audience responded to me at the first challenge proved it. So, then . . . what if I presented him with a performance? Something with music and dance, that tells the story of our two nations coming together in triumph?"

Fatimah gave her a nod of approval.

"I like it," Aladdin agreed. "Malik and I can recruit street performers we know. Some of the best musicians, dancers, and mime artists perform at the bazaar."

"Perfect." Jasmine felt a flicker of excitement. "Maybe I could rewrite the lyrics of a folk song or two to adapt to our tale."

"And I will design you a showpiece of a stage," Fatimah said, her silver-gray eyes twinkling.

"Between all of us, we can help you make it a tough fight for Karim," Malik said. "Speaking of . . ." He lowered a canvas sack from over his shoulders, filled with two dark-wood curved bows, unexpectedly small in size, and a quiver of arrows. "We'd be wise to continue your *actual* fight training. I would expect one of the final challenges will test those particular skills."

"Yes, of course. But I'm hoping those bows aren't so tiny on account of my size?" Jasmine arched an eyebrow at him.

"Of course not," Malik said with a laugh. "On the contrary, it's a composite bow that is meant to be small. That's part of what makes it so lethal."

"Today, we're teaching you the Parthian Shot," Aladdin said with a mischievous grin.

"The what?"

"It's an advanced fighting technique that comes from the early nomads. *Not* the upper class or organized military," Malik said pointedly. "Which means we'll catch Karim off guard with it. Of course, you're not close to advanced when it comes to fighting, but you are an expert rider... so this just might work. Now, can we borrow a couple of horses to demonstrate?"

Jasmine nodded, feeling a rush of anticipation. She returned to the stalls, releasing the chestnut mare Aladdin rode most frequently, Sahla, and leading the horse by the halter to join the others.

"You can ride Midnight," she told Malik. "He always treats my friends well."

Malik climbed onto Midnight's back armed with a bow and arrow, while Aladdin followed suit on his horse. Jasmine watched, riveted, as the two men rode toward each other from opposite sides of the courtyard, shooting a barrage of arrows while galloping at an ever-quickening pace. When they were mere inches apart, Malik executed a quick pivot turn while firing three arrows over Midnight's backside while galloping away. The arrows shot through the air at the exact same time, in a straight line, aiming directly for Aladdin. Fatimah let out a low whistle as they watched.

If Aladdin hadn't been prepared for this, if he hadn't moved out of the way at just the right time, it could have all been over.

"Show me again," Jasmine said, her heart pounding faster. "And then I want to try myself, as many times as it takes to get it right."

. . .

Jasmine returned to her bedroom suite glistening with sweat and still grinning from the rush of training. When she saw Princess Shirin and Nadia waiting by her door, she remembered with a jolt her planned tea with the princess—and what she needed to say.

"I'm sorry I'm late! Come in." Jasmie hugged Shirin, and the two of them followed Nadia into the room.

"You look rather . . . disheveled," Shirin remarked, raising an eyebrow at Jasmine.

"Just a bit of sport." Jasmine laughed, swallowing her guilt at the lie. Shirin was one of her best friends; she should have been able to tell her the truth. And yet, all she had to do was take a closer look at Shirin to know that something was different today—and that *something* had to do with Karim.

"He asked you, didn't he?" Jasmine blurted out as soon as they were alone and seated around the low dining table, with two porcelain cups of tea and a tray of baklava between them.

Jasmine could tell Shirin was holding back a smile as she nodded.

"It's all rather sudden, of course, so I know it's more about him needing to choose the right woman for the sake of the challenge, as opposed to having a real interest in me." She gave Jasmine a conspiratorial wink. "This could be a good thing. If I can get close to him, then anything you need to know, I'll find out."

Jasmine studied Shirin.

"You're not upset about this. Not even a little." She felt a knot form in her stomach. "You like him."

Shirin looked away as her expression grew defensive.

"No, of course not! I mean . . . Well, I don't know. Sometimes I can't help enjoying his company. And there's no denying how handsome he is. He might be the most handsome man I've ever seen."

"That isn't saying too much for the men of Numan," Jasmine said dryly.

"And he talks to me like I'm important," Shirin said, in a quieter voice. "He's nothing like Rashid. He acts like everything I say or do matters."

"That's because you *are* important. He knows full well that having you by his side would elevate his status." Jasmine exhaled in frustration. "Karim isn't some harmless nobleman, Shirin. He's trying to steal my *throne*."

"I'm still on your side, Jasi, you know I am," Shirin insisted. "But you have to understand that me attending the reception as his chosen consort means . . . well, it means I'll no longer be invisible. I don't have to just stay in the background as the silent, dutiful princess, there to prop up her father and brother. I can't help it if I enjoy that one brief sliver of feeling something like power." She smiled sadly, and Jasmine felt a twinge of regret.

"But, Shirin," she said gently. "It's only another form of propping up yet another man."

Shirin set down her teacup with a deep breath. "No. It's not the same thing."

Jasmine could see that her friend didn't want to believe her. There was no use arguing over it. She reached across the table to clasp Shirin's hand.

"All right. I won't try to change your mind." Shirin looked up, her expression contrite. "Maybe . . . well, wouldn't you say Karim has played right into our hands by asking me to attend the reception with him? They say to keep your enemies close, after all."

"I don't know. It's hard to imagine a version of events where Karim doesn't win this one now." Jasmine looked at Shirin with a rueful smile. "As much as I love Aladdin, there is no chance that he'll measure up in the judges' eyes. They'll always see him as a street rat. I know the only choice they would respect is a consort who is politically advantageous."

Shirin hesitated. "What if . . . what if you *didn't* bring Aladdin?"

"What?" Jasmine stared at her. "You mean trot out another man, instead of the one I'm meant to marry?"

"Just as a ruse, for the tournament," Shirin said hurriedly. "You could pretend that the ministers' words really did influence you, and that your determination to win the tournament and take the sultan's place outweighed your desire to marry Aladdin. Of course, you would tell Aladdin the truth. And as soon as you win the tournament and have the crown on your head, you could 'realize' the error of your ways and recommit to him." She shrugged her shoulders. "Seems to me like the perfect way to outsmart the ministers."

Jasmine's heart started ticking faster, playing out the possibility in her mind. What if Shirin was right? What if she really could have it both ways—do what she needed in order to win, and then still marry Aladdin in the end?

"*If* I were to humor this idea," Jasmine said slowly, "there's still the matter of which man I would pick as my pretend consort."

"You conveniently have a palace full of royal guests right now," Shirin reminded her.

"Yes, but aside from your brother and Achmed, most of them are a good twenty years older than me or already married, or both. Not to mention, this plot would require a very specific sort of man, since I don't want to hurt anyone," Jasmine said. "It would have to be someone who wouldn't take it to heart . . ." She stopped midsentence as the name presented itself. He was *right there*.

Part of her was repulsed by the thought, but the other part couldn't help picturing how it would look if she swept up to the reception with the pompous prince of Batana on her arm. The same prince her ministers were so eager for her to make nice with, from the kingdom whose alliance with Agrabah was so crucial to their prosperity . . . maybe even more than the alliance with Azra.

There was no doubt that Achmed as her consort would impress the ministers and the king of Azra, and make Karim look that much smaller by comparison. She wouldn't have to worry about hurting an innocent nobleman with her false motives either, seeing as she was fairly certain Achmed didn't *have* any genuine feelings.

"You're considering it!" Shirin cried gleefully, pointing at Jasmine's face.

"Well. Maybe," Jasmine admitted. "I can't argue with your logic. The question is . . . could I bring myself to do it?"

CHAPTER TWENTY-THREE

As the day of the challenge drew closer, the palace was transformed into a bustling hub of activity, with a parade of vendors streaming in and out of the service doors. There were canisters of sweet wine and cases of fresh-cut lamb, veal, and ox to deliver for the feast; there were elaborate flower displays and performance stages to erect in a matter of hours. The most difficult part for Jasmine was managing to keep her plans hidden when all Karim needed to do was walk into Crystal Hall to see her progress. She had to resort to covering their unfinished decorations with tarps and rehearsing their entertainments in the Forest of Sands, a tree-lined expanse behind the palace gardens that went on for miles before leading to the dunes that formed the backdrop of Agrabah.

Meanwhile, Nadia slipped into the banquet room a few times to spy on their opponent, reporting back to Jasmine on the dramatic new painted stone reliefs on display and the new elaborate marble fountain that spewed wine instead of water. Between these and Shirin's whispered updates—that Karim was planning a horse-mounted archery exhibition to follow dinner, with himself as the star archer; that he'd commissioned a sword made of rare materials for the king—her temptation to surprise them all with the powerful Prince Achmed as her faux consort began to grow. If she was going to have a fighting chance against Karim, then she had to play to win. Surely Aladdin would understand . . . wouldn't he?

The day before the banquet, she asked Nadia to deliver a secret message.

"Please ask the prince of Batana to meet me for a walk in the orchard garden. Make sure Rajah stays behind, so we don't have another . . . incident with the prince. You can accompany us, of course, so that there's no chance of any misunderstanding."

Nadia couldn't hide the look of disapproval on her face. She'd been against this idea since Jasmine had first broached it in private. Still, she nodded and turned for the door, setting the plan in motion despite her misgivings.

• • •

As soon as Prince Achmed came plodding down the gravel walkway leading to the orchard garden, twirling his mustache with a self-satisfied smirk, Jasmine started second-guessing her decision. She squeezed her eyes shut and thought of her father, imagined him watching from above, aghast, as his crown was placed on the head of a lying usurper. She pictured being forced to flee Agrabah, leaving her country in danger as the darkness that befell Orostan started to spread across the kingdom. It was enough to firm up her resolve, to fix a smile on her face for the prince.

"Thank you for coming," she greeted him. "Walk with me?"

Achmed winked at her and held out his arm. She accepted tentatively, as if his arm might sting her if she got too close. Nadia kept pace a few steps behind them while they walked, her eyes low.

"You have likely guessed why I called you here," she began. "Seeing as you know of my predicament."

Achmed gave her a sidelong smile, licking his lips.

"You've come to your senses, haven't you?"

Jasmine's skin crawled as she answered, "Y-yes. I was wrong before to refuse you in the way that I did. You see, I—I fell in love with someone else." She stopped, swallowed the lump in her throat. "But now I realize that love might not be the most important thing when a kingdom is at stake. I need the right consort to rule beside me."

Those were clearly the magic words. Achmed's eyes glittered, his nostrils flared, and she could practically see the power-hungry excitement dripping from his skin.

"Well, well. We are on the same page, then, Princess."

Jasmine felt a jolt of shock as he called her "Princess" in the same way Aladdin always did.

"You understand what I'm asking, then?" she pressed him, her voice coming out almost harsh. "Until now, it seems to me you've been supporting Karim's claim. I'm asking you to switch teams, so to speak. To back me, to attend the banquet tomorrow at my side. After that, if all goes well"—she exhaled—"*maybe* we can revisit the topic of . . . engagement." She nearly choked on the word.

"Oh yes. I understand. I've been waiting for this, you see, waiting for you to come to your senses." Achmed flashed his teeth in another slimy grin. "I just hadn't expected it to take so long. You certainly know how to make a man wait, don't you, Princess?" He eyed her as though she were an appetizing dish instead of a person, and it took all Jasmine's self-control to not swat his hand away from her arm.

"I'm not sure what you mean," she said, forcing another laugh. "Come, let me show you the pond—"

"After I had to leave so unceremoniously that day, I asked myself countless times: *What* could have possessed you to turn me down? You must know, Jasmine, that I have my pick of the ladies back home. Nothing like that had ever happened to me before," he said, wide-eyed. "And then I had the answer." He snapped his fingers.

"Oh, really?" Jasmine arched an eyebrow. "What was it?"

"Why, it was your *womanly time*, of course." He lowered his voice to a stage whisper. "That explained your outlandish response to me. You were simply not well! I can only imagine how much you've replayed that moment over in your head ever since, wishing you could go back and undo it." He sighed dramatically. "And now look! You found your way to a second chance."

Achmed pretended to applaud and then chortled heartily at his own antics. Jasmine fought the urge to make a run for it, to disappear rather than spend another second with this pig in a prince's clothing. *This was a mistake, a terrible mistake. . . .*

But there was no backing out of it now.

. . .

The Forest of Sands had always seemed to Jasmine like a forgotten parcel of land, untouched by city architects or gardeners. Patches of rough, overgrown grass blended with sand underfoot, while date palm trees rose overhead with their long, wild leaves. This uncultivated spot was usually empty and easy to get lost in, which made it the perfect place for Jasmine to meet with her team in secret. It was here that she practiced sparring with Malik and Aladdin, or sat nestled against a tree to soak in Fatimah's knowledge. Today, a little over twenty-four hours before the King's Banquet, the forest was busier than usual, with more than a dozen of Agrabah's street performers gathered to rehearse for tomorrow night.

Fatimah had woven a magnificent set with her fingers, and it stood proud and bold in the middle of the forest—a set that moved on its own as it shifted seamlessly between depicting the mountainous landmarks of Agrabah and the bridge-covered rivers of Azra.

Watching the performers rehearse a song with her lyrics in front of Fatimah's magic-touched set, Jasmine should have felt exhilarated by what they were creating. But instead, there was only a gnawing sense of dread as she looked at Aladdin.

Tell him. She had made enough excuses to put this moment off; now she was just being cowardly. But every time Aladdin came close and Jasmine opened her mouth to speak, she pictured the hurt in his eyes, the betrayal she knew he would feel—and she kept quiet. Until the moment came when she had no choice.

"They look amazing, don't they?" Aladdin said beside her, nodding at the performers. He smiled down at her, a flirtatious spark in his eyes. "Almost as amazing as I'm going to look in the new formalwear Tarek designed for me for tomorrow night. He said it was a gift, after all you'd done for him at the tournament. Expect me to look as princely as you've seen me yet!"

Jasmine's heart skidded to a stop.

"What is it? Did I say something wrong?" He peered closer at her.

"I—well, it's just—" she stammered, glancing between Aladdin and all the people around them. "Can we go somewhere to talk? In private, I mean."

Aladdin's smile slipped. It was as if he already knew what was to come. Jasmine couldn't meet his eyes, her stomach in knots.

"Carpet," he called, looking up to the sky. In seconds, Magic Carpet appeared behind one of the trees, waving a tassel in greeting.

Aladdin and Jasmine ducked away from the rest of the group, climbing onto Magic Carpet when no one was watching. And then Carpet spirited them off the ground, up to the domed golden rooftops of the palace. For the first time, Jasmine was numb to the thrill of flying, barely noticing the wind whooshing beneath them as they dipped and soared.

Carpet landed smoothly in a partially enclosed balcony at the top of one of the palace's teardrop-shaped towers. Hardly anyone at the palace would have dared venture so high, but then, none of them had a magic carpet to shield their fall. Up here, she and Aladdin would be safe from any prying eyes or ears.

"You look nervous," Aladdin said, his brow creased with concern as they rose to their feet. "You haven't even acknowledged Carpet."

The rug's tassels drooped in response.

"You're right—I'm sorry." Jasmine bent down to give Carpet a gentle pat, and the fabric perked up instantly.

"What did you want to talk about?" Aladdin asked.

Jasmine drew in a deep breath, bracing for the words she had to say.

"I . . . I did something to help me win tomorrow." She dropped her gaze. "And I'm so afraid you'll hate me for it."

"I could never hate you," he said, lifting her chin to draw her eyes back up to his. "Just tell me."

"Um . . . I invited Prince Achmed to go with me to the banquet," she blurted out in a rush. "It's only a trick, of course. When the ministers said we'll be judged on who we present as our intended consort, I knew I had no choice but to bring someone these pomp-ous, snobbish men couldn't find fault with. So you see, it's only for tomorrow night—well, actually a bit longer, until the tournament is over. And then we can go back to how everything was before!"

Jasmine glanced up at him hopefully, but she could see in his eyes that she had hurt him. She felt her hope turn to dust.

"It's only a ruse, for the tournament," she insisted.

"How do you plan to explain it, then?" he finally responded. "What will you tell everyone tomorrow, when there's another man at your side?"

He turned away before she could answer, hiding his face as he gripped the balcony railing. Jasmine's heart twisted. She stepped up behind him, reaching for him, but he moved away from her touch.

"It would only be a lie," she said in a small voice. "You and I would know the truth, and that's all that matters."

"No, it's not." Aladdin shook his head. "You're clearly so—so embarrassed by me that you're willing to fabricate a relationship with someone else, someone you hate. How can you expect me to stand by and watch it happen?"

"I've never been embarrassed by you!" Jasmine protested. "I'm only thinking of *these* small-minded men who are judging me, and the need to protect my crown from this usurper who is intent on stealing it—"

"What happened to the Jasmine who put love and freedom above all else?" Aladdin interrupted. "Why would you lower yourself, all for some stupid crown?"

Jasmine stared at him, stung.

"The *stupid crown* you refer to is my father's legacy. I may not have cared as much for it before, but can't you see that everything's changed now? We can't just go flying off into the sunset and allow this imposter to take over the kingdom!"

"I do see that everything's changed," Aladdin said, his voice tinged with regret. "You've changed." He looked behind her, at Carpet cowering on the ground. "Carpet, take us back. Back to the palace for the princess, and home for me. My real home."

But Aladdin was already taking her hand and leading her onto the carpet.

"I will miss you every day," he said. "But I can't watch this happen."

He brushed his lips across her hand one last time, and Jasmine felt the wrenching pain of separation as he let her go.

"Good-bye, Princess," he said softly, an ache in his tone. And then, before she could stop him, Aladdin and the magic carpet lifted off into the air, leaving her behind.

CHAPTER TWENTY-FOUR

You did the right thing. Really, Jasi, stop being so hard on
yourself."

Jasmine looked up from her slumped position on the settee in
her bedroom, where she'd been sequestered with Rajah for the last
hour. Shirin had come as soon as she heard the rapidly traveling
news of Aladdin's departure.

"The banquets are to take place in less than twenty-four hours,"
Shirin reminded her. "You need to pull yourself out of this and get
your focus back if you are to win."

Jasmine rolled over, resting her head on her arms.

"Winning doesn't seem as important anymore," she said quietly.
"I don't want to be sultana without him by my side."

Nadia was hovering behind Shirin, and her face softened for the
first time since their walk with Achmed. Nadia had made it quite
clear how much she disapproved of what Jasmine had done, but she
was here all the same, checking to make sure the princess was all
right.

"It's not important?" Shirin echoed. "So does that mean we can drop this competition? Let Karim win—and let me be his queen?" She gave Jasmine a pointed look.

Jasmine flinched. *No.* As much as she hated everything about the choice she'd had to make, as much as she longed to be with Aladdin right now, the words she had said to him were still true. There was no way she could hand over her kingdom, her father's legacy, to someone else—someone who didn't deserve it.

"I thought as much." There was a wistful note in Shirin's voice, and it hit Jasmine with a pang of guilt: how much brighter her friend's future might be if Jasmine did let Karim have the throne. Instead of living in Prince Rashid's shadow back home, under his control and at the mercy of his whims, Shirin would become queen consort of Agrabah.

But she would have to marry Karim, Jasmine reminded herself. A man who was quite likely a fraud, and conniving and untrustworthy either way.

"You deserve better than him," she told Shirin. "Still . . . I know this is complicated for you. Once I win the tournament and take back my rightful place, I promise, I'll make sure you stand to benefit from it too."

Shirin gave her a small smile.

"Now you sound back in fighting form. As you should be."

Jasmine stood up from the settee, stretching her arms overhead.

"I'm going to win," she repeated, speaking to herself as much as to Shirin. "And as soon as I do, I'll make it right with Aladdin. I'll bring him back."

This wouldn't—*couldn't*—be the end for them.

. . .

The only perk of the King's Banquet was that it freed Jasmine from having to attend another tension-fueled court dinner the night before. With the palace in the throes of preparations, the ministers instructed the staff to deliver trays to all the royals and guests in their rooms instead, giving Jasmine the relief of being alone with her heartache. She could only imagine how all eyes would fixate on her when she did venture out of her suite in the morning, what with all the gossip circling around Aladdin's sudden departure—not to mention how the court would react to the upcoming surprise of Prince Achmed on her arm. Jasmine would need every spare moment to prepare herself to face it all. So when Nadia knocked on the door to announce she had a guest waiting, Jasmine's spirits took another dip, until she saw who it was: Fatimah.

There was something surreal about seeing the enigmatic afsungar here in Jasmine's own room, away from the stars and trees she seemed to belong to. Rajah crept to the doorway to inspect the newcomer and Fatimah greeted him like an old friend, bending down to stroke his fur and murmur in his ear. It took a few moments of staring before Jasmine remembered her manners, ushering Fatimah inside and offering her a seat and a cup of tea. But Fatimah declined both, retrieving a small parcel from her cloak.

"I had brought something for you today, but you left the forest so suddenly." She gave Jasmine a knowing look, and Jasmine felt her cheeks flush as she wondered what Fatimah thought of her now. She couldn't possibly approve of the way Jasmine had hurt

Aladdin—but the compassion reflected in her eyes made it seem as though maybe she did understand, after all.

"I'm sorry," Jasmine began, but Fatimah was already lifting a horn-shaped piece of pottery from the parcel. *A wine horn,* Jasmine realized, remembering the decorative drinking vessels her father collected. It was painted in black and white stripes, its handle sculpted in the shape of an animal's head. Jasmine studied it as Fatimah spoke.

"I've seen how seriously you are taking this tournament challenge, and I thought I might help a bit more," she said. "You can present this gift to the king tomorrow evening. The striped hyena is the national animal of Azra."

"Thank you." Jasmine took the wine horn from Fatimah, touched that she had thought of it. "Did you make this?"

"I did." A secretive smile flashed briefly across Fatimah's face. "And there's something else. This one is for you."

Fatimah handed Jasmine a lotus flower carved out of willow wood, with a magnetic needle inserted into its center and sealed with wax. As Jasmine gazed down at the wooden flower in her palm, the needle started to . . . twitch.

"A compass," Fatimah explained, "to guide your way through the tournament and beyond."

"Is it magic?" Jasmine asked, watching the needle's strange movements.

"You might call it a natural source of magic. The needle is made of lodestone, a mineral that aligns with the magnetic field of the earth. See that compass rose in the center?" Fatimah pointed to a faint circle surrounded by a few dozen points. "It will direct you north, south, east, west—and anywhere else you need to go."

"Aren't those the only four directions?" Jasmine raised an eyebrow.

Fatimah didn't answer. She was glancing around the room, her eyes landing on the pile of books, with *The Emerald Tablet* and *The Rubaiyat of Omar Khayyam* at the top. And with a rush, Jasmine realized there was no better time than now to confide in Fatimah about her father's warning messages, the poem, and the dreams. They were finally alone.

Fatimah listened carefully to Jasmine's story, her eyes revealing no hint of surprise.

"Well? What do you think?" Jasmine asked breathlessly.

"I think your instincts are worth following," Fatimah said, looking at her with a glint of approval. "While a poem may be just a poem to some, it can represent the lifelong answer to a riddle for others."

"So . . . so you think there *is* a place he was trying to lead me to?" Jasmine felt her heartbeat pick up speed. "The door with no key, the veil—are they real, and more than just a metaphor?"

"I think you ought to look," Fatimah said simply. She glanced down at the willow-wood flower in Jasmine's hand. "Take this flower. The compass can be your guide."

Take this flower.

Jasmine drew a sharp breath. What were the chances that Fatimah would quote the last words of her father's message—words Jasmine hadn't shared?

"Is this the—"

"I should go," Fatimah interrupted, turning her gaze to the window and the darkening night sky. "I will return tomorrow."

"Wait. Before you go, there's something else. It's about Aladdin." A lump rose in Jasmine's throat as she said his name. "Will you make sure he's . . . all right?" *And convince him to forgive me?* she wanted to add.

"He's stronger than you know. He'll be all right." Fatimah looked at her kindly. "As will you."

Jasmine blinked back tears. When she looked up, Fatimah was already gone from the room. The only sign of her was the raven, fluttering its wings above her balcony as it climbed higher in the sky.

· · ·

Jasmine was wide-awake when the water clock struck midnight, as she waited for the palace to become still. The smarter way to spend this night, she knew, would be to get her rest for the high-stakes day ahead . . . but with the flower compass staring at her from the bedside table and Fatimah's words ringing in her ears, Jasmine had to make the most of the quiet palace. Rajah, ever vigilant, stirred awake and hopped off the bed to follow as she crept out of the suite.

She had to go searching.

After pulling on her dressing gown and sliding her feet into a pair of woven slippers, Jasmine reached for the torch illuminating her bedroom. She gently lifted it from its sconce on the wall, holding it in front of her to guide her way.

Tiptoeing through the royal household wing, her footsteps silent on the carpeted floors, Jasmine had the sudden, overwhelming urge to run to the opposite side of the staircase, where Aladdin's bedroom was located. Was there even the slightest chance that he'd had a change of heart and come back? Or even simply returned in the night for his things? But when she reached the fork in the landing, she paused only briefly before moving on to the grand staircase. She wasn't sure if her heart could take seeing his empty room—and she also couldn't risk Karim hearing her outside the door.

At the bottom of the staircase, Jasmine pulled the compass from the pocket of her robe, studying it under the torchlight. But the magnetic needle didn't move so much as a flicker.

"Where should I go?" Jasmine whispered. She glanced up above. "What are you trying to show me, Baba?"

Still no sign of movement. Jasmine proceeded through the Grand Atrium into the next marble-pillared room, following the labyrinthine layout of the palace's main floor. Every few steps, she would shine her torch on the walls around her, searching for a door with no key. And then, in a flash, she remembered—the hidden chamber where the sultan's fire once burned. She had written off the possibility of any connection between that secret, compact space and her father's message, especially since there was no veil to be found within it . . . but what if she'd been wrong to take the word so literally? What if the "veil" referred to anything that could obstruct what was behind it—like a fire's leaping flames?

With a shot of energy, Jasmine raced forward, retracing her steps from the night of the funeral. Now, when she looked down at the compass, the needle was pulsing—leading her north.

The same direction as the room with the fire.

There it is. The wall at the end of the corridor, with the turquoise-and-gold mosaic pattern. Jasmine was raising her hands to the tiles, trying to remember which squares the high elder had pressed to open the passageway, when she felt it: the compass twitching in her hand, drawing her away from here. At the same time, Rajah turned his head and let out a low growl.

Jasmine stared down at the magnetic needle, which spun west now at double speed. Slowly, she backed away from the mosaic wall and followed the compass's lead toward the Grand Atrium, then into Crystal Hall. There, her torchlight bounced off the room's mirrors to reveal glimpses of decorations for tomorrow: the serpentine table and marble chairs she'd selected, the performers' stage with Fatimah's magic-tinged set. Yet in the dark, with no guests to fill the vast, vaulted space, Crystal Hall felt more chilling than beautiful. And when Jasmine's torchlight swept across the oval mirror opposite her, she saw something that made her stumble backward in panic, fear seizing her heart in a cold grip.

It was a flash of yellow eyes. Eyes like the snake from Orostan.

Jasmine bit back a scream and sprinted from the room, Rajah thundering behind her. She scarcely dared to look behind them until they reached the Mirrored Terrace, a decorative passage leading from Crystal Hall to the gardens. A slatted roof revealed glimpses of the night sky, while floor-to-ceiling gold-framed mirrors lined one side of the walkway. Opposite the mirrors was a long open-air archway of carved pillars with sheer silk panels hanging between them. As the silk danced in the wind, Jasmine could have sworn she heard something behind it. A whisper . . . no, *whispers*. Inaudible at first, and then:

"This is where our tale concludes . . . for tonight."

Jasmine froze in place. That was—that was *her*. The same unfamiliar voice she'd heard in the middle of the night. The ghost in her bedroom.

"Wh-who's there?" Jasmine stammered. And then, looking wildly around her, she felt her heart stop as everything came into focus.

A door to which I found no key. The archways. *A veil past which I could not see.* The silk panels.

The blood rushed in her ears as she stepped forward, toward the billowing fabric—to the voice.

And then she lurched backward in shock as a different voice echoed beyond the arches, replacing the whispers. A voice she recognized. Rajah started forward and Jasmine grabbed his fur, motioning for him to stay put.

"You're certain you don't know where it is?" the man hissed from the other side of the hanging silk.

"N-no, I already told you—"

Holding her breath, Jasmine flattened her body against the pillar and peeked through the silk to look. She should have expected them, after hearing their voices—but it was still a shock to discover Karim and Payam, their faces furious under the light of hanging lanterns as they faced each other on the lawn. Jasmine quickly returned to hiding behind the pillar and signaled for Rajah to be quiet, listening to the men's voices with a rapidly racing heart.

"And I told *you* that we need the book," she heard Karim snap. "It's the only way in."

Jasmine stifled a gasp. *What book?* Was he after the same one the sultan had urged her to find?

A gust of wind muffled their voices, and now Jasmine could only make out snatches of the conversation. *"He's waiting..."* *"Looked everywhere..."* *"If you want to stay, you had better prove your—"*

Jasmine leaned forward as far as she could without revealing her hiding place, desperate to hear them more clearly. Then—

"Did you check her room?"

"Of course I did. I've checked every time I found it empty, but—"

Jasmine felt her body sway against the stone. *Her room.* They were clearly talking about her. They'd searched her things. Which meant that either Payam was too dimwitted to find where she'd hidden the books—or none of them was the book he was looking for.

"What was that?" Karim's voice echoed sharply.

"What?"

"I heard something," Karim said slowly, and Jasmine clamped a hand over her mouth to muffle her breathing. "It came from back there."

He was pointing in her direction—she knew it. Jasmine looked frantically at the door, but there was no way to make a run for it without being seen through the silk, especially with a tiger at her side. Part of her wondered if she should step out from behind the pillar, reveal herself, and demand to know everything. But for the first time, instead of pure anger toward Karim, she felt a burgeoning sense of fear—a fear that kept her rooted to the spot. There was something more to him now than the cocky usurper she thought she knew. Something darker. She could hear it in the ice-cold tone of his voice, devoid of any humor or humanity, as he berated Payam.

"You fool. You said we'd be alone at this hour."

Then came the sound of heavy boots crunching against leaves as Karim marched toward the arches and silk. Toward *her.* Jasmine's thoughts became a blur of panic, wondering what to say, what to do, especially as Rajah was struggling to keep still—the tiger shook out of her grasp, bolting forward through the arches seconds before Karim could discover them.

"It was the princess's tiger you heard!" Payam shouted, and Jasmine's muscles clenched with fear as she listened to the men scramble away from Rajah. If they wondered what he was doing there in the middle of the night or if Jasmine was with him, Rajah didn't give them a chance to stay and find out. Karim's and Payam's footsteps grew fainter as the tiger chased them off, until Jasmine could finally exhale again. She took off at a run, skidding against the marble in her haste.

Every creak in the walls, every rustle of wind or fabric, sent Jasmine's heart into her throat as she moved stealthily through the chain of formal rooms and up the grand staircase. At last, she reached the door to her suite and raced across the threshold to safety, collapsing onto her bed in relief and exhaustion.

Yet the relief was short-lived. Her mind was still running in circles, replaying everything she had just heard. What else was Karim after, and how was Payam—someone who was sworn to protect her—involved? What more could Karim *want*, besides her throne? Or was it that this elusive book held the key, somehow, to the crown?

CHAPTER TWENTY-FIVE

How many people are left whom I can trust?

The thought ran through Jasmine's mind the next morning as she sat in front of the mirror with Nadia dressing her hair. The King's Banquet was only hours away, and somehow, before then, she would have to transform herself into a capable, winning sultana *and* convince the gathered crowd that she was actually considering Prince Achmed to be her future consort. Yet all she could think about was last night, and the dangers all around her.

"It'll be all right," Nadia said quietly, catching Jasmine's eye in the mirror as she wove the gold band through her braid. "He'll come back."

Nadia, Jasmine answered her silent question. *She might be the only person from the palace whom I can trust now that Baba and Aladdin are gone. And maybe,* maybe, *Arman.* She loved Shirin, but even her close friend had to look out for herself first and foremost.

"I hope so," Jasmine said with a weak smile.

"If I may speak out of turn . . . I do worry about Princess Shirin's influence on you. Anyone who would encourage you to drop a man like Aladdin can't be a real friend. Not in my mind, anyway."

"But it's only a ruse, remember? Shirin was just trying to help me regain my crown, and at a cost to herself. Remember, if Karim wins"—Jasmine shuddered at the thought—"then Shirin could become queen. Her suggestion might have been a painful one, but it was for a greater good. Besides"—she lowered her eyes—"I'm the one who thought of Prince Achmed and invited him into this plot. Which is something that I don't know Aladdin will ever forgive."

Nadia placed a comforting hand on her shoulder.

"I can't imagine him not forgiving you one day. He loves you so much."

"When this is all over, I'll bring him back," Jasmine vowed. "Even if he's given up on me by then, I still have to try." She looked into her own eyes in the mirror. "I'll do whatever it takes."

. . .

"Your Royal Highness! This is a surprise."

Arman rose hastily from his seat in his private office and folded into a bow as soon as he saw Jasmine in the doorway. "To what do I owe the honor of your presence?"

"I needed to talk to you alone, and it couldn't wait."

Jasmine took a deep breath, pausing to study Arman. How could she be sure he was trustworthy when so many around her clearly weren't? She knew she was still clinging to memories of the different times he had protected Jasmine and her father, but there was more to it. Maybe it was the barely concealed smile on his face when she found a way to set Tarek free, when it appeared she might win that challenge. He was proud of her then—she felt it. And so Jasmine took a chance now that maybe, hopefully, he was on her side.

"It's Payam. I overheard him speaking with Karim late last night, and it became clear that Payam is his accomplice in some sort of scheme. They were talking about searching my rooms for a valuable book—and he admitted to Karim that he's entered my suite when it was empty and gone through my things." Jasmine's face heated up with fury as she relayed the words. "Since he is the one who's been guarding my room, which has already been broken into under his watch, I fear for my safety."

She watched Arman's expression shift into shock.

"Are you *certain* it was Payam's voice you heard?" he asked, furrowing his brow. "I haven't known him to break a single rule since he joined us. He knows as well as I do that ransacking the princess's belongings would get him thrown out of the palace. I can't imagine why he would take the risk."

"I didn't just hear him. I saw him." Jasmine paced the room, thinking quickly. "Could it be that Karim has something he's holding over him? A promise to elevate his standing or make Payam one of the ministers if he were to succeed in taking my crown?"

Arman let out an involuntary chuckle.

"Payam may be perfectly satisfactory as a guard, but a future minister he is not. The man can barely string three sentences together."

"And yet somehow Karim finds him so useful." Jasmine frowned. "It doesn't make sense."

"We did assign Payam to be his personal valet once we—well,

once we determined Karim would be staying awhile," Arman said, diplomatically dancing around the reason her cousin was still here. "It could be that they simply developed a rapport."

"I know what I heard."

"Is there no chance you misheard your name, or anything else, while you were listening in?" Arman arched an eyebrow at her.

"I wasn't *listening in* so much as stumbling onto the conversation. And . . . well, they didn't say my name specifically, but it was clear that the 'her' they spoke of was me." Arman still looked skeptical, but Jasmine pressed on. "I don't trust Payam. I want him to go."

"I'm afraid it's not that simple, Your Highness," Arman said, though his expression was sympathetic. "Until you or Karim succeeds to the throne, Commander Zohar controls who works within the palace. Knowing him as I do, I can tell you he would be highly unlikely to dismiss Payam, particularly over this. I can remove him from guard duty on your room, however."

Jasmine nodded and slumped into an empty armchair before the fireplace.

"It feels like I am a hostage," she said bitterly, "forced to live among all these men who want to hurt me."

"Not all," Arman replied, his expression softening. "There is a faction of us in the palace who would like nothing more than to see you become sultana."

Jasmine managed a grateful smile.

"Thank you, Arman. I'm glad to know there are a few people I can still count on." She paused. "I only wish I knew what Karim and Payam were speaking about last night, and what they were looking for. It feels like there is so much—so much darkness and mystery everywhere I turn."

"Darkness and mystery?" Arman echoed, dubious.

"What we saw in the council chamber is a perfect example," Jasmine pointed out. "That, and what happened in Orostan. Did the troops you sent uncover any survivors there, or any answers?"

Arman gave a slight shake of his head, and was about to say something more when he was interrupted by the blare of trumpets outside the window. He and Jasmine exchanged a bewildered look before following the sounds of fanfare out onto his small balcony.

A cavalcade of horses, draped in the flags of Agrabah and Azra, was riding through the palace gates ahead of a twelve-soldier military corps marching on foot in the decorated uniforms of the Caspian army. Jasmine craned her neck to find the king of Azra standing on the Sultan's Balcony one floor above, already in his full crown and regalia, smiling down at the display in his honor. Jasmine's heart sank.

"I see Karim started our challenge hours ahead of schedule."

"Ah, yes. The morning-of parade." Arman's mouth was set in a thin line. "The crown ministers were all instructed to attend, with the exception of me." He glanced back at Jasmine. "Though it's my job to remain impartial in this, I think Karim suspects where my loyalty lies."

At least Jasmine knew she had been right to come to Arman—though it was only a slight lift to her mood, knowing there was nothing he could do about Payam, and that Karim was already out there showing her up.

"Welcome, King Mahmoud, to a day in your honor!" Karim's voice bellowed from the Great Courtyard up to the Sultan's Balcony as he doffed his cap and bowed. He sounded entirely different, and far more cheerful, than the sinister voice she'd heard last night. "Before the evening festivities begin, it would be my great privilege to showcase the strength and prowess of the Caspian army, in which I serve as general. . . . "

Jasmine rolled her eyes and stalked back inside. The very last thing she needed was to watch this ridiculous display. But there was no avoiding the sounds of applause from the Sultan's Balcony and cheers from onlookers on the ground as the cavaliers performed their tricks and the swords swung and clashed in a propulsive dance.

"I suppose I might as well tell you now how I plan to beat Karim at his game," Jasmine said miserably. "I've invited Prince Achmed to the banquet tonight."

"You did what?" Arman stared at her in astonishment.

"To present as my intended royal consort." Jasmine swallowed hard as she practiced the lie for the first time. "I'm afraid I had to—to end things with Aladdin. For the sake of the tournament, and the crown."

Arman was silent for a long moment, and then he placed a hand on her shoulder.

"That must have been very difficult, Your Highness. But if I may say so, I believe you made the right decision . . . for the *crown*."

Not for you, came the unspoken part of his sentence.

"Now, you should be up there with the king of Azra too." Arman offered her his arm and a conspiratorial smile. "I have to admit, I'm looking forward to seeing the expressions on a few particular faces when you tell them the news."

. . .

Jasmine was stepping out onto the Sultan's Balcony, gearing up for the performance of her life, when she heard Prince Achmed call from below: "I am here once again seeking the hand of the beautiful Princess Jasmine of Agrabah, your future sultana."

Heads turned on either side of the king of Azra as she swept forward, pausing on her way to the balcony's edge to bow and smile to the king. Then she looked out at the Great Courtyard, forcing a delighted smile onto her face.

"Prince Achmed, welcome. It brings me . . . great joy to tell you that, should these next few days go well between us, I will be glad to accept your offer." The words were like a knife scraping her throat—but the stunned looks on Karim's and Commander Zohar's faces made the ploy almost worth it.

While Achmed made a show of blowing exaggerated kisses up to the balcony, Jasmine turned back to the king and her ministers.

"The prince of Batana is currently my choice for a royal consort." Her insides clenched as she delivered the lie. "Aladdin may have been a girlhood infatuation, but he is not a suitable partner for a sultana. While I will always care for him, I do understand I need a man of Achmed's stature to rule alongside me when I take my father's crown." It was all she could do to keep from choking on the sentence.

The king of Azra studied her with newfound respect.

"You are wise to make this choice, Princess. There would be enough obstacles against a woman sovereign as it is, without adding a pauper as your consort." He chuckled, then surveyed Prince Achmed and his retinue with an approving nod. "A shrewd decision indeed."

Jasmine smiled through gritted teeth. The only thing that made this moment bearable was catching the flustered look that passed between Karim and the commander. At least now the tables had been turned. She was the one showing them up.

CHAPTER TWENTY-SIX

"Princess Jasmine, my beauty!"

Jasmine winced at the sound of Prince Achmed coming up behind her in the Grand Atrium, his long velvet-and-silk cape sweeping the marble floor after him. She closed her eyes with dread and took a deep breath before plastering a smile on her face and turning to him. After she gave the obligatory curtsy, Achmed took her hands and pulled her close. So close, she could smell the garlic on his breath.

Jasmine hid her face, instantly queasy. It wasn't just the stench of him but the idea of being this close to another man that turned her stomach. She carefully extricated herself from his embrace.

"We'll have plenty of time for all of ... *that* if we're to marry," she said with an awkward laugh.

She was saved from continuing the nauseating conversation by the six ministers walking together into the foyer. As they bowed to Prince Achmed, Jasmine noticed the deferential way the ministers spoke to him, looked at him. Markedly different from how they behaved toward her.

So it wasn't a mistake to pick him, then, Jasmine thought gloomily. *Just torture.*

. . .

The palace was aglow with lights when night fell, echoing with the strains of music and the intermingled chatter of the court and its guests. From the banquet room, where Karim lorded over his reception, the percussive beat of tablas accompanied the plucking strings of the lute, while in Crystal Hall, Jasmine's chosen trio of lyre, oud, and harp players performed a selection of classical melodies in advance of the surprise show to come. Jasmine's long serpentine table was finally uncovered and piled high with the finest meats, stews, breads, and wines in Agrabah, while a display of climbing flowers, including her signature white jasmines, was revealed in all its glory. Surveying the scene from her gilded chair at the head of the room, Jasmine couldn't help but smile in approval. For her first banquet, it looked and sounded divine. There was just one flaw: the prince seated next to her.

"A dance for my future bride?" Achmed offered now, rising and extending his hand.

"I would love to, but I was told by my advisers that I must save the first dance for the king." Jasmine tried her hardest to look regretful about this. "In fact, it has been taking quite a while for him to join us. I'm going to go ask Arman for an update."

As she stood, Achmed grasped her elbow to stop her.

"Let one of the servants handle that," he said dismissively. "You belong here, seated in comfort beside me."

The words sent a tremor of revulsion through her. However

difficult she thought it might be to pretend with Achmed, the reality was infinitely harder—and she had a feeling that getting him to leave once this was all over would prove an even bigger challenge.

"I know, but I'm—I'm impatient," Jasmine improvised. "I prefer to get things done myself. I'll only be a minute."

She shook off his arm as gently as she could manage, and then made her way through the small crowd to the door. Jasmine followed the sound of the tablas to the banquet room, where she found the marble doors flung wide open, giving her a full view of the king of Azra laughing and toasting with Karim in front of a flowing fountain while beautiful dancers gyrated around them. Jasmine could see the king eyeing the dancers up and down, but Karim seemed surprisingly oblivious. He had a beauty of his own on his arm, and as the two exchanged a flirtatious glance, Jasmine did a double take. Shirin looked different tonight, older. Dark kohl lined her eyes, and her lips were stained pink. With her striking red gown and the tiara sparkling against her auburn hair, Shirin looked more like a queen than any Jasmine had ever met. Watching her and Karim together, like they *belonged* together, Jasmine felt momentarily dizzy, as if she'd lost all her bearings.

Just then, Shirin glanced up toward the doors. Her face flushed as she caught Jasmine's eye, her expression shifting to an unmistakable look of guilt. She must have known what she was doing—charming Jasmine's rival, helping him win over the king just by being at his side—and from the looks of it, she was enjoying herself.

Jasmine turned quickly, before Karim could spot her too, and headed back toward Crystal Hall. There was no point in asking for

Arman's help to speed along Karim's banquet and hurry the king to her own. It was perfectly clear how well things were going for her opponent. Now, instead of itching to prove herself tonight, Jasmine fought a creeping feeling of defeat.

She returned to Crystal Hall moments before a dozen costumed figures filtered through the doors, Nadia leading them inside. The street performers were here. As she recognized Malik's profile among them, Jasmine's heart lifted with hope. Maybe Aladdin was with him . . . ? But as she scanned their faces, her spirits fell. He wasn't there. Of course he wasn't.

Jasmine swallowed the lump in her throat and joined them, greeting the performers with an awkward smile. These were Aladdin's people more than hers; surely they would despise her for the way she'd seemingly replaced him with a prince. But if they did, they didn't let it show. It wasn't until she came face-to-face with Malik that she felt any hint of a chill.

"How is he?" Jasmine whispered while leading the performers behind the curtain of the stage Fatimah had built.

"He won't speak about it," Malik said stiffly. "But he did make sure to tell me I should come tonight as planned. In spite of . . . well, everything, he still wants this to go well for you. He knows you would be the better ruler."

Jasmine's heart seized. There was so much she wanted to say, to explain, to relay to Aladdin through Malik. But then, as if on cue, a coarse hand gripped her arm. Prince Achmed was right behind them.

"There you are. Where have you *been*? I thought that was only supposed to take a minute," he huffed, ignoring Malik and the performers as they bowed to him dutifully. "Come, they say the king is on his way. Which means as soon as you get your dance over with, the night will be ours."

Jasmine couldn't bring herself to look at Malik after that. She reluctantly accepted the prince's arm, telling him as they walked back to their seats, "I had to get my performers ready. We have a surprise planned for the king."

"All this fuss to impress the ruler of a kingdom that boasts only a shadow of the splendor our two nations will have when combined," Achmed remarked. "The vision of the two of us at our thrones should be all he needs to see."

Jasmine was saved from replying by the entrance of the king. His soldiers preceded the ministers of Agrabah and then King Mahmoud himself, who was wearing a full-body silk brocade formal dress robe in the green and white colors of Azra. The jewels in his crown gleamed atop his head as everyone in Crystal Hall lowered to their knees, bowing and curtsying. When she rose from her curtsy, Jasmine noticed the redness in his face and glassiness of his eyes, no doubt from Karim's indulgent wine fountain. Her heart sank as she wondered if the king would even notice all the work and detail that had gone into her banquet—or if Karim had already won, simply by virtue of buttering him up with drinks.

"Now, then," the king said, rubbing his hands together and taking his seat on the largest marble-and-gold chair in the room, between Jasmine and Achmed. "What do you have in store for me?"

Jasmine cued the musicians to resume playing and then said, "First, a feast. Then a show."

"I think you mean first a *drink*!" King Mahmoud slapped his leg as he laughed heartily. . . .

"You're right, Your Majesty," Jasmine replied with a grin. "And I have a special gift for you to drink from."

She reached for the parcel tucked beside her chair and handed it to the king. As he opened it, taking in the intricate woodwork and striped hyena design of the wine horn Fatimah had made, he rewarded her with a genuine smile.

"Well done, Princess. Now, how about that drink?"

Jasmine signaled to one of the palace staff, who hurried over with a flask and carefully poured the red liquid into the wine horn. As he lifted it to his lips, the king let out a cry of delight, and Jasmine gasped. The carved hyena was *moving*, opening its own mouth in tandem with the king as he drank.

"How clever!" he cried, studying the wine horn more carefully. "How did you do it?"

Quickly remembering that it wasn't supposed to be a surprise to her, Jasmine said coyly, "Just a bit of magic I thought Your Majesty might like."

"Quite right. My grandchildren at home will be enamored of this."

Thinking on her feet, Jasmine said, "There are more treasures like these to be found in Agrabah. We have the finest craftspeople creating the most unique, cutting-edge wares for our bazaars, not to mention the historic collection of riches found throughout Agrabah. With a new trade agreement in place, Azra could share in this prosperity."

"You don't waste any time, do you?" The king chuckled, pointing a stubby finger at her. "I will admit, you have given me something to think about."

They gathered around the serpentine table, with the king at the head and Jasmine and Prince Achmed seated on either side of him, and the feast began. As much as she'd been dreading Achmed's company, Jasmine had to admit he was proving useful here, as he and King Mahmoud shared the same boorish sense of humor and boastful storytelling style. Strangely, though the king kept refilling his wine horn and seemed more jovial with every sip, he appeared far more sober than when he had first entered Crystal Hall. Jasmine eyed the wine horn curiously, wondering what other magic Fatimah might have infused it with.

After a decadent dessert spread of baklava, date-and-cardamom cake, qurabiya shortbread cookies, and rice pudding, it was time for the show to begin. Jasmine directed everyone's attention to the stage as the performers emerged from behind the curtain dressed in traditional costume, from the jewel-toned multilayered skirts and matching headdresses native to Agrabah to the brocade trousers and metal cummerbunds worn by the men of Azra. Jasmine stepped onstage to join them.

"When our tale begins, Arabia is under siege," she said, infusing her voice with drama. "Not from fighting between warring countries—but from a war waged by our own earth. You see, it hadn't rained in any of our Arabian countries in two long years. Some said the Arabian Drought was a message from a higher power; others said it would go on forever. But there were two individuals who understood what was needed to save their earth: a young nomadic princess from Agrabah, and the first king of Azra. . . ."

For twenty minutes, Jasmine spun her tale to an engrossed audience, while musicians and dancers performed against the backdrop of Fatimah's revolving set. The show concluded with Agrabah's young princess and Azra's first king joining forces to tend to their struggling earth, offering it a form of tribute in a bridge between their two lands—not unlike the bridge recently proposed by Agrabah's government under her father's regime. As it appeared, shimmering, on Fatimah's backdrop, a mist of water sprinkled through the room. At last, in the story, they had rain—and in real life, a dash of magic.

The king rose to his feet in applause, and the rest of the guests quickly followed. A celebratory chain dance marked the end of the performance, and Jasmine boldly offered the king her hand. "Shall we?"

The king's eyes sparkled with delight, and the audience cheered as the real-life king of Azra and princess of Agrabah joined their counterparts onstage, circling their wrists and moving their hips to the rhythm. "Now all of you!" Jasmine called, beckoning the rest of the guests.

Chairs scraped against the floors as the audience rose from their seats and joined in the dancing. Everyone around her was smiling, especially the king. The night was going so well, she didn't even mind when Prince Achmed attempted to pull focus with his over-the-top hip moves. Jasmine beamed as she looked around the room. For the first time in days, she felt something resembling hope.

And the only person she wanted to tell was Aladdin.

· · ·

"I've made my decision on tonight's winner," the king said in her ear at the end of the dance. "Let's see if your minister of Arabian nations and the high elder agree with my choice."

Jasmine's stomach fluttered in anticipation. She watched hopefully as the king sauntered up to Khaleel and the high elder, his fellow judges in the tournament's second challenge. They conferred in a brief huddle and then took the stage.

"Princess Jasmine, you have exceeded my expectations tonight," the king began. "I look forward to continuing our conversations and building a bridge between our nations . . . with you as sultana. In a unanimous decision, you are the winner of tonight's challenge."

Joy and relief bubbled up within her at his announcement and at the realization that—for a second time now—her storytelling had helped her achieve the impossible. It had secured her the win.

Jasmine curtsied in gratitude to the king before instinctively turning to look for an ally to celebrate with. Of course, Aladdin wasn't there. She didn't see Nadia anywhere either, and Shirin was with Jasmine's opponent in the opposite room.

As gratifying as it was to win, there was something hollow in her victory without the people she loved most there to share in it.

• • •

As soon as the king retired to his chambers for the night, Jasmine took it as her cue to pry Prince Achmed's hand from hers and tell him she was off to bed.

"Let me escort you," he offered, and Jasmine hastily shook her head.

"It wouldn't be—be proper if you were seen near my room

before we're married," she improvised. "You stay here, enjoy yourself. I'll see you in the morning."

If the prince noticed the lack of enthusiasm in Jasmine's voice, he didn't seem to notice. He kissed her hand good night, and then joined the table of half-drunk noblemen, helping himself to another flask of wine.

Once she had passed through the doors and was blissfully alone in the palace corridor, Jasmine let out a long exhale. She'd done it. She had established herself as a force to be reckoned with in the tournament. Hurting Aladdin had been the only flaw in the plan—but if she could just win the next two challenges, she would have her title and her crown back. And then she would win him back too.

At the foot of the grand staircase, Jasmine spotted a huddled figure, head in her hands. It took a few moments before she recognized the figure as Princess Shirin. With her gown crumpled around her and a face stained with tears, she couldn't have looked more different from the glowing, regal vision at Karim's side earlier in the night.

Jasmine joined her on the bottom stair, wrapping an arm around her friend. Shirin's shoulders stiffened, but she didn't push her away.

"What's wrong, Shir?"

Shirin wiped her eyes with the back of her hand.

"I'm happy for you. I wanted you to win, really. It's why I gave you the advice I did, to bring forth a more suitable man of whom the judges would approve."

"So then why does it feel like you're trying to convince both of us right now?" Jasmine asked gently.

"Because even though the loss wasn't mine . . . it felt like it."
Shirin sighed. "For one brilliant, shining moment, I got to experience what it would be like to have it all: a position of prominence among a roomful of princes and kings, not just as my father's daughter or my brother's sister, but as—"

"Karim's intended?" Jasmine interrupted, pointedly.

"A future *queen*," Shirin said. "And the way he was looking at me and speaking to me . . ." Her cheeks flushed. "I'd never felt so admired, least of all by a man so handsome and clever. But as soon as the ministers came in to announce he'd lost the challenge, it was like he didn't see me anymore. He just . . . left. And, of course, Prince Rashid let me have an earful over how I clearly didn't do enough, how I *wasn't* enough to help Karim win the way Prince Achmed helped you."

"I'm so sorry, Shirin." Jasmine's chest constricted as she looked at her friend. "I hate this. I hate that they made you feel that way. I only wish we could be on the same side, like we were before."

As Jasmine took Shirin's hand, and thought of Aladdin and her own broken heart, it occurred to her that men of privilege like Rashid, Achmed, and Karim could sail through life, making demands with every expectation they would be met, while women were forced to sacrifice so much of themselves just to survive.

Even for two princesses, it was still a man's world. . . .

CHAPTER TWENTY-SEVEN

The next few days in the palace felt like an exercise in dodging vipers. Jasmine's win had only heightened the tension between her and Karim and the infighting between her crown ministers, so that every time she left the bubble of her bedroom, she felt it: a target on her back. The conversation she'd overheard between Karim and Payam had her perpetually on edge, suspicious of everyone around her. If her father's sworn protector could sneak into her room and search her belongings, how could she trust anyone? There was no longer the feeling of sanctuary in her room, and she found herself too anxious to sleep, afraid she would wake up to find Karim and Payam in the darkened suite with her, prying into her things while she slept.

Then there was Achmed, a viper of a different stripe. The balancing act required to keep up the facade with the prince—listening to him drone on about his many "accomplishments" while she tried to look remotely attentive, then peeling his hands off her when he got too close—left Jasmine exhausted at the end of each day. With

Aladdin long gone, Shirin growing distant, and Nadia increasingly busy with her duties in the palace, Jasmine felt more isolated as time dragged on. So it came as an unexpected relief when she and Karim were called down to the council chamber to hear their next challenge. *The closer we get to the end of this tournament,* she thought, *the sooner I can have my life back. If I win.*

"This week, you will prepare for two challenges concurrently," Commander Zohar announced once they were all seated. "As minister of war, I will outline a hypothetical attack coming from Greece, and each of you will be tasked with assembling an infantry and counterattack strategy—which you will demonstrate for me in a battle enactment on the Great Courtyard, one week from today."

A confident grin spread across Karim's face, while Jasmine's stomach dropped. This challenge would play right into his strengths.

"In the meantime"—the minister of the treasury, Majid, spoke up—"I challenge the two of you to locate the most precious, prized object in all of the Palace of Agrabah. Search high and low, through every nook and passageway. The item you choose will show us what you value most—and whether you can grasp the true value of your kingdom."

The book, Jasmine thought with a jolt of energy. Could this be the reason her father had urged her to seek it out? Especially if Karim was looking for it too, there had to be something clearly valuable held within it. What if this book ended up being not only the answer to her father's riddle—but her key to winning the tournament?

One thing was certain: She had to find it before anyone else did.

. . .

Late that night, while everyone else in the palace slept, Jasmine sat up in bed combing through both *The Rubaiyat of Omar Khayyam* and *The Emerald Tablet* for what felt like the hundredth time. Rajah, a tiger who once prided himself on sleeping a solid twenty hours a day, had taken to Jasmine's insomniac ways ever since the night of the intruder. He refused to leave her alone, and was now resting his chin on her knee, watching as she flipped back and forth between the two texts and her parchment of notes, searching for more clues she might have missed. Just when she was about to pack the books away and close her eyes, she saw—something. It was subtle enough to be missed at first glance, but as she grabbed a magnifying glass from her desk to double-check, there it was: a faint circle surrounding the words *underground vault*.

The words were from the frame story of *The Emerald Tablet*, which told of its text being discovered in a vault beneath a towering statue depicting the god of wisdom and communication. Inside the vault was an ancient corpse on a golden throne, holding the titular tablet in its skeletal fingers. The tablet's stories and teachings were soon transcribed to paper, into books all across Arabia and the Mediterranean—like the one in Jasmine's hands. And her father had made a point of circling not just *underground vault*; as she looked closer, she saw the faint outline around the word *corpse* as well.

Jasmine froze as the answer came to her in a rush. An underground vault, where a corpse would be found . . . There was only one place that could be. The dark, windowless room where her father's body was prepared for burial. The same place where he had urged her to *Find the book*.

. . .

Jasmine could feel her heart clanging in her chest as she tiptoed through the corridor to the Grand Staircase, gripping her torchlight with white knuckles and silently praying Karim wouldn't wake up and see her. She felt a twinge of guilt for feeding Rajah a sleep-inducing herb, but it was the only way to get her overprotective tiger to stay behind. She couldn't exactly sneak through the tight confines of the palace underground with him lumbering beside her.

Jasmine turned to glance behind her every few steps, aiming the lantern to check for Karim. But though there was no one in sight, she still had the eerie sensation of being watched—a feeling that caused the hairs to rise on the back of her neck and goose bumps to prickle across her skin.

Down on the main palace floor, she retraced her steps from that fateful day when she'd last heard her father's voice. She felt her way along the walls, waiting until her hand closed around the knob that opened the camouflaged door into the palace's hidden lower chambers. When her fingers scraped against a keyhole just above the knob, Jasmine's spirits sank. This wasn't the door with no key, then . . . and if there was a key, she had no idea where to find it.

She turned the knob, just in case. To her amazement, the door creaked open. The last person who walked this passage had left it unlocked . . . by mistake, or on purpose?

Across the doorway hung a heavy damask curtain, a barrier

between the upstairs and downstairs worlds. Jasmine pushed past the fabric and began the cold descent underground.

The stairs ended in a dark, bare stone hallway, a chilling contrast to the lavish, gleaming palace interiors above. Through her torchlight, Jasmine could see that she was in a narrow warren, with a row of doors on either side of her. But which one was *the* door? They all looked the same to her, and when she closed her eyes and tried to remember entering and exiting the room with her father's body . . . it was all a blur.

With her heart ticking at an ever-faster pace, she aimed her lantern across the row of doors, waiting to find an anomaly or missing keyhole among them. But what she found instead was over a dozen identical doors—none of them built for keys.

Jasmine didn't know whether to laugh at the irony or scream in frustration. She would have to enter the rooms one by one, opening each door that she suspected contained remains of the dead. After all, only a monarch could be buried at Sultan's Peak, the mountain facing Mecca miles from the palace. She had always known somewhere in the back of her mind that the wives, siblings, and children of sultans past were likely buried here on palace grounds. But she'd never had to think about them or face those ghosts. Until now.

With a shaky breath, Jasmine tentatively turned the knob on the first stone door—and found herself somewhere wholly unexpected.

There were no tombs or dead bodies here. Instead, she stood in a room of gray cobblestones, with a pair of dark stone pillars flanking the entrance. The image of a snake and the letter *J* were carved into the pillars, and as Jasmine slowly circled the room, she felt the same creeping sensation of dread that her body and mind associated with him—Jafar.

He had built this lair.

A rickety birdcage sat empty on a pile of gray bricks, a stray red feather the only remaining trace of Jafar's parrot, Iago. A bronze orrery hung in the center of the room, a mechanical model of the solar system. Jasmine could so clearly picture Jafar standing beneath it, plotting his own takeover of the universe, that she shuddered at the sight. And as her eyes adjusted to the dim light, she saw something else. Something suspended in midair beneath the orrery.

It was a round brass bottle, dark and rusted. Jasmine peered closer, frowning as she tried to recall what it reminded her of. She reached for the bottle, and as her hand brushed the brass, smoke puffed out through its opening—creating a screenlike effect in the middle of the room. A screen with shadows moving across it. And then Jasmine recoiled in shock, her heart clambering into her throat.

Something was crawling across the smokescreen. It was a scene in silhouette, a sight that filled her with a familiar gripping fear: the giant shadow with the knife, creeping toward her bed curtains. Her intruder.

Jasmine stumbled backward, looking around the room wildly, wondering *how* it was possible her moment of terror could be replaying itself here in Jafar's lair. But then the shadows curled together and shifted, revealing a new image—then another.

The dead woman with the frozen scream, lying in the forest of bare leaves. The snake slithering among the fallen animals in

Orostan. Its yellow eyes, somehow glowing bright through the smoke, while everything else existed only in gray.

All her visions, the terrible things she'd seen, were reflected back at her in the smoke from Jafar's suspended brass bottle.

Jasmine backed away in fear, tripping in her haste and bumping into a row of shelves behind her. Old scrolls and jars of strange liquids clattered onto the cobblestones at her feet, and as she crouched down to clear her path, her fingers froze on another brass bottle. This one was a murky gray, but as soon as she touched it, the bottle's surface turned clear and shadows began to move within. The shadows shifted and grew, forming three distinct shapes. Three adolescents: a boy in a crown, and another boy and girl in plainer clothes standing behind him.

"Tell me again, Jafar."

Jasmine's head snapped up in shock. The voice—where was it coming from? She could hear the youthful, boyish tone coming from everywhere and nowhere, all at once. Was it in her mind? Or seeping through the bottle's twisted magic, echoing off the cobblestone walls?

"Tell me about the realm of the dead," the shadow boy needled. "Please?"

"For starters, my liege, it's called the City of Brass," a different, haughty voice replied. Jasmine's breath caught as she recognized the term by which Jafar always addressed her father. Which meant . . . the boy in this magic shadow show was the young sultan, known back then as the crown prince.

"He's not the one you should be listening to," the girl interjected. "Jafar has never even *been* to the other realms."

"And you have, Taminah?" the young sultan breathed.

Taminah. The only person Jasmine ever knew with that name was her childhood tutor, the one who used to read her those addictive, frightening folk tales. She had grown up at the palace, Jasmine remembered now, a child of one of the courtiers, who would go on to work there herself. Just like Jafar.

The young Taminah nodded. Jafar ignored her, addressing the sultan as he said confidently, "She isn't the only one who can cross the realms, my liege. I will too, and I'll do so much more. Just wait and see."

The shadows melted, the bottle's contents turning murky once again. Jasmine shook it desperately, trying to bring it back to life, to see her young father again. Without him, there was nothing in this room but a thick current of fear—of danger. But the bottle remained dark, and Jasmine tripped forward, hurrying from the lair and back into the corridor of identical doors.

Jafar's secret chamber couldn't be the place where her father had meant to lead her. He likely never even knew of its existence. She could feel herself drawing closer, like a magnet, to the true destination. Steeling her nerves, Jasmine opened another door . . . into a room of marble tombs.

It was cold enough to see her own breath leave her body as she circled the room, shining her torchlight across the names carved into the tombs. Ancient names from history books like Achaemenes and Parmys. The daughters and younger sons of the early kings . . . all but forgotten in this hidden place.

Staring at the sealed slabs of marble before her, Jasmine had the sinking realization that her plan would never work. If the book really was hidden in one of these tombs, there was no way of knowing which one—and the last thing she intended to do was go around opening up and possibly desecrating multiple tombs of her ancestors.

"Where is it, Baba?" she whispered into the room of the dead. "Please, show me."

There was no response, no familiar voice or otherworldly light to guide her way. Instead, all she felt was another gust of cold. It was strange how chilly it was down here, even though the desert was just outside the door. Jasmine was hugging her arms to her chest, trying to warm up, when she felt something in her pocket poke at her skin. *Fatimah's compass.* The wooden lotus flower.

If Fatimah could build a wine horn with carved creatures that came to life, if she could transform herself into and out of a raven . . . then certainly she could infuse this compass with magic. A navigational magic.

Jasmine pulled the compass from the pocket of her dressing gown, watching as its magnetic needle twitched to life.

"Lead me to the book," she whispered. "Please."

The compass went stock-still—and then the needle suddenly skated to the left, urging Jasmine to move. Which meant the book she was looking for wasn't in this room.

Holding the compass in one hand and her lantern in the other, Jasmine proceeded slowly past the doors. When she reached the end of the mazelike hallway, the compass started twitching in a frenzy, pointing her toward the second-to-last door. Jasmine gripped her lantern tighter, trying to keep her fear at bay as the moment when she would have to open one of the tombs drew closer.

This chamber was nearly identical to the others, but with a new set of names etched across the marble slabs. *Mandana. Shapur. Artystone. Bahram.* And then the light of her torch landed on one of the older tombs, its marble crumbling at the edges with age. *Atossa,* Jasmine read. *Daughter of Cyrus the First.* In a land where royal daughters normally faded into obscurity, Atossa was one of the few names Jasmine recognized from her tutor's teachings: a daughter and later wife of influence in the old Achaemenid days. And suddenly she knew, without even needing to glance at her compass, that this was the one.

Atossa's tomb was the door with no key.

With her heart in her throat and excitement mingling with terror, Jasmine placed her lantern on the edge of the tomb and began the work of lifting the heavy lid. The marble had been sealed shut for so long, she had to use the small knife from Malik to ease it open. Sweat dripped from her brow as she worked to loosen the lid, so focused on her task, and so elated when she felt the marble finally pry loose, she was scarcely aware of anything else.

Using all her strength, Jasmine lifted the lid of Atossa's tomb with a cry of exertion. And then, bracing herself, she peered inside.

Instead of the skeletal remains or rotting flesh she feared, Jasmine was staring at a dark staircase within the tomb. It beckoned her forward, a terrifying invitation. Gathering her lantern and all her courage, she climbed inside.

Jasmine was three steps down into the tomb when she heard it: a creak behind her. And then she felt a warm breath on the back of her neck. A scream lodged in her throat as she turned.

Payam.

Jasmine stared at him in shock. His eyes glittered as he looked back at her—eyes that seemed to glow almost *yellow*.

"Wh-what are you doing here? Why are you looking like that?" Jasmine sputtered. "Were you following me?"

"I'm only doing the same thing as you, Your Highness," Payam said coolly. "Looking for the most valuable object in the palace."

His voice, his demeanor, were jarringly different than before. There was none of his usual quiet awkwardness, and it occurred to Jasmine with a jolt that *this* was the real Payam. The other, deferential figure was an act.

"Why are you doing this?" Jasmine's voice shook. "Why would you go so far to help Karim of all people, a usurper you hardly know? Didn't my father mean something to you?"

Payam's eyes flashed, his pupils dilating. Jasmine's heart thudded in her chest. *Those eyes*. Like the eyes of the snake, the eyes from the mirror . . . how was it possible?

"Neither of them means anything to me," Payam hissed, his voice now matching those snakelike eyes. "The only person who promised me more if I served him well, who offered me the chance to share the riches and spoils of Agrabah and its parallel realms, was Jafar." Payam's lip curled. "He may be lost to the world now, but it doesn't matter. I'm still here to claim my prize, and if I could avenge him along the way?" The corners of his mouth turned up in a mirthless, chilling smile. "I was glad to do it."

"Avenge him?" Jasmine repeated, the hairs rising on the back of her neck. "Do you mean by helping Karim steal my throne? Or . . . something else?" *Something even worse?*

"Who says it's one or the other?" Payam let out a cruel laugh, and Jasmine gasped as she recognized something in his voice—the snatches of the conversation she'd overheard the other night.

"I told you that we need the book. It's the only way in." "He's waiting . . ."

That cold, harsh voice she had so easily assumed belonged to Karim, her enemy, had been Payam's all along. He must have been manipulating Karim, directing him to do Payam's bidding—*"search her room," "find the book"*—all under the guise of helping him win. And now Jasmine knew with a sick certainty what else he had done.

"It was you," she whispered. "You killed my father—didn't you?"

Payam opened his mouth to answer, and his eyes suddenly rolled back, before flashing a burnished, blazing yellow. Jasmine screamed, trying to scramble away from him, but she found herself trapped; he was blocking her path. And then he blinked, his expression momentarily dazed as his cold eyes turned brown once more. That's when it hit Jasmine that *something had happened to him.* He wasn't human—or if he had been once, he wasn't anymore.

Jasmine gripped the stone wall to keep from falling, terror flooding her veins as she realized the danger she was in. She looked wildly over Payam's shoulder to the top of the stairs. If she could get past him, if she could get away—

She would be handing him the book. She couldn't run, couldn't let him take what she'd been searching for, the same elusive object *everyone* seemed to be searching for. So instead, Jasmine darted forward.

She was fast, but so was he. They were neck and neck as they ran down the remaining steps, each one trying to shove the other out of the way as they landed in another, smaller chamber. A room just large enough to fit an aged golden throne, preceded by a path of turquoise stones. From the back, Jasmine could see an unmoving, shrunken figure seated on the throne.

Terror gripped her insides as she gingerly circled the throne—and let out a choked scream.

A corpse was sitting upright before her, with hollowed-out eye sockets and a waxy skull for a face. Its skeletal remains were dressed in royal robes, the silk fabric still preserved, as it sat on its golden throne—just like in *The Emerald Tablet*. Only this wasn't the male figure from the story, but the female form of Atossa, hundreds of years past her death.

And she was holding a book.

Payam followed Jasmine's gaze, his eyes widening at the corpse and then zeroing in on the book. The two broke into a sprint, fighting each other to be first to seize it. They were close enough now that Jasmine could just make out the unfamiliar title, scripted in calligraphy across the book's spine: *One Thousand and One Nights*. But while the book was in Atossa's hands, Jasmine knew it was impossible for it to have been hers. In her day, the advent of paper hadn't even arrived from China yet. Which meant this was a newer treasure, stowed here for safekeeping.

Jasmine's and Payam's hands grasped the book at the same time, yanking it from the skeleton's grip. As they each pulled one half of the book, desperate to claim it—the delicate binding ripped in half.

Jasmine's eyes had only a second to register the chapter title at the top of the torn page in her hands—"The City of Brass"—before everything around her disappeared.

CHAPTER TWENTY-EIGHT

Jasmine opened her eyes in a new land. A place where fog fell like a curtain, blurring her vision as she climbed up from the dirt. Fog like the gray mist that had blanketed Orostan back home.

"The veil past which I could not see," she whispered. Fear shivered its way down her spine as she struggled to get her bearings, trudging through the endless heavy cloud that surrounded her on all sides. Her only relief was that Payam was nowhere near.

Finally, after what felt like hours, something emerged through the fog. It was a forest of leafless trees—the same forest she'd seen in her dark vision in the mirror just before her father's funeral. Jasmine looked around wildly for somewhere to run and spotted a wrought-iron gate in the distance. It wasn't until she got closer that she noticed the marble tablet posted at the bottom of the gate.

CITY OF BRASS, it read in faded lettering. *CAUTION TO ALL WHO ENTER HERE.*

Jasmine froze. The City of Brass … the chapter title from Atossa's book. The name of the realm Jafar spoke of in the magic shadow show she watched from his lair. Did she dare to enter? But her hand was already lifting the latch on the gate, her body knowing before she did that she had to see this journey through.

The dirt path snaked ahead, surrounded by more bare trees, but the sight of rooftops in the distance gave her a sprig of hope. Where there were roofs there was a town, and people who could help her make sense of where she was. She quickened her pace.

As the town drew near, Jasmine noticed strange, menacing statues cropping up along her path. There was a giant, its mouth open to bare its enormous teeth, a gargoyle, a demonic creature. She shuddered.

Finally, a small town stretched out before her: a modest place, with a stone fountain and bell tower at the center, surrounded by one-story homes and merchants' shops. Yet the town square was eerily empty, its cobblestones littered with brass bottles strewn across the ground. *Brass bottles*—another eerie similarity to her vision in the mirror, and to the bottles in Jafar's lair.

Jasmine turned her frantic gaze to the shop and house windows, relieved to find that it wasn't the abandoned town it appeared to be at first glance. She could see a few merchants standing stiffly at their shop counters, an old woman sitting by her front window, a younger couple in their kitchen. But they were all oddly still.

Jasmine nearly tripped over another brass bottle at her feet. She lifted it, examining the bottle curiously. And as she touched it, she felt a strange pull—compelling her to open the lid.

Red smoke came rising out of the bottle, and Jasmine scrambled backward, crying out in panic. Something fiery within was pulling itself free, and though she tried to slam the lid back on, she was too late. The fire had escaped. It was growing larger and larger before her eyes, forming a shape as enormous and towering as Aladdin's genie, but the opposite of the Genie's comforting blue appearance. This creature had spotted red skin and flaming yellow eyes; it had claws longer than Jasmine's arms and dark hooves for feet.

Jasmine had never seen anything so terrifying in her life.

She trembled, staring up at the demon, which looked like it had crawled off the pages of one of Taminah's books. "The Story of Dahish the Ifrit." She could almost hear her tutor's voice again now. "A tale of a jinn who chose darkness."

It was real . . . all of it.

There was only one thing this demonic creature looming above her could be could be: an ifrit, evil jinn of the underworld. Just like the creature Jafar had turned into when he made his fateful final wish on the lamp—the Genie's malevolent opposite.

As it roared in triumph at being freed from the bottle, Jasmine whipped her head around in panic, searching for a place to hide. She dashed to the nearest merchant's shop, a grocer's, throwing open the doors while the ifrit's bellowing laugh echoed behind her.

The shopkeeper stood frozen behind the produce counter, his arm resting limply on top of the display case. His eyes were glassy, as if in a daze; he didn't so much as blink. Jasmine glanced at the counter below him, and her stomach turned.

The pomegranates, pears, and apples lining the shelves were rotted black, crawling with worms.

That was when she understood the terrible truth.

He was dead. *All of them were.*

And now the ifrit was right behind her, snarling an incantation.

The shopkeeper's eyes flashed to life, blazing yellow—and the corpse began to move.

Jasmine let out a bloodcurdling scream as she raced out of the shop, quickly discovering she was no safer outside. Everywhere she looked, the ifrit was raising the dead. Spirits crept out of the brass bottles on the ground, the shopkeeper and old lady and the couple in the window came lurching out of their doors ... all of them advancing on Jasmine. These demons and corpses were going to kill her, a world away from home. Now she would never have a chance at fulfilling her destiny, for there would *be* no destiny—

The compass in her pocket dug sharply into her skin, just as she heard an unexpectedly familiar voice. *The* voice. Soft yet strong, far away but still audible enough for Jasmine to hear her words.

"And then the ifrit, whose name was Dahish, betrayer of King Solomon, raised all the dead in the City of Brass, leaving the princess with only one slim chance for survival: the marble wall."

Jasmine shook her head. What—*who*—was that? Was this a panic-induced hallucination? But as Dahish and his corpses closed in around her, she realized it didn't matter whether what she heard was real or not. It was her only hope. The ghostly voice that had frightened her when she heard it back home was almost a comfort here in this terrifying place, like the voice of a friend. Somehow, some way, she knew she had to get to it. Somehow, some way, she knew she had to get to the voice.

Following the direction of the compass's needle, which ticked frantically against her skin, Jasmine ran south, fighting past the skeletal hands clawing at her, toward the outline of a marble wall in the distance. When she was close enough to touch the wall, the ifrit suddenly raised its massive arms overhead, transforming in an instant into a towering serpent. The snake from Orostan...magnified. With its tongue and teeth lashing at her, Jasmine had to fight for her life, using every bit of speed and strength she possessed to reach the wall.

Finally, just inches from defeat, she grasped the stone. Her skirts tore as she climbed, blood spilling across her skin as she fought off the skeletons and serpent pulling her back—until, at last, she was over the edge, falling to her knees.

• • •

Jasmine landed in a foreign room. It was a bedchamber as sumptuous as her own back home, with velvet and gold furnishings and jewel-toned silk fabrics everywhere she looked. A crowned man reclined against a sea of pillows as a young woman about Jasmine's age who must have been his bride recited to him . . . telling a story Though it looked like a peaceful picture from afar, a stench of danger and dread poisoned the atmosphere.

Jasmine backed away, and then stopped when she noticed the book—hovering in midair under a glass case, its pages open. It bore the same title as the one she had found in the tomb, *One Thousand and One Nights*, only this book seemed alive, and writing itself. Words dashed across the page from a floating raven-feathered quill as the woman on the pillows spoke them aloud. Jasmine watched in astonishment. *What kind of magic is this?*

The young queen looked up just then, catching her eye. Jasmine felt a shock of recognition. There was something in the woman's expression that reminded her of a young Taminah . . . but then she shifted in the light, and now it was Fatimah she resembled, a spark of silver in her beautiful dark-gray eyes. The king followed the woman's gaze, but he looked straight through Jasmine without seeing her. While he ordered his queen to continue the story, she stared at Jasmine a moment longer and mouthed, *Wait.*

"And the diamond in the rough thought quickly, devising an ingenious solution for ridding Agrabah of the evil Jafar, proving himself worthy of the princess in the process. While they all exhaled in relief that the vizier-turned-jinn was gone, trapped in a dark and rusty lamp, the Genie took the lamp and flung it overhead, hurling it out of Agrabah for good." The young queen paused her story, and the king leaned forward, urging her to go on.

"When the Genie threw the lamp, his all-powerful strength sent Jafar's lamp flying, not just far from Agrabah, but out of their world . . . into another realm entirely. Of course, what none of them realized—what they could never have known—was that at the moment of his banishment, Jafar's dark magic left an opening. A passage formed between two realms, Agrabah and the dark underworld. The place where creatures of nightmares live, the worst among them being Dahish the ifrit, and his army of flesh-eating ghūls."

The king's eyes were wide as he hung on her every word . . . just like Jasmine, who was too stunned to speak as she realized from the very first line that the story being told was hers.

"That wretched fool, Payam, searched the desert for Jafar's lamp, desperate to find him and unlock his wish-granting jinn power for Payam's own gain. But instead, what he stumbled upon was the glowing gateway between realms that Jafar's dark magic left behind."

The queen lowered her voice to dramatic effect.

"And the ifrit of the underworld possessed Payam's spirit. Made him do terrible things, commit the worst of sins—regicide. And through the now-open passage between realms, the realm of the dead was able to infect Agrabah with its malevolence, starting with Orostan. Soon, however, the darkness and death would spread throughout the kingdom. Once the princess crossed out of her realm, leaving the protective charm of her tiger behind, she came face-to-face with the ifrit. And now the ifrit could at last enter her world, free of any spells or barriers against it. . . ."

Jasmine listened in horror, her insides turning to ice. If this was real, if the rest of the story was as true as the beginning—then that meant everyone she loved was in danger.

"This is where our tale ends for tonight," the young woman said, and the floating raven-feather quill stopped in midair. The king grumbled in disappointment.

"You'll finish it tomorrow, then?" he demanded.

"I will." She smiled. "Good night."

As soon as the king swept out of the bedchamber, the young queen exhaled in relief and motioned for Jasmine to come closer.

"You must be Princess Jasmine," she said, gazing at her in awe. "You look exactly as I pictured . . . every last detail of you." She reached for Jasmine's hand. "My name is Scheherazade. I have been telling your story for days now." She paused. "You might say I called you into existence."

"What do you mean?" Jasmine shook her head, perplexed. "Are you saying that I . . . I'm not *real*? Just some figment of your imagination? Or am I the one imagining you?"

"Imagination is what gives rise to reality," Scheherazade answered. "So you see, it doesn't matter whether I dreamed you up, or you me. We are both real in our separate realms: you in your world of Agrabah, and I in mine."

Scheherazade looked at Jasmine in wonder.

"I've often wished to escape into the stories of my making. Who would have guessed that you would instead travel to me?"

"But—but what is this place?" Jasmine asked. "And how can I get home to Agrabah?"

Scheherazade raised an eyebrow.

"Are you certain you want to go home? Did you not hear what's waiting there at the palace? Dahish the ifrit and his ghouls, the dark magic spreading across Agrabah. King Shahryar's palace is a treacherous place too, but you would still be safer even here."

"If that's true, then all the more reason I need to get back, *now*," Jasmine pleaded. "My people are in danger. I don't want to be safe if they're not. Can you help me?"

Scheherazade was quiet for a moment, thinking.

"The truth is, I would be dead myself if it were not for the king's fascination with your story. And it is my imagination that spun you into this," she acknowledged. "Yes, I will help you. Tell me, Jasmine: How do you want your story to end? How do you want to be remembered, long after you're gone?"

"I . . . I just want to do right by Agrabah," Jasmine realized. "I want to be known as someone who made life better in my kingdom, especially for the overlooked. I want to be the light that drives out the darkness." She paused. "But I don't know how. It all seems so impossible now, with forces both human and inhuman alike against me."

"The times we live in are cruel to women, especially those who dare to defy norms and traditions," Scheherazade said. "I know that better than most. But remember: You reinvented your future once, when you fell for the character even I wasn't expecting you to fall for; when you petitioned the sultan to change Agrabah's laws so you could marry for love. I'm rewriting my future here too, by keeping myself alive through stories. You can do the same." Scheherazade clasped Jasmine's hands. "From here on out, Princess Jasmine, I cede control of the narrative to you. Use your mind, your voice, to create the ending of your story that *you* choose."

"I want to . . . but how?"

"By forgetting everything you've ever been told about what is and isn't possible," Scheherazade said simply. "In fact, stories themselves are what help us to open our minds beyond what we ever imagined possible for ourselves. It was a story I myself heard, about a girl who became empress of China, that inspired my tale about you."

"I haven't heard that one," Jasmine said. "How did she become empress? Was she born into it?"

"Quite the opposite. She was a female warrior of humble origins. When the army conscription came to China, demanding that each house send one of their men to fight the Huns in the emperor's war, this young woman knew her father would never survive it," Scheherazade began. "He was far too old and weak. So she decided to save his life—by disguising herself as a man and taking his place."

"She sounds like the bravest woman in the world," Jasmine marveled.

"Yes." Scheherazade smiled. "But she wasn't only brave—she was also skilled, a far better fighter than most men. She achieved great honor on the battlefield, helping China win their victory. Later, after everyone learned the astonishing truth that their decorated comrade was actually a woman all along, the emperor chose Mulan to be his successor."

"Even though she was a girl?"

"Even though." Scheherazade looked deeply into Jasmine's eyes. "You can be a hero too. I see it in you. One day, your story could inspire countless girls to rise up and rule."

Jasmine felt unexpected tears brimming in her eyes.

"Thank you, Queen Scheherazade. Your words are a gift I'll never forget." She took a deep breath. "I'm ready now. Ready to fight for my home, my people."

"I know you are."

"But will I see you again?" Jasmine asked.

Scheherazade placed a gentle hand on her shoulder.

"Well. I might have woven a piece of myself into your story too . . . only in a different form than this one."

Jasmine's heartbeat quickened.

"How do you mean?"

"Someone who has been there to guide you, helping you discover your true potential and unlocking the ruler you can be." Scheherazade gave her a knowing look. "Does a name come to mind?"

Yes. And yet . . .

"I don't understand." Jasmine shook her head, studying the enigmatic woman before her. "How can you be both there and here?"

"The storyteller makes the magic," she said, smiling at Jasmine's surprise. "In my world I might be trapped in this palace, but in yours, I am part of the Queen's Council: a mystical entity that can take on many different forms, with one sole purpose—to help women rise and become leaders across the realms. We appear to the ones we believe in and who need us the most, in a form they will respond to. And that is how, even before today, you had already found me."

Jasmine's chest swelled with emotion.

"You were my raven," she whispered. "Fatimah."

Scheherazade clasped her hand. "Because I believe in you."

And though Scheherazade was still the only crowned queen among them, she lowered to her knees then, curtsying to Jasmine with eyes full of pride.

• • •

Scheherazade led Jasmine down a carpeted corridor awash with paintings and tapestries, some that Jasmine recognized from her own palace of Agrabah, and through an arched doorway to a terraced garden. A white stone pond was the centerpiece of the garden, its crystal water filled with the most vibrantly colored fish Jasmine had ever seen. Seated on a marble-and-stone bench before the pond was a middle-aged couple with their arms entwined, the woman's long black hair falling in waves against the man's shoulder. Watching them, Jasmine felt a profound sensation of homesickness. They were so familiar—and yet . . .

"Who are they?" Jasmine asked as Scheherazade led her closer.

"Hamed and Roxanna," Scheherazade replied, and the color drained from Jasmine's face. "They used to work for Shahryar's father, the late king. They met and fell in love here at the palace, and when they married, the former king gifted them a home on palace grounds." She watched them fondly. "They are both retired now and seem to spend the most blissful days together, just doing nothing at all . . . as if catching up on lost time."

"Those were my parents' names," Jasmine whispered.

Scheherazade's expression changed as she nodded for Jasmine to go to them. Jasmine raced toward the couple, hopeful tears blurring her vision. Her heart swelled as she stopped before the bench, drinking in every familiar line in their faces.

"It's really you!" she cried. "Baba, Maman—I'm here."

But they gave no indication of seeing or hearing her. The sultan continued stroking his wife's hair while she nestled in closer to him, their eyes on the pond beyond Jasmine.

Scheherazade joined them, gently pulling Jasmine away from the couple as she pleaded, "What's wrong with them? Why aren't they responding to me?"

"Because you are not a part of this world," Scheherazade whispered. "You still belong to the other."

"But my parents *were* my world," Jasmine protested. "How is this possible?"

"I often get inspiration for my stories from the people around me," Scheherazade said. "Hamed and Roxanna are the only people I've felt truly safe with in Shahryar's palace. I suppose that's why I reimagined them as the mother and father of your story."

Jasmine gazed back at them, feeling her heart break all over again.

"But my father—he was leading me here. He somehow knew about the book, about *you*, about all of this." She looked at Scheherazade through her tears. "Why would he want to send me here, if he wouldn't even know me when I arrived?"

Scheherazade followed her gaze, thinking for a while before answering.

"There is only one true way to live forever, and that is to be immortalized in stories. As he grew older and closer to the end of his life, your father started to believe that the tales he'd heard as a boy from Taminah were true. That there was a magical book with worlds that could be reached within its pages, that there was a place where he and his beloved wife could find immortality. He was leading you here to join them . . . and yet he never thought through the fact that you too would have to die in order to exist here."

Jasmine closed her eyes, letting the tears spill down her cheeks.

"Is that what you want?" Scheherazade asked softly. "Remember, I've given you control of the narrative. What do you choose?"

Jasmine looked longingly at her parents on the bench, before forcing herself to tear her eyes away.

"If I stay here, the people I love—Aladdin, Nadia, my kingdom—they'll all be destroyed," she said. "I have to go. There's just one thing I need to do first."

Without waiting for Scheherazade's reply, Jasmine turned toward the bench. She walked slowly at first, and then broke into a run, until she was close enough to throw her arms around the two of them.

Jasmine's mother gasped, and then looked at the sultan with a smile.

"I just felt the strangest, most wonderful thing," she said.

Jasmine held her breath while still holding her parents.

"That's funny," the sultan chuckled. "I felt it too."

Jasmine's mother closed her eyes happily, tilting her face up to the sun. And as she stretched her arms, she unknowingly wrapped her daughter in an embrace.

I'll remember this forever, Jasmine thought gratefully, giving her parents one last hug. *And it will be enough.*

She stood from the bench, joining Scheherazade at the edge of the pond.

"Before you go," Scheherazade said, "I think you might need this."

Jasmine saw a glint of metal as Scheherazade slipped a dagger into the belt of her trousers.

"Now close your eyes, and let me lead you."

Jasmine squeezed her eyes shut, and then felt hands pushing her forward. There was the sensation of falling, clawing at air, the splash of warm water. And then everything went dark.

CHAPTER TWENTY-NINE

J asmine opened her eyes. She lay flat on her back on the stone floor of Atossa's tomb.

Home. She was home. Had it all been a dream? But then she glanced down and saw Scheherazade's dagger, still tucked in her belt—and above the tomb, coming from the palace, was the thick stench of smoke. *Fire.*

She clambered to her feet, grabbing her lantern, which was miraculously still lit. Racing up the steps and out of the tomb, she fled the chamber. The smell of smoke was even more palpable out in the warren, and she realized in horror that it was coming from upstairs . . . where nearly a hundred people currently slept.

Jasmine thundered up the passageway steps, pushing past the hanging curtain and the hidden door until she was back in the main palace interior. A cloud of gray smoke rushed to meet her, burning Jasmine's throat and stinging her eyes as she fought through it, as she tried to scream a warning to everyone upstairs.

Except . . . no one was upstairs or asleep. Not anymore. The main floor looked nearly unrecognizable since she last walked these steps. She blinked rapidly, wondering if she'd been transported back to her waking nightmare in the City of Brass—only it was infinitely more terrifying now, because it wasn't just Jasmine under siege. From the visiting royals to the ministers and staff, all the palace's inhabitants were out of their beds and surrounded.

Pale-skinned ghūls stalked them across the Grand Atrium, half men, half beasts, baring sharp claws and teeth. A swarm of serpents wrapped their scales around their victims' throats, while Dahish the ifrit loomed high above them all, breathing fire. At the ifrit's side, Payam watched with wide-eyed glee.

As the scene swam before Jasmine's eyes, the front doors were flung open. Two familiar figures broke through the smoke, and her hand flew to her chest.

Rajah . . . and *Aladdin*. He'd come back—and he'd brought a small army with him. Through the firelight, Jasmine recognized so many faces from the marketplace: Malik and Fatimah, Tarek the tailor, Omar from the tannery, Babak, who had taken refuge with his family in Aladdin's broken tower, the street performers from the banquet.

None of them had shied away from the terror of what was unfolding in the palace of Agrabah. Everyone Aladdin had befriended or helped was here with them now. Jasmine flew into his arms.

"I'm sorry—for everything," she said, choking through the smoke.

"It's all right, Princess." He squeezed her hand. "Let's go. We have a battle to win."

Aladdin unsheathed his sword, Malik nocked an arrow, and

their group of street fighters jumped into the fray. Omar hurled a bucket of water at the ifrit's fire, and the water soared above the flood of arrows that came firing from Malik's and Babak's weapons.

Jasmine's eyes swept quickly across the carnage of the atrium to see where she was needed most. Aladdin was dueling Payam across the hall, while the rest of the street fighters were firing arrows at the ifrit or joining the crown ministers and guards battling the ghūls and snakes with their swords. She spotted a particularly large serpent holding Prince Achmed in a tight grip, and Jasmine quickly grabbed Scheherazade's dagger. While Achmed wailed, she crept behind the serpent and lifted her dagger—slicing off the monster's head.

It screeched in agony, spinning wildly before falling to the marble floor in a pool of blood. She and Achmed both stared in astonishment, and then the trembling prince stumbled to his feet.

"This is a monstrous kingdom you have, Jasmine," he spat. "I'm leaving."

"Before you go, please, you can help us!" she cried. "Remember everything you told me, all the battles you've won? Now is your chance to win the biggest fight of them all, to have epic stories and verses written in your name—and then you never have to see any of us again."

Achmed took one more look up at the fire-breathing ifrit and shook his head.

"You are on your own, Princess." And with that, he ran like the coward he was—straight out of the palace doors.

There was no time to react. Jasmine rushed back into the thick of the fighting, crossing paths with the commander and Karim as they dueled two ghūls each. As much as she loathed the two men, she realized now that they were never the real enemy. It was Payam—it was the ifrit—and it was the lingering stain of Jafar's dark magic.

Just then, a two-headed serpent lunged at Aladdin, and Jasmine cried out to warn him. He dodged its sharp teeth with a jump, wielding his sword against the monster. Like the fearless young man she first saw leaping across rooftops and dodging guards in the marketplace, Aladdin led the serpent on a chase, battling him to the top of the grand staircase, ducking and swinging until he pierced the serpent between its eyes. But what he didn't see, right behind him, was Payam.

Jasmine raced forward, and suddenly she felt something strong take hold of her, whisking her onto its back. *Rajah.* As the tiger sprinted toward Payam, they passed Malik, who tossed a bow and a handful of arrows into her arms. And in that moment, Jasmine knew just what to do.

"Payam!" she shouted, distracting his attention from Aladdin. As the enemy lunged toward her, Jasmine signaled Rajah to make a quick turn, firing three arrows from across the tiger's back. Payam fell to the ground with a shocked sputter and a cry.

Jasmine couldn't resist punching the air in triumph. She had done it; she had executed a near-flawless Parthian Shot when it mattered most. But her relief was short-lived.

Across the atrium, a wolflike ghūl seized two bodies, one in each of its massive hands.

Jasmine squinted, realizing in horror that the ghūl had Rashid— and Shirin.

"No!" she screamed, sprinting toward them, leaving Malik and the street fighters to finish Payam. Aladdin heard her cry and rushed into the fray ahead of her, brandishing his sword at the ghūl and stabbing it from the back. The ghūl dropped Shirin and Rashid from its grip and Jasmine ran to her friend, the two clutching each other in relief. Rashid spun around, and as he raised his sword Jasmine could see in his eyes that he didn't want to be saved by Aladdin—he wanted to defeat the ghūl himself. As he aimed for the ghūl's chest, the monster reached forward, digging its claws into Rashid's torso. Killing him on the spot.

Shirin's bloodcurdling screams pierced the air. Jasmine grabbed her hand, pulling her away from the carnage while Aladdin fired his arrows at the ghūl.

"You'll be all right," she said into her friend's ear, fighting the urge to sob along with Shirin. "We'll get through this."

From the corner of her eye, Jasmine spotted a different creature, a walking corpse like she'd seen in the town square of the City of Brass, closing its bony fingers around Karim's neck. She quickly readied her bow and arrow, shooting at the corpse. Karim looked at her in astonishment as it dropped to the floor with a chilling screech.

"Wh-why did you help me?" he asked. "I'm your enemy."

"No, you're not." Jasmine gestured to the monsters surrounding them, wishing Karim were her biggest threat. "I did what a good leader would do. Now it's your turn. You say you want to rule Agrabah? That means defending *all* of its people. Fight with us."

Karim nodded, raising his sword and running into the fray. As he, Jasmine and Aladdin, Shirin and Nadia, Malik and Arman, and

Majid and Parisa banded together with the street fighters, they succeeded in fending off most of the monsters on the ground. But the biggest remained, and it was soon overpowering them again as the ifrit hurled breaths of fire down toward them.

A shout echoed behind them, pulling Dahish's focus away. Jasmine turned to see Fatimah, who was chanting something in an unfamiliar language, her eyes locked on Dahish's. Jasmine's mouth fell open as Fatimah's body jerked forward and began to spin, shedding her mortal skin . . . and revealing herself to be a magnificent blue genie.

Dahish roared in fury, focused solely on the genie now. Fatimah extended her arm, sparks flowing from her fingertips as she fought Dahish's breaths of fire with flashes of lightning. While the genie and the ifrit battled on the landing above, and Aladdin and the street fighters defended the palace from the ghūls and monsters, Scheherazade's words echoed in Jasmine's ears.

Create the ending of your story that you *choose. Forget what is possible. . . .*

And with the power of her conviction, Jasmine raced up the staircase two at a time to where the ifrit and the genie battled. Taking a steely breath, she leaped up onto the ifrit's fiery back, catching it by surprise—and with Scheherazade's knife, Jasmine stabbed Dahish in the eye.

Dahish flailed blindly, tumbling to the floor. Fatimah swooped down next to him and something materialized in her palm. *His brass bottle.*

The atrium echoed with the sound of his defeated screams as Fatimah captured Dahish and forced him back into his brass bottle, throwing it into the last flames of the fire with Payam's bloodied body. As they burned, the remaining ghūls and snakes disintegrated before Jasmine's eyes, turning to ash now that the ifrit who controlled them was gone.

Jasmine and Aladdin ran into each other's arms, exhausted and elated. The battle was won. Fatimah floated toward them, bowing gracefully, as if they hadn't all just been through a war.

"Well done, Sultana."

She approached Karim next. Everyone watched in stunned silence as Fatimah the genie brushed her blue hand across Karim's cheek while whispering a chant in Agrabah's old, forgotten language. And then, before their eyes . . . Karim's entire body turned to stone. He was nothing more than a statue.

"*What*—what is this?" Jasmine gaped at the man of stone in disbelief. Across the room, she heard Shirin cry out in shock.

"He was never real, Jasmine," Fatimah revealed "At least, not in this form. The true Karim was indeed only your cousin, a benevolent young man who died tragically in battle months ago. It was never about him—it was about you. He was the test."

"I don't understand. . . ." Jasmine shook her head, unable to tear her eyes away from the statue that was once Karim. "A test of what?"

"Were you ambivalent about taking your father's place, or were you willing to *fight* for Agrabah, for your people? Were you ready to do whatever it took to be the sultana you were born to be, regardless of all those who doubted you? Could you weed out the enemies in your midst, surround yourself with the right people, and be a leader of change? *That* was the test." Fatimah smiled. "And it's quite clear that you passed with flying colors."

"If Karim wasn't real . . . what about all of this?" Shirin gestured at the carnage around them, her gaze lingering on Rashid's body. "Can you bring my brother back?"

Fatimah's expression grew somber.

"I'm afraid Karim was the only illusion here. The threat to Agrabah, and the realm of the dead seeping into your world, was in fact real. Which is why I needed to know we had the right leader to pull Agrabah out of the darkness." She gently touched Jasmine's cheek. "You."

Fatimah turned back to Shirin, her eyes warm with empathy.

"I can't bring your brother back, but I can promise that by defeating Dahish today, the window between worlds is closed. You are safe."

"If you can't bring Rashid back, then how did you resurrect *him*?" Arman spoke up now, gaping at Karim with wide eyes.

"A genie can't reveal all her tricks," Fatimah said, arching an eyebrow. "But what I can say is that it wasn't a resurrection, it was a magic trick. An enchanted statue that assumes the identity I give it . . . only for as long as the spell lasts."

The crown ministers edged forward, wearing a range of stunned expressions. Commander Zohar and Hassan, minister of law, looked thunderstruck at being duped by Fatimah, while Arman, Majid, and the others appeared almost impressed.

"Well. Now that there is apparently no challenger for the throne, it's quite clear Jasmine is our sultana," Arman declared.

"Hear, hear," Majid agreed with a smile. "Though I must add that in my book, she won both of the final two challenges right here in this battle." He lowered to his knees, and the other ministers followed suit, joined by Aladdin and the street fighters, until Jasmine was the only one left standing.

"Long live Sultana Jasmine!"

"Blessed be her reign."

EPILOGUE

Moments before her coronation was due to begin, Jasmine stood hand in hand with Aladdin, the two of them alone in the marble hall that led to the Sultan's Balcony.

"I'm so proud of you, Princess," his warm voice murmured in her ear. "Sultana." Jasmine slid closer to him, tilting her face up to his.

"And I am proud of you. It was you who rallied the people of Agrabah to fight with us, and who fought heroically yourself. I'm lucky to have you as my newest crown minister, representing the people . . . and I'm even luckier to have you as my husband-to-be."

Aladdin grinned down at her, resting his forehead against hers.

"Six more weeks." He brushed his lips against her cheek, then lower, meeting her lips with his. Jasmine stood on her tiptoes, pressing against his chest as she kissed him back.

"Just imagine," she murmured between kisses, "a lifetime of this."

"A lifetime isn't nearly long enough," he replied.

At the sound of footsteps behind them, Aladdin squeezed her hand and gently stepped back. Her new lineup of crown ministers—Arman, Khaleel, Majid, Parisa, and now Aladdin—preceded her onto the balcony, where the people of Agrabah were waiting in the Great Courtyard below.

Jasmine stepped out onto the balcony to thunderous applause and exalting cries of "Long live Her Majesty, Sultana Jasmine!" She smiled at the sea of faces before gently motioning for silence.

"Now that our great battle with the underworld is won, I realize that what truly mattered was never about securing the throne—it was being worthy of it," Jasmine declared before her people. "If I am truly worthy of being your sultana, I must leave the choice to you. Do you, my beloved people of Agrabah, wish to continue our monarchy, with me as sovereign? It's in your hands. The story of our kingdom is yours to write as much as it is mine."

The roar of assent was loud enough to be heard all across the empire. Jasmine was moved to tears as she smiled at her people, and the high elder stepped forward, placing her father's treasured crown atop her head.

Up above, a silver-eyed raven perched on one of the rafters, watching the celebrations.

The bird's presence went unnoticed by most of the guests, but Jasmine glanced up at it more than once, smiling at the sight. And as the coronation ceremony drew to a close, the raven met Jasmine's eyes and bowed its head ever so slightly before disappearing into the sky.

Somewhere, far from here, another future queen was in need of counsel.

THE END

ACKNOWLEDGMENTS

This project is quite possibly the most meant-to-be of my career thus far, and I'm so incredibly grateful the stars aligned! Anyone who knows me even a little knows that I'm a Disney superfan at heart; some of my earliest memories revolve around Snow White, Cinderella, and Ariel, but it was the movie *Aladdin* that really changed the game for me. From Alan Menken's glorious music to the thrill of me and my brother finally seeing characters onscreen who looked like our family, it remains *the* movie of our childhood, and Jasmine has always been my favorite princess. So when I received a surprise email from my agent saying that Disney was interested in me possibly writing a Princess Jasmine YA novel, all I could say was OMG. I must have pinched myself countless times since to make sure it wasn't a dream! ☺ To everyone at Disney who had a hand in making this dream come true, I thank you with all my heart, starting with:

Jocelyn Davies, my absolutely brilliant editor! I can't thank you enough for believing in my vision and choosing me to tell Jasmine's story. Thank you for helping me make this book so much better with your genius notes, for all those inspiring phone calls talking through the plot, and for being such a supportive champion of this project. It's an honor to work with you!

Elanna Heda, thank you for your wonderful help along the way and keeping everything on track! Thank you to Karen Krumpak for your copyediting wizardry, and Martin Karlow for your eagle-eyed proofreading. I'm grateful to have you both looking after my words.

Many thanks also to SILA Consulting for your authenticity read and insightful notes!

Crystal McCoy, Kaia Hilson, and everyone in publicity & marketing who helped send this book out into the world with a big splash: thank you, thank you, for everything! Crystal Patriarche, Hanna Lindsley, and Leilani Fitzpatrick at BookSparks, thank you for being such a dedicated publicity team and helping readers find Jasmine!

Marci Senders, thank you for designing such a beautiful cover, and Scott Altmann, thank you for your gorgeous rendering of Jasmine!

To my wonderful agent, Joe Veltre: thank you for being such a rock in my career. I'm so grateful for your steadfast support and for making so much business magic happen! ☺ Thanks also to the rest of my dream team at Gersh, Greg Pedicin and Lynn Fimberg. You three are the very best! And to the best lawyer, Chad Christopher: thank you for always taking great care of me and my contracts.

So much love and thanks to my fellow Disney queens, Emma Theriault and Livia Blackburne. Our sisterhood is one of the biggest gifts this project has given me! Thank you for your friendship and your beautiful books—it's an honor to share this series with you.

To the rest of my incredible author friends, especially Livia, Tess Sharpe and the Trifecta group, Romina Garber, Gretchen McNeil, and Abdi Nazemian: thank you for your amazing support, for all the great chats, and inspiring me every day with your brilliance. Thank you to my best friends Mia Antonelli, Roxane Cohanim, and the Bratman family for all your love and support.

Pamela Lopez, thank you for being a beloved member of our family and making it possible for me to have the time and space to write—I couldn't do this without you!

I was fortunate to have a wealth of Persian mythology to draw from while writing this book, and I give my heartfelt thanks to my ancestors and all the Persian storytellers who came before me, especially the authors and scholars who contributed to *One Thousand and One Nights* and the translators who brought these special folktales to the world's attention. Thank you to the team of John Musker & Ron Clements, Ted Elliott & Terry Rossio, Alan Menken, Howard Ashman & Tim Rice, for taking a centuries-old story about a young man and a magic lamp and turning it into the most fantastic movie that enchanted my heart and captivated my imagination at such a young age. It's the honor of a lifetime to get to write in your world.

My biggest thanks and inspiration on this project are due to my amazing mother, the brilliant recording artist ZaZa. Your albums *Nights One and a Thousand* and *Book of Kings* are what made me fall in love with Persian mythology, and your gorgeous music is both the soundtrack to my childhood and the songs I listened to every day while writing this book of my heart. I'm so lucky to have you as both a mom and a muse!

To my incredible father, Shon, first and forever love—thank you for being the biggest champion of the arts in our family, and for giving me the confidence and the wings to chase after these dreams. ILYSM! To Arian, the best big brother in the universe and the first person I think of when I think of Aladdin: This book is for us!

Endless thanks to my readers—those who have been with me since *Timeless* and those who are just finding me now. Thank you so much for welcoming my stories into your lives. Thank you to all the dedicated librarians and booksellers for championing books far and wide!

Lastly, for the three loves of my life: my true prince of a husband, Chris, and our treasures, Leo James and Jordan Rose. Every day is happily-ever-after with the three of you.